"IT'S TIME YOU START THINKING OF YOURSELF, MISS JONES. START MAKING THINGS RIGHT FOR YOURSELF. I THINK YOU'LL DISCOVER WHAT I MEAN AFTER YOU'VE THOUGHT ABOUT IT."

Sara stood at the corner of the house for a long time, almost until dark had fallen, just standing there thinking. She tried to make sense of Emrys' words, but images of the man kept intruding: his smile, his eyes when he was angry and they were like ice chips, his eyes when he was happy and they were like liquid caramel, his hands with the strong fingers, his expression. Darkness fell, and Sara finally went to sit on the bench in the front garden. She pulled Lucy up to sit beside her and put her arms around Lucy's neck, burying her face in the familiar fur as she finally figured out what Emrys meant. "For myself," she said, "Lucy, just thinking of myself, I know what I want and I want Emrys." She rubbed her cheek against Lucy's soft, floppy ear. "Oh," she whispered as realization sunk in, "I think I'm in love with Emrys."

WATCH FOR THESE ZEBRA REGENCIES

LADY STEPHANIE   (0-8217-5341-X, $4.50)
by Jeanne Savery
Lady Stephanie Morris has only one true love: the family estate she
has managed ever since her mother died. But then Lord Anthony Rider
arrives on her estate, claiming he has plans for both the land and the
woman. Stephanie soon realizes she's fallen in love with a man whose
sensual caresses will plunge her into a world of peril and intrigue . . . a
man as dangerous as he is irresistible.

BRIGHTON BEAUTY   (0-8217-5340-1, $4.50)
by Marilyn Clay
Chelsea Grant, pretty and poor, naively takes school friend Alayna
Marchmont's place and spends a month in the country. The devastating
man had sailed from Honduras to claim his promised bride, Miss
Marchmont. An affair of the heart may lead to disaster . . . unless a
resourceful Brighton beauty finds a way to stop a masquerade and
keep a lord's love.

LORD DIABLO'S DEMISE   (0-8217-5338-X, $4.50)
by Meg-Lynn Roberts
The sinfully handsome Lord Harry Glendower was a gambler and the
black sheep of his family. About to be forced into a marriage of con-
venience, the devilish fellow engineered his own demise, never having
dreamed that faking his death would lead him to the heavenly refuge
of spirited heiress Gwyn Morgan, the daughter of a physician.

A PERILOUS ATTRACTION   (0-8217-5339-8, $4.50)
by Dawn Aldridge Poore
Alissa Morgan is stunned when a frantic passenger thrusts her baby
into Alissa's arms and flees, having heard rumors that a notorious
highwayman posed a threat to their coach. Handsome stranger Hugh
Sebastian secretly possesses the treasured necklace the highwayman
seeks and volunteers to pose as Alissa's husband to save her reputation.
With a lost baby and missing necklace in their care, the couple embarks
on a journey into peril—and passion.

*Available wherever paperbacks are sold, or order direct from the
Publisher. Send cover price plus 50¢ per copy for mailing and
handling to Penguin USA, P.O. Box 999, c/o Dept. 17109,
Bergenfield, NJ 07621. Residents of New York and Tennessee must
include sales tax. DO NOT SEND CASH.*

SAINT'S HAVEN

Dawn Aldridge Poore

Zebra Books
Kensington Publishing Corp.

http://www.zebrabooks.com

ZEBRA BOOKS are published by

Kensington Publishing Corp.
850 Third Avenue
New York, NY 10022

First Printing: August, 1997
10 9 8 7 6 5 4 3 2 1

Printed in the United States of America

Chapter 1

Parson Grimm brought Jack and James in, bloody and bruised, and tossed them in a heap at Mrs. Jones's feet. "I was able to save them this time, but I may not the next," he said, knotting up his huge fists. "This one took it in his head to fight me when I cotch'd them and t'uther one took it up."

Mrs. Jones closed her eyes in despair and sat down in her chair while James stood shakily in front of her. Mrs. Jones was as shaky as James. She turned to Sarafina. "Sara," she said faintly, motioning with her pale hand.

Sara stepped over to where Jack was still down and pulled him up to a sitting position. He had a cut lip and the beginnings of a fine black eye. "Thank you, Parson Grimm. We'll see to the boys." She frowned at the two, and they averted their eyes. "Just what did they do this time?"

Parson Grimm was an ex-boxer and still looked more fit for a cockpit than a pulpit. "Pickpockets!" he spat. "I saw them do it myself. I made them give the gen'nulman's watch back to 'im and apologize. He wanted to press charges, but I talked him out of it." The parson looked hard at the boys. "You can do what you want, Miz Jones, and I know how hard it is on a woman alone, especially trying to raise boys what ain't your own; but I'd take them away from London. This ain't no fit place to raise a boy, I tell you. Every time they get on the street, they get into the devil's work. Caring for orphans is God's work, all right, but not even the good Lord"—here Parson Grimm paused and raised his eyes to the ceiling—"could watch for every orphan in London. These boys need som'thing to do."

Aunt Zell was busy knitting a winter cap for Matthew, no matter that it was early May. She nodded and agreed. "Idle hands are the devil's workshop, I've told you before, Sophie," she said to Mrs. Jones. "We need to move out to the country. I've said that before as well and you've ignored me, so you see what's come of that."

Mrs. Jones, seldom one to make decisions, brushed her blond hair, so unlike Sara's dark curls, back from her forehead. In dismay, she looked around at the others. Parson Grimm was blocking the door, Sarafina was in the middle of the room, and Aunt Zell was in her rocking chair knitting. The six orphans looked at them warily. Jack was still on the floor, James was leaning groggily against a table, while Briget, John, and Matthew were standing round-eyed by the kitchen door. Mary, Matthew's twin, was pulling at Sarafina's skirts while Sarafina dabbed at James's cuts. "What do you all say?" Mrs. Jones asked, very pale. "Oh, I do wish Clayton were here!"

"He isn't here, Mama, except in spirit," Sarafina said, picking Mary up and handing her off to Briget. "We're going to have to decide this on our own." She walked to the sideboard and poured her mother a glass of sherry. "I think Parson Grimm is right," she said, handing Mrs. Jones the glass. "We've been talking about moving to the country for over a year, and it's high time we did something about it. It's May now, and spring would be a good time to go. We could plow a garden and raise vegetables and herbs, we could ... we could. ... There are all sorts of things we could do." Sarafina was at a loss as to what else could be done in the country. Even though she had been born in the country, she was, for all her talk, city-bred. Country life and country ways were alien to her.

"All right," Mrs. Jones said weakly, gulping down the rest of the sherry. "Will you help us, Parson Grimm?"

"The whole church will help, Miz Jones, and I'll see to it that the church back at ... where?" He looked at Sara as Mrs. Jones said nothing.

"The village of St. Claire," Sara answered. "Our house, Saint's Haven, is there."

"St. Claire. I've heard of someone there, although I've never met him." He scratched his massive head. "I'll see what I can do." He patted Mrs. Jones's hand and nodded encouragingly. "Don't you worry about a thing." Parson Grimm's pulpit voice rumbled from deep in his chest. "Moving's the right choice. That's the only way you're going to keep from having gallows bait on your hands."

The sherry was working. Mrs. Jones stood and smiled beatifically. "That settles it, then. We'll start packing tomorrow."

Sara stopped dabbing at the boy's cuts long enough to stare at her mother. "You're really going to move?"

"Of course, Sara. It's what Clayton would want us to do." She swept her arm to include the children. "The whole lot of us—we'll all move to Saint's Haven."

Chapter 2

The road was a muddy mess and so were Sarafina's clothes. The twins, Matthew and Mary, had fallen from the wagon into the mud and were covered with dirt in varying stages of dryness. They no sooner got dry than the wagon mired again and they were, once more, treated to muttered curses from Garfield, the man who had lived with them and watched after the horses and the orphanage since they had first come back to London.

They were all exhausted, and the recent heavy spring rains had soaked every mile of the road from London, leaving huge boggy patches and deep mud. It was unseasonably hot today, and by tomorrow, Garfield had said, the road would be dry enough to travel; but they had opted to continue on to Saint's Haven today. The wagon was heavily loaded and had been mired down almost continuously, it seemed. Sarafina stood beside the puddles and watched Garfield and the boys work to get the wagon out yet again. This time their predicament looked worse than the others, she thought, as she held Mary up to try to keep her out of the mud. Matthew was a muddy mess, beyond help until they could find a tub to dunk him in.

According to Garfield, they were not far from Saint's Haven now, and they could get there none too soon. They had been unable to find an inn the night before and had slept in the wagon with the boys and Garfield standing guard. James and Jack had thought that was a fine adventure and fell into the spirit of things, but Garfield and Sara knew how dangerous the roads could be at night. Fortunately, nothing had happened, much to Jack and John's disappointment. They had been ready to fight either footpads or highwaymen. At the inn where they had stayed the night before that, Jack had talked to a stableboy who had told him of a dangerous felon named Perkin who preyed on this stretch of country. Jack could hardly wait to meet him face-to-face.

The wagon wheel moved in the mud with a sucking sound and almost broke free, but rolled back again, buried almost to the axle. Garfield and the boys tried again and almost got it out, but the wagon teetered on the edge of firm ground, then fell back into the mud. The boys grunted and strained, but they needed just one extra little push. Sara handed Mary to Aunt Zell, pulled her dress up as much as she decently could, and tied it to try to keep the hem out of the mud. Then, over Mrs. Jones's objections, she waded out into the mud to help push. John and Garfield got on one side, and she got on the other with Jack and James.

The wagon made a sucking sound and began to move. Sara almost slipped, and mud splattered the front of her dress. She felt the sleeve seam rip as she pushed and strained, and sweat began to run down her neck into her dress. "Once more," Garfield said with a grunt. "Heave on three. One, two—" He stopped as a horse and carriage came around the curve behind them, the horses prancing and shying as they saw the wagon blocking the road.

"What the hell are you doing in the middle of the road?" It wasn't a question; it was a roar.

Sara, Garfield, and the boys stopped pushing and looked behind them at the fine carriage and black horses. The carriage was black, with trim picked out in red and gold, and the horses had harnesses trimmed in silver and red tassels. A man leaned from the carriage window, a frown on his face. He was dark, with almost black hair and an olive complexion. Right now his dark brows were furrowed, and there was an angry set to his mouth. He looked at them with what Sara thought was disdain as he knocked on the side of the carriage to get the driver's attention. The man didn't wait for an answer to his question but looked up at his coachman. "Can you get around this, Bevan?" he demanded.

"Aye," Bevan answered, moving the prancing horses up to the side of the road where the land was firm. The man in the carriage looked at them as they passed, and Sara met his eyes as he went by them. A frown crossed his face as he looked at their decrepit wagon and at each of them covered with mud. As the fine carriage moved on, he closed the window.

"Of all the . . . the supercilious . . . the . . .," Sara said through clenched teeth.

"Turn the other cheek, my dear," her mother said. "Remember that we must make allowances for others."

Sara glanced at her mother before she put her shoulder to the wagon again. "Some people, Mama, don't need allowances. Rather than turning the other cheek, a good, swift kick in the *other* cheek would be more appropriate." She ignored her mother's shocked gasp as she leaned against the wagon and pushed hard on Garfield's, "All together, ready . . . NOW!" The wagon didn't budge.

"It's going to take something under the wheels," Garfield said, wiping sweat from his forehead. "I'll see what I can find." He took Jack and went off in search of some limbs.

It was the better part of an hour before they returned, an hour filled with John teasing Briget until she cried, James muttering that he was grown up enough to go with Garfield, and Matthew and Mary whining that they were hungry. Sara didn't want to clamber into the wagon to find anything to eat, so she finally convinced the children to follow her into a nearby field where she saw some berries. When she reached them, the red berries turned out to be unripe and inedible. She did, however, find a fine apple tree limb on the ground. She, James, and John dragged the limb to the wagon and put it in front of the back wheels. Garfield and Jack came up just as Sara was crawling from under the wagon, muddy from the waist of her gown to her bare feet. She had taken off her shoes and stockings before she tried to put the limb under the wheel, right after one of her shoes had been sucked off in the muck and it took several minutes to locate it. She had quickly decided that bare feet could be washed easier than shoes and stockings.

Garfield stood back and looked at the heavy limb under the wheels and then at her. "Good job, missy," he said as he and Jack put more limbs in front of the wheels. "This should do us. Let's push together. One, two, NOW!"

The wagon pulled onto the limbs and over the muddy spot. Sara was pushing with all her strength when she heard a shout from the front. She looked up for an instant, but could see nothing over the top of the wagon. The horses pranced and surged forward. Crunching out of the mud and over the tree limbs, the wagon moved forward with a sudden lurch. Sara had put all her weight against the wagon, and when it surged free, she teetered and lost her balance. She tried to step forward, but tripped over one of the limbs. Feeling herself begin to fall, she grabbed unsteadily for the back of the wagon; but her fingers just grazed it, and with a *splat!*, she fell face first into the soupy mud. For a moment, she thought she was going to suffocate, but then she was unceremoniously jerked back by the hair on her head. She gasped for air, yelped in pain, and tried to turn around. "Let go of me!" she screeched. "Jack, James, you devils! You'll pay for this." She twisted around and raked the mud out of her eyes. To her horror, she was looking right into the face of the man who had passed by in the carriage.

"I think you'll live," he said, grabbing her hand and pulling her to her feet. "I came back to try to pull you out, but I see you've managed on your own." He looked at Garfield. "Is there anything else we can do for you? The road gets better from here on up, as far as my place anyway. I hear it's fine on to the north."

"About time it firmed up." Garfield nodded. "Been muddy all the way from Lunnon."

"A wagon that heavy ain't made for roads like these." This was from the coachman who accompanied the stranger. He and Garfield looked at each other and nodded in understanding.

"Not much to be done about it." Garfield nodded again.

"If you need nothing else, we'll be on our way," the stranger said. "Good day." He nodded at Sarafina and then at Aunt Zell and Mrs. Jones. "Have a good journey, ladies." With that, he was back on his horse, another glossy black, this one with a white star on its forehead. Sara noted with satisfaction that he had gotten mud on the gleaming leather of his boots and on his impeccably tailored clothes. He looked down at her and tried to suppress a smile, but laughed aloud in spite of himself, his teeth a flash of white against his dark complexion. Before Sara could say anything, he had given them a wave and was off down the road toward the village of St. Claire. The coachman, Bevan, followed him, leading two strong work horses that he had brought to help pull the wagon out.

"See, Sara," Mrs. Jones said, looking after the man, "you shouldn't have had hard thoughts about him. The man was a gentleman after all."

Sara gritted her teeth, but tasted nothing but mud.

Chapter 3

It was late afternoon by the time they passed through the village of St. Claire and reached its outskirts where Saint's Haven was located. Sara was looking forward to something hot to eat, a bath, and a good night's sleep. "It's the next house," Mrs. Jones said eagerly. "Lord Emrys owns this parcel"—she gestured toward an expanse of well-tended fields—"and the land behind us. I heard he bought the land on the other side as well from Squire Marston."

"I'm surprised Emrys hasn't tried to buy Saint's Haven," Sara said. "That would give him the whole stretch on this side of the village."

Mrs. Jones chuckled as she moved forward so she could be the first to see. "All he'd have to do is look at the place and realize I'd never sell it. Saint's Haven is such a beautiful little place."

Garfield walked beside the tired horses while Jack held the reins. Sara, Aunt Zell, and the rest of the children looked eagerly as they rounded a curve for their first glimpse of Saint's Haven. "I do hope," Mrs. Jones said, "that Mr. Bekins has kept my flower gardens intact. My mother gave me the roses."

They rounded a bend in the road as Mrs. Jones pointed ahead. "Right around here," she said eagerly. "Clayton loved this spot so. He—" She stopped, her voice choking as they rounded the bend in the road. They all stopped abruptly and looked in shocked silence as the house came into view.

"Is *that* it?"

That was a tumble-down structure with sagging doors, broken windows, and outbuildings that looked perilously close to collapse. The front garden was a mass of tangled weeds, and the remains of a burned-out stable stood off to one side. One shutter banged against the side of the house as the breeze caught it. The shutter for the other side of the window was missing.

Garfield pulled the horses and wagon to the side of the road, and they all climbed down and stood silently looking at the ruins. Finally, Mrs. Jones began to wail. "My roses! Clayton's garden!" Her voice was stricken. "He was so proud of his garden."

"Perhaps you've forgotten, Mama," Sara said, putting her hand on her mother's shoulder. "Perhaps Papa's garden was in the back of the house."

Mrs. Jones shook her head and looked at the tumble-down house in silence. Sara felt disappointment well up inside her and moved away so her mother wouldn't see the tears in her eyes. Quickly, she let go of Mary's hand and walked back toward the house. She had given up walking in her thin shoes and had hunted up a pair of brogues from her box in the wagon, so she didn't mind trampling through the weeds. She had pulled her almost black curls back and tied them with a bit of ribbon.

Standing in the weedy patch that was the front garden,

she took a deep breath as she tried to remember her times here. There was nothing—no memories at all except a vague impression of flowers, sunshine, and her father tossing her up in the air while he laughed. Certainly, she thought, as she looked around at the ruin and the weeds, there was nothing happy or cheerful about this place.

She rounded the corner of the house and looked on the destruction at the back. Two of the outbuildings—a chicken house and one other small building—had been torn down, and recently from the look of them. A rock wall along the back had also been torn down and the rocks piled in heaps. The field beyond had been cleared, and several large apple trees had been cut and chopped up. Sara moved slowly forward and almost tripped over the remains of a bird house that had been cast aside. She looked back at the main house to discover that most of the glass was missing from the windows at the rear and the back door was gone. A thin, mangy-looking dog—an emaciated beagle from the looks of it—came out of the house, wagging its tail so hard that it shook all over. The dog came over to her, sniffed at the mud on her dress, and recognizing one as dirty as itself, wagged its tail again, whined in a friendly way, and licked her hand. Absently, Sara patted its head and went back to the forlorn group standing beside the road.

"Mama," she said gently, "are you *sure* this is the place?"

"I'm sure." Mrs. Jones stared at the scrawny dog, its ribs making a pattern on its sides. "What is that creature? It looks almost dead."

"I think it lives here." Sarafina gestured toward the house. "Mama, someone seems to be dismantling the buildings in the back. Are you *positive* this is Saint's Haven?"

"Of course," Mrs. Jones snapped. "Wouldn't I know my own house?"

"But it's been twenty years, Mama," Sara said gently. "Perhaps . . ."

Mrs. Jones shook her head. "There's no perhaps, Sara. I know my own house, and I know this is Saint's Haven. I've sent Mr. Bekins money regularly for all these years to watch the house and take care of the repairs. I know your father sent him money for a new roof just before he died, and I sent money to repair the outbuildings. Mr. Bekins even wrote your father that there was an excess of funds and he had invested it, reaping even more profit. Things should be in perfect order."

"Well," Aunt Zell said briskly, "they're not, but we have nowhere else to go. We might as well go inside and see what we need to do. This may be our cross to bear."

"Devil of a cross," Garfield muttered as he moved the wagon and horses toward the house. The track was so overgrown that the task was difficult. "Don't know where I can stable the horses."

"There's one shed left standing. You might use that."

Garfield snorted. "Not much of a stable, I tell you."

"It's better than nothing for tonight, and we can make better arrangements for tomorrow," Sara said.

Garfield looked at her, started to say something else, then changed his mind. "True enough," he said gruffly. "We've always made the best of things."

Sara gave him a small smile and went to the front door. It opened with a creak at just a touch of her fingers, and she stepped inside, almost holding her breath, as the others followed her. Inside, there was little furniture. It appeared that the chairs had been broken up and burned in the fireplace. Dust was everywhere, dancing in the light coming through the dirty window. There were birds' nests on the windowsills and clumps of dirt caught against the inside walls. Weeds were growing in the clumps of dirt that were inside the room in sunny patches next to the walls. Mrs.

Jones stood in the middle of the room and looked around slowly. "I think I'm going to faint," she gasped.

"Don't you dare, Mama," Sara said, scooping up Mary before she fell over some rags that the dog was using as a bed. "There's no place for you to rest except the floor." She motioned to Briget to get a box for her mother and sat her down. Aunt Zell was there with the vinaigrette. Garfield came in and grimaced as he looked around. He opened his mouth, but at Sara's frown, he said nothing. Sara looked at the once shiny staircase. "I'm going upstairs."

"I'd best go with ye, missy," Garfield said, picking up a stray chair leg. "Don't think there is, but there may be something up there. Bats, if nothing else."

Sara shuddered but went up the steps carefully. They seemed sturdy and in good repair, other than a broken post or two. At the top, everything was dark. Garfield went ahead of her and threw open the heavy drapes that were over the windows at the end of the hall. Dust flew everywhere, and Sara was taken with a sneezing fit. When she could finally catch her breath and look around her, the dust had settled, and light was coming in through the broken panes of the window. Sara gasped as she saw a crooked picture on the wall. It was a small painting of her father, the bright blue eyes so like hers and the same almost black curls. With a small cry, she took the picture from the wall and held it as she and Garfield looked at the rooms.

The bedrooms still had furniture, although everything was filthy and there were no sheets to be seen. The curtains were still in place, although some of them were in shreds and were falling down. Everything was covered with dust. Evidently someone had been staying in the house as there were dirty dishes scattered around. What was left of Mrs.

Jones's furniture was covered with old candle wax. Mold and even more candle wax lay atop a heap of garbage.

"Don't say a word," Sara told Garfield as she tried to keep from crying. "We'll just have to clean it up."

"Be a job." Garfield looked around. "Looks like a tribe of gypsies have been here."

Sara swallowed her tears and nodded as she put the picture of her father carefully down on a small table. "I don't want to take this down and overset Mama any more than she is," she explained as she wiped the front of the painting with her fingertips. She looked at Garfield and rubbed at her eyes. "Put on a good face, Garfield."

Sara smiled brightly at everyone as she came down the stairs. "At least we'll have a place to sleep," she told them. "Although I don't think we should try the beds tonight. We'd best clean up down here and try to sleep here tonight. The beds are filthy, and we'll have to air everything before it can be used."

The twins started to cry as Mrs. Jones gave in to tears. "Now, Mama," Sara said as cheerfully as she could, "in a day or two we'll have everything right again. Tomorrow you can go see Mr. Bekins while we clean up. I'm sure there's some explanation."

Sara and Aunt Zell took charge and tried to turn cleaning up the front room into a game so the children wouldn't see how bad things really were. Sara quieted Garfield's grumbling with a look and began hauling broken furniture out the back as the dog stayed right at her heels, its tail wagging all the while. Garfield, Jack, and James set to work repairing what windows they could, taking glass from the windows of the upstairs bedrooms to fix the panes below. They repaired the front door and managed to find the back door in the weeds. By the time Aunt Zell and Mrs. Jones had laid out the last of their food as a cold supper, Sara and the children had finished what they could do to fix up the front room. It resembled nothing so much as a gypsy's camp with bedding on the floor and a small fire in the fireplace to ward off the chill of the spring night. At least, Sara thought to herself, it was a roof over their heads. There wasn't much more to say about it.

She directed James and John to bring in some chairs and tables from anyplace they could find something that wasn't broken. She went with them upstairs to search.

One room upstairs looked as if it had been used for conferences of some sort—card games, Jack said knowledgeably, as Sara gave him a quelling glance. A table stood in the middle, surrounded by most of the usable chairs in the house. The boys carried everything downstairs to the empty room Mrs. Jones said was the dining room. There they heated water for tea and made a picnic out of supper.

"At least," Mrs. Jones said as she sat in front of the blazing fire and looked around, "it's our own." Sara poured them another cup of tea and gazed around the room. The children were snuggled under blankets on the floor, the dog was draped across Sara's feet, and the fire made the room cozy. It didn't really matter what lay beyond the pool of cheerful light. "Yes, Mama, you're right. We're home," she said.

Sara had a terrible night. She slept on a pallet on the floor next to the twins. The beagle sniffed all over, then curled right up against her back. She chased it off several times, then finally gave up. The next morning, she woke from sleep dreaming that soft raindrops were falling on her face. It took her a moment to realize that the dog was licking the side of her cheek. With a sniff of disgust, she pushed it away and sat up. That was a mistake—she ached all over and her back hurt in places she didn't know she had. Worse, in the light of morning, she was dirtier than ever—a condition she hadn't thought possible—and she smelled like a beagle. She gave the dog a disgusted look and tried to shove it away, but it ignored her, hopped onto her lap, and tried to lick her face again.

Sara put the dog firmly on the floor and stood up as quickly as she could. Every bone and muscle in her body protested as she tottered to her feet, trying to keep from groaning. When she finally got upright, she stood there a moment until she was sure her body would work. Then she tiptoed around the sleeping twins and looked across the floor. Garfield had placed himself across the front doorway, making sure, as he said, that no one bothered them. Jack had done the same at the back door, and Sara carefully stepped across him and went out. Jack didn't move. The dog sniffed Jack, jumped over him, and followed Sara outside.

The early morning sun hadn't yet burned off the morning moisture, and everything sparkled. The dew clinging to the thin strands of cobwebs in the grass and weeds caught the light and glistened like a field of diamonds. Sara had never seen anything like it. A rabbit munching grass stopped what he was doing and looked warily at the beagle. The dog was busy lapping at Sara's fingers and didn't even notice it. "A fine hunter you are," Sara said, stooping to scratch the dog behind its ears as the rabbit hopped off behind the shed. The beagle promptly fell on the ground and rolled over with all four paws in the air, presenting its bony ribs and stomach for scratching. "Enough," she said with a laugh. "No more until you've had a bath." She looked down at her dress. She had knocked off most of the mud, but the dress was beyond help. "Mama said there was a pond out here, whatever your name is. If we can find it, both of us could use a cleaning."

She started off across the rubble of the rock wall and

through a freshly ploughed field as the beagle trotted along beside her, occasionally sniffing here and there. In the distance Sara could see some trees and, as she got closer, the glimmer of a small pond.

The pond was completely sheltered by willows on one side, and there were tall reeds and grasses along the rest of the marge, except for some large, flat rocks that dipped into the water. Sara made her way to the rocks and sat down, holding her knees under her chin. The pond was beautiful in the morning mist that was rising from the glistening surface in puffy wisps. Sara slipped her shoes off and touched a toe into the water. It was cold; but her feet soon became accustomed to the cold, and she inched farther into the water, washing mud from her legs and arms. The dog sat beside her and watched, wagging its tail all the while. She sniffed as the ripe hound scent wafted her way. "You need a bath as much as I do," she said, eyeing the dog. With a quick look around, she stood and stripped off her dress, then waded out into the water, carrying the dog. "Be still," she muttered to the wriggling animal as it snuggled against her and lapped at her face with its rough tongue. "You're going to drown the both of us."

Waist-deep in water, she wet the dog and tried to rub some dirt from its short fur. It jumped from her grasp and splashed in the water, finally swimming in circles around her. Sara grabbed for it, but it eluded her. "If you're not in the mood for a bath, then I am," she said, splashing water toward the dog as she gave up trying to catch it. She held her breath and ducked her body under the water, almost gasping with the shock of the cold water, then came up shaking her head. "All this bother and no soap," she said to the dog.

She had just washed yesterday's mud away when she heard a noise. Through the willow fronds, to her horror, she could see a horse and rider approaching. Quickly she made her way to the verge of the pond and snatched her clothes from the log. There wasn't time to do anything with her clothes except hold them under the water with her. She could hear the horse's hooves and the tuneless whistling of the rider as she settled down in the water behind a fallen log and sank down as far as she could, leaving only her face above the water. As the horse drew closer, the rider dismounted by the far edge of the flat rocks and led the horse to the pond to drink. Sara edged her face up so she could see over the fallen log and looked at the rider. It was, she realized to her horror, the man who had come back to help them the day before.

"What are you doing out there?" She froze at the words, then realized the man was speaking to the dog, who was still swimming in the pond. "I thought I'd gotten rid of you, you mangy cur." The man squatted down and threw a stick into the middle of the pond. "Fetch," he commanded. The dog looked at him, then at the stick, and with a joyous bark, ignored the stick and paddled toward the man. "No, fetch the stick," the man said. Instead, the dog leaped from the water right onto the man, knocking him backward into his horse.

"Damnation! You stupid cur, get off me!" The dog had placed itself on the man's head and was licking his chin. The man spluttered and tossed the dog aside, then got up. "Ruined! Another coat ruined! And for what? Every time I get around you and try to make friends, you do this." He turned to look at the dog, his fist raised. The dog looked back with trusting brown eyes and wagged its tail at him. The man lowered his fist and shook his head. "This isn't the first time, you devilish hound," he said, brushing at his face to get the water off. "What did I do to deserve this? I should know better." He got back on his horse, dripping water from his soggy cravat, and looked down at the beagle. "You've got to be the devil's own spawn," he said, shaking his head. "Lucifer incarnate." He turned the horse and looked back at the wriggling beagle. "Well, I'm through with you. Go back where you came from." With that, he was off, riding slowly around the edge of the pond. Sara slid as far down into the water as she dared without getting her mouth and nose covered. The dog came around the edge of the pond and began wagging its tail at her and making excited noises. "Get away," she hissed, one eye on the figures of the horse and rider as they rode slowly away. "Not now!"

It took forever, it seemed, for the man to disappear from sight, and Sara was blue from the cold by the time she scrambled from the water. With her teeth chattering and goose bumps on her arms, she tried to get back into her wet clothing. It took her an eternity, she thought, but finally she was covered enough to make the dash from the pond to the house. She ran through the newly ploughed field, getting dirt on her shoes again, but paying no attention. She had to get to the house and some dry clothes, no matter what.

The beagle ran along beside her on its short legs, thinking this was a new game. It darted in front of her and then behind, barking all the while. Just as she was almost out of the ploughed field, she tripped over the beagle, sending it rolling down a furrow, while she landed face first on the damp earth. "Dear God," she muttered, "he was right. You *are* the devil's own spawn."

She had started to rise when she heard the voice behind her. "This seems to be our customary way of meeting," a man said. Sara turned her head to the side and saw a horse's legs in her field of vision. As the rider dismounted, these were joined by a pair of Hessians which had been shiny this morning, but were now covered with dust, mud, and paw prints. Sara moaned ruefully as she recognized the stranger. He pulled her to her feet, his eyebrow raised as he looked at her from top to bottom. She looked down and saw that her dress was dripping water and was covered in mud. Worse, in her haste to get dressed, she had buttoned it askew. With a muddy hand, she pushed her soaking hair off her face and looked at him. She was covered in mud again. She touched her face and felt it completely coated with the freshly ploughed dirt.

The man laughed, pulled a handkerchief from his pocket, and rubbed at her face. "There, is that better?"

Sara looked at him closely. He was dark, as though he spent a great deal of time in the sun, and his eyes were light brown, almost an amber color. He was laughing at her again, and there was a dimple in his cheek. He would have been exquisitely dressed except for the dust, the water, and the dog hair on his clothes.

"Is that better?" he asked again.

Sara nodded. "Yes, thank you." She was going to say more, but he spoke again. "What are you doing here?" His tone was pleasant, but she sensed something else under it—a layer of annoyance, perhaps.

"We're staying here now," she said.

"Here? You just moved into this house without so much as a by-your-leave?"

"Yes, but—"

"And you're staying here. In that house?" He pointed toward Saint's Haven.

"Yes." Sara nodded. "You see, my mother and the children—"

"You'll have to leave," he said flatly, no longer smiling. "I've had enough trouble with this place. First there was Mr. Bekins, then Ned Perkin and all that bunch of cutthroats he ran with. When we finally got rid of them, I thought that was the end. No more. I'll have no one in that house. I'm going to tear the damn thing down anyway." He looked at Sara, his amber eyes not warm now, but rather like chips of hard, yellow quartz. "You'll have to move on. I'll give the lot of you until midmorning to get out and move on or, by God, I'll have the sheriff on you." He stepped back toward his horse. "You may be able to turn your situation, whatever it is, to an advantage with most people, but I'll not have this on my land."

"Your land?" Sara gasped. "What do you mean, your land?"

He mounted his horse and stared coldly down at her. "I mean just what I said. This is my land. I own it; I bought it in fee simple. It belongs to me and I'm telling you to leave. It's that uncomplicated. Remember what I told you—I expect you to be gone by midmorning." With that, he turned his horse and rode off, leaving Sara standing there, staring at him.

Chapter 4

Sara watched him go out of sight and, with a frown on her face, turned toward the house. The dog barked at the retreating horse and man, just to establish its territory, then turned to Sara to be petted for its good work. She patted the animal absently on the head as it tried to jump up on her. "No," she said sharply in the same tone she used for the twins.

She looked at the dog as it stood and wagged its tail at her, so excited that the whole back half of its body wiggled. "I do believe we've acquired a pet," she said aloud as the dog ran in circles around her feet. "Come on." She went into the house, the beagle following at her heels, its tail wagging all the while.

"Time to get up, Jack," she said, rousing Jack as she stepped over him. He sat on the floor and looked around, confused. "Do you want out?"

Sara laughed. "I've been out, thank you. The beagle and I took a walk this morning."

Jack sighed and leaned against the wall. "I see I'm going to have to practice staying awake."

"Nonsense." Sara turned as she heard wood splintering in the front of the house. "Everyone always sleeps better in the country. Aunt Zell says so." She and Jack laughed as she pulled Jack to his feet and they went to the front to see what was happening. Garfield was there, searching for wood to build up the fire. "I thought we might as well finish off these chairs," he said as he picked up some splintered wood that had once been chair legs.

"Burn anything that can't be saved," Sara said, stooping down by her mother and shaking her shoulder. "Mama, I need to talk to you."

Mrs. Jones sat up groggily. "What an unpleasant night, Sara," she muttered, pushing her blond hair from her face. "I don't know when I've had a worse time." She peered at Sara, then looked again. "Heavens, child! What happened to you? Is it raining?"

"No, Mama." Sara pulled her up to a sitting position. "I, uh . . . I was in the pond."

Mrs. Jones looked perplexed. "Why on earth would you do that, Sara?" She tried to rise and held her hand out to Sara. "Oh, dear, my back! Do help me."

Sara helped her up and hurried away up the stairs to change before Mrs. Jones or Garfield could ask anything else. She stopped to pick up the picture of her father from the small table. "We're going to stay here, Papa, I promise." She walked down the hall to the small room she had chosen for herself and propped the picture up on a small, rickety table beside the bed. "Mama's right— no matter how it looks now, this is home, and we're going to stay here. I promise that, and I promise I'll take care of Mama." She ran her fingers over the portrait and smiled. Finding her father's picture in the house proved it was Saint's Haven—and home. No dark stranger was going to make her leave. If he believed she would give in to his threats, she thought to herself, then he certainly didn't know Sarafina Jones!

Quickly she scrambled into a clean shift and an old blue round gown, then ran down the steps just as Garfield began brewing some tea. "We might as well wake the others," Sara said, going around and waking everyone except the twins. She wiped the teacups out and helped Garfield with the tea. As soon as everyone had a cup, she stood and tapped on a glass. "There's something we must discuss," she began, not knowing how to tell them of the stranger's claim. "I suppose the best way is just to say it." In as few words as possible, she told them of her meeting with the stranger, his claim to the property, and his order for them to move.

Mrs. Jones was incensed. "How could he?" she demanded. "I know my own house, Sara."

"I know, Mama." She hesitated. "I found proof. I found a picture of Papa upstairs."

"The little portrait his cousin Mae painted." Mrs. Jones smiled softly, remembering. "I knew it was here someplace."

"Fine," Aunt Zell said briskly, "but I doubt that a court of law would accept that as proof." She gestured to a caricature in a frame by the door. "May I remind you that we also have a drawing of King George, but the house certainly doesn't belong to him."

"I have the papers to prove it," Mrs. Jones said. "Not that it belongs to King George, but that it's ours." She looked around vaguely at the boxes and crates piled in the middle of the floor. "They're in here somewhere."

"Then I suggest we find them, Sophie," Aunt Zell said, pouring each of them another cup of tea. "We may have to produce them today when we refuse to leave. If Sara's stranger is of any consequence, he'll have the local constable on his side.''

"As arrogant as the man is, I'm sure he must run the entire village." Sara grimaced, thinking of those cold amber eyes. "I got the impression that he'd do what he thought necessary."

"Then we must find those papers." Aunt Zell put down her cup and began shoving boxes around. "Do you remember where you put them, Sophie?"

Mrs. Jones frowned as she thought. "I think they're with my knitting. I've kept Clayton's papers for years in that small carpetbag with my knitting. The deed must be in there." She frowned again and waved vaguely in the direction of a tumbled pile of possessions. "But then, it could be in the box with Sara's school papers. I don't know— I've never looked. Clayton took care of those things."

The deed wasn't in the carpetbag, or in the knitting, or with any of Sara's things. Sara divided all the possessions into piles and tore off a sheet of paper about the size of a deed to show the children what they should look for. Then she gave each of the children a box to search while she and Aunt Zell searched the trunks. Mrs. Jones was too agitated to do anything except sit and moan. "If it's here, Mama, we'll find it," Sara said grimly as she lifted the lid of a small trunk. "If you're sure you have the papers proving this place is ours, no one is going to chase us off."

"I'm sure," Mrs. Jones said in a faltering voice. "At least, I think I'm sure."

By midmorning, the room was a jumble of possessions thrown every which way, and there was still no deed. "Think, Mama," Sara implored. "Where would you have put it? Where was it when you last saw it?"

Mrs. Jones put a hand to her head. "I simply can't think, Sara dear. I need to lie down for a while, and then perhaps I can think about it."

Sara resisted the urge to shake her mama. "Please, Mama, we must—" She stopped as she heard a noise outside. Rushing to the window, she saw the stranger and another man. Her heart sank to the floor. "They're here!" she said, turning around.

"Let me at him." Jack walked toward the door, his fists held up. "I'll make him sorry he ever tried to shove us around."

Sara stepped in front of him. "That's no way, Jack." Quickly she looked around. "Aunt Zell, you stay here with Mama and take care of her. The rest of you come with me." She marched them out the front door to face the stranger. Once outside, she picked up Mary and held her. Sara and the children lined up across the front, staring defiantly at the two men.

"I see you're still here," the stranger said, raking her with a gaze. "I warned you."

"We're here and we're not leaving." Sara lifted her chin. "We own this place and we intend to stay here. You can't chase us from our own property."

"*You!* You own this!" To her surprise, he threw back his head and laughed, then turned to the other man. "Have you ever heard such gall, Chiswick?"

Chiswick grinned at them. He was older, in his fifties perhaps, heavy-set although not at all fat, and looked as though he were accustomed to having his orders obeyed. He looked like retired army to Sara from the way he sat in his saddle. "Gall's hardly the word," Chiswick said. "Why don't you tell them?"

"Tell us what?" Sara asked coldly.

The stranger ignored her. "I've told them once, but it looks as if I may need to say it again," he said to Chiswick. The tall stranger leaned over his horse's mane to look right at Sara, his eyes hard. "As I told you before, this is *my* property. I bought it and paid for it."

He looked so angry that Sara felt her heart drop to her shoes, and she involuntarily held so tightly to Mary that the child began to whimper. She forced herself to take a deep breath and loosen her hold. "I don't believe you."

His face closed and grew dark. "It matters not to me whether you do or not," he said, turning his horse. "I own this; I have the deed to prove it. I want you out of here by this afternoon."

"We're not leaving." It took every ounce of Sara's courage to face him and keep calm.

He gave her a measured look, then turned to Chiswick. "Come on, Chiswick. There's no point in wasting our time. We'll let the magistrate handle this."

"Wait!" Sara tried unsuccessfully to keep the panic out of her voice. "I'm telling you that we own this place and we can prove it. My mother has the deed for it. Saint's Haven belonged to my father."

Chiswick stopped and turned with an amazed expression on his face. "Jones?" he said, peering down at her. "You're Clayton's daughter?"

Sara tilted her chin and met his eyes. "I am. And this is our house."

Chiswick looked at her slowly, from her head to her toes and back again. "Aye, you do have the look of the Joneses. I should have seen that. You're the very picture of Clayton when he was young."

"Do you know my mother? My father?"

Chiswick nodded. "Know them well. I was able to verify Clayton's signature on the deed when I saw it. We grew up together."

The tall stranger moved on his horse again. "No matter. The place is mine now and I want to clean it up. I expect you to be out."

"We're not going." Sara made herself stand tall and look at him. If it hadn't been for the children around her, she doubted she could have done it. "Saint's Haven was my father's and it still belongs to us. We intend to stay here and turn it into an orphanage."

Chiswick laughed as he turned to the stranger. "Well, Emrys, she's got you. How are you going to turn out a house full of orphans?"

"You forget I hold the deed." Emrys looked at her coldly. "You *will* leave here."

A thought terrified Sara. What if he asked her to produce the deed she claimed to have? She decided to attack instead. "If, as you say, you own the place, I want to see your deed. My father never signed such a document, sir, and I think you're trying to steal our property."

"What!" It wasn't an exclamation; it was a roar.

"Tsk, tsk," Chiswick needled, thoroughly enjoying this. "Stealing from orphans. What next, Emrys?"

Sara pressed her small advantage. "If you have a deed, produce it, sir. This is our property, and we intend to stay here. I don't believe you have papers on it."

"I have, and I'll go get the damned things and show them to you. And the magistrate." He scowled darkly at her. "Are you coming with me, Chiswick?"

Chiswick barely glanced at him, then looked back at Sara. "Where's your mother?" he asked with a smile. The question seemed innocent enough, but Sara detected another question in it, one that wasn't asked aloud.

"She's inside. I will not allow you to disturb her." Sara glared at him.

"As I said, we're old friends," he said, still smiling. "I'd like to see her." He looked at Emrys again. "Go ahead, Emrys. I'll stay here and get reacquainted. I haven't seen . . ." His voice trailed off.

Emrys looked at Chiswick in surprise, glared again at Sara, and rode off without looking back.

Chiswick looked down at Sara. "He has a deed, you

know. I've seen it and even verified Clayton's signature on it. Unless I had some proof, I'd start packing. Emrys isn't a man to cross."

"If you knew my father as you say you did, you'd know that he loved Saint's Haven. He'd never sell it." Sara looked at Chiswick. "My mother has never signed the place away either. She has the deed."

"Your mother." A strange, small smile briefly crossed his face. "It seems strange for Sophie to have a grown daughter." He hesitated a moment. "Is she . . . is she well? I haven't seen her in many years."

"She's inside." Sara paused while Chiswick regarded her. "Would you like to come in and visit with her? I can't offer you much in the way of hospitality. It seems someone ransacked the house before we got here." She turned and marched inside, herding the children in front of her. She could hear Chiswick behind her, but didn't turn around.

Chiswick stopped, stood in the door, and looked at Mrs. Jones. He didn't seem to notice the mess. "Sophie," he said softly. His voice had an odd tone in it. "Sophie, you haven't changed at all." He stepped inside and looked around as though looking for someone. "How is Clayton?"

Mrs. Jones looked at him slowly, then smiled. "Roger?" She stood and held out her hands. "Can it really be you? What a surprise!" She stepped over some jumbled clothing and walked to Chiswick. "It's been years."

"Yes." Chiswick's voice was even. "How is Clayton?" He looked around the house.

"Clayton's been dead for a while," Mrs. Jones said softly. "I thought you knew. I wrote to Gwen."

"I'm sorry. I didn't know. Gwendolyn didn't . . . didn't mention it." He fumbled for words. "I was gone for some time. While I was away, Gwendolyn had . . . Gwendolyn has . . ." He paused and swallowed hard. "Gwendolyn has had some problems for many years. She stays at home in her room most of the time. It's often difficult for her . . . to talk very much.''

"I'm sorry to hear it." Mrs. Jones turned. "Sara, meet your father's greatest friend, Roger Chiswick."

"We've met," Sara said briefly. "Mr. Chiswick accompanied the man who was demanding that we leave." She looked at Chiswick, but he said nothing. He was still looking at Mrs. Jones in that odd way. Sara stepped between them. "Mama, we've got to find that deed. You must remember where you put it last. The stranger—what did you call him, Mr. Chiswick?"

"Emrys."

"Old Lord Emrys?" Mrs. Jones asked, surprised. "Lord, he must be, what now, seventy? I recall that he didn't get married until he was in his forties and then only because he came into the estate."

"The old lord died in 1810," Chiswick told her, pulling up a chair. He put it on the floor and shook it to see if it would hold him, then offered it to Mrs. Jones. "This is his son, Evan. A sad case if there ever was one." He sat down opposite her and looked at her, the strange, small smile on his face again. "And have you come to stay, Sophie?"

"Yes. We intend to turn Saint's Haven into an orphanage."

"Your daughter mentioned an orphanage." Chiswick looked around with a grin. "I was afraid for a moment that all these were yours. Do I take it that you brought the orphans with you?"

Mrs. Jones laughed. "Sara is mine. Don't you think she looks like her father?"

Chiswick nodded. "I noted it when she first told me her parentage." He looked carefully at Sara. "She has Clayton's blue eyes and dark hair, Sophie, but I think she has your mouth. And your charm." He stopped, and there was an embarrassed pause as he turned his hat in his big hands.

Mrs. Jones smiled at him and touched his arm lightly. "Where are you and Gwen living now, Roger?" Sara kept making faces at her, trying to get her attention, but Mrs. Jones ignored her.

"In the old house near the bridge. The house we had— the big house—burned while I was away. I joined the army right after you left."

Mrs. Jones nodded. "Clayton told me that you planned to join. I always hoped the best for you, Roger, as did Clayton." She smiled at him. "I was so pleased when I heard that you had married Gwendolyn and settled into your father's house."

"When it burned, Gwendolyn barely escaped." He paused and grimaced at the painful memory. "Instead of trying to rebuild, I just redid the old house. We have no children, so we really didn't need anything larger. I left the army and came home to live as that was the time when . . . when Gwendolyn was having some difficulty. We've lived there since. That way, I can keep a watch on her."

"Is she in poor health?" Sara asked politely, hoping to get rid of Chiswick so she could get her mother back onto the topic of the deed.

"You might say that." Chiswick turned his hat in his hands again. "Emrys says he owns this place, Sophie. I believe him."

Mrs. Jones laughed. "Don't be silly, Roger. I know Clayton didn't sign the place away, and I certainly haven't. We'd never sell Saint's Haven."

"Emrys bought it," Chiswick said doggedly. "I saw the deed myself when young Bekins brought it by with Clayton's signature on it."

"Bekins?" Sara was horrified as she turned to her

mother. "Mama, did you sign anything for Mr. Bekins? Anything at all?"

Mrs. Jones frowned. "Of course I did, Sara. Mr. Bekins is always sending me things to sign—or at least he used to. I haven't received a thing from him for a long while." She frowned and looked up in amazement. "It must be a year or more."

Chiswick looked troubled. "There's a reason for that. Bekins—the old man—has been dead for over a year. His son, a sorry lot if there ever was one, took over his management, went through everything Bekins had managed to save. There was talk about it, but I never really heard anything except innuendo." He shrugged. "At any rate, young Bekins spent everything his father had and then left the country."

"But not before he sold Saint's Haven to Emrys," Sara said slowly.

Chiswick nodded. "Aye, I'm thinking that's what happened."

"Impossible. Mr. Bekins had no authority to do anything of the sort." Mrs. Jones shook her head. "And I'd certainly know if I signed anything as important as a deed, Sara. Do give me some credit. Saint's Haven is ours and that's all there is to it. Lord Emrys will just have to accept that fact."

"He's gone to get *his* deed," Sara said hollowly.

"No matter." Mrs. Jones reached for her knitting and began to knit and purl. "Our deed is perfectly good."

"Perhaps it would be—if we knew where it was," Sara said. "Mama, for heaven's sake, put that down and try to think. Where was the deed the last time you saw it?"

When Mrs. Jones declared that she had no idea at all, the entire family began another search through their possessions while Chiswick stood by, offering his assistance. After a futile half hour, Sara was ready to cry. "Mama, do try to remember! When did you see it last?"

Mrs. Jones frowned and put her knitting to one side. "I think it was right after Clayton's funeral. Yes, I'm sure it was. I had wanted to wear my black dress, and I did, but it was so very hot that day. I remember looking for my handkerchief and seeing the deed in the drawer." She paused and smiled briefly at Sara. "You looked so perfect in your dress that day. Your father would have been proud."

"The deed, Mama. It was in with your handkerchiefs?"

"Yes, let me think. I was looking for that linen handker-chief." She shook her head. "I got out the deed and put it on top of the dresser. I can almost see it in my mind."

There was a muffled shout outside, and Garfield leaned over to look out the window. "Ye'd better be seeing it in more than your mind, Miz Jones. Here comes Lord Emrys with a paper in his hand, and he looks fit to fight with the devil!"

Chapter 5

Sara dashed to the door and flung it open, running outside to intercept Emrys before he could come inside and overset the others. The beagle ran outside with her, but this time, it sat down on its haunches on the weedy walkway and looked warily at Emrys.

"Packing, I trust?" Emrys asked, catching a glimpse of the jumbled interior of the house.

"We don't intend to leave. This is our home." Sara caught a faint tremor in her voice and could have kicked herself for it. She hadn't felt afraid at all when she ran out. It was, she told herself, just that Emrys looked so forbidding on his black horse. He was all dressed in black as usual, and his expression, as Garfield had pointed out, did make him look as if he was ready to take on the devil. Sara took a deep breath and squared her shoulders. She wasn't afraid of Emrys or any man, she reminded herself.

Still, she was relieved when Garfield came out of the house and stood beside her. Just knowing he was there made her feel better.

Emrys dismounted lazily, glancing with what appeared to be amusement at Chiswick's horse still tethered to a bush. *"Your home?"* He walked over to stand in front of her and smiled at her. The smile didn't show up in his eyes—they were still yellow-rock cold. "We'll see about that," he said, drawing a small packet of papers from his waistcoat. "What I have here, madam . . ."

"It's miss, if you please. Miss Sarafina Jones."

He gave her another cold smile. "Very well, Miss Jones. What I have here is the deed to Saint's Haven, duly signed by the owner, Clayton Jones, and witnessed by Geoffrey Bekins. As a precaution, before I actually made the purchase, I asked Roger Chiswick to verify the signature since he had been well acquainted with Mr. Jones. Mr. Chiswick said he believed the signature to be genuine." He handed her the packet of papers which was secured by a black ribbon.

Sara pulled at the ribbon and snarled it, drawing it into a knot. After two or three attempts, Emrys reached for the papers. His fingers touched her hand, and she looked up at him in surprise, his eyes once again reminding her of cold chips of ice. "Let me do it, Miss Jones," he said impatiently.

"I'm perfectly capable of opening a packet, my lord," Sara said through gritted teeth as she pulled at the ribbon. It wouldn't budge; all she was doing was pulling the knot tighter. With a flash of anger, she jerked the ribbon, still knotted, from the packet, taking off the corner of one of the papers. Emrys picked up the scrap that floated to the ground and looked at it. "No harm done," he said silkily. "It's blank."

It occurred to Sara that Emrys thought she was trying to shred his so-called deed, and she started to deny it. She caught herself before she spoke—if Emrys thought that, nothing she could say would change his mind, and she wasn't going to get involved in an argument with him. Any more of an argument, she amended to herself.

She forced herself to look at Emrys and smile. "Good, I was afraid I had damaged it."

"Heaven forbid." Emrys smiled again, not pleasantly.

Sara gritted her teeth as she ignored him and began looking through the papers. She handed the under papers, which looked rather like maps, to Garfield and opened the top paper. Her heart sank as she glanced at the bottom and saw her father's familiar signature. As she looked at it, she felt the blood rush from her face. "It can't be," she muttered to Garfield, "it simply can't be!"

Emrys reached for the deed, but she turned away, the paper in her hand. "My father would never do this. We certainly didn't receive a penny for the property. Something has to be wrong." She looked up at Garfield. "Go get Mama and Aunt Zell. They need to see this." Garfield rolled up the map and silently went into the house. Sara forced herself to look Emrys right in the eyes as she waited. He was smiling smugly.

Mrs. Jones came out accompanied by Mr. Chiswick. Without a word, Sara handed her the deed, pointing to the signature. Mrs. Jones looked shaken. "Clayton did sign this!" she gasped. "It can't be! Clayton would never do such a thing without telling us!"

"It appears he did." Emrys' voice was smooth as silk, and there was a hint of a triumphant smile playing around his lips. "Now, if you'll just give me back my deed, I'll leave and let you attend to your packing. I want you out of here before nightfall."

"But where will we go?" Mrs. Jones wailed. "Roger, how can you let him do this?"

"If he has a good deed, Sophie, there's not a thing I or anyone else can do. It's his property." He looked helplessly at Mrs. Jones. "I verified that signature myself. I was certain it was Clayton's, but to be sure, we compared it to some old letters I had. It looked just the same." He turned, his hands palms up. "Saint's Haven belongs to him, Sophie."

Emrys moved back a step, his newly polished Hessians picking up dust from the weeds. "Yes, and I think I'll not wait to tear this place down. After all this rain, I can burn the thing tomorrow and nothing else will catch. Yes, that's what I'll do."

Mrs. Jones collapsed in Mr. Chiswick's arms.

Sara glanced over at her mother to make sure she was all right. Mr. Chiswick held her and was picking her up to take her into the house as the dog began wriggling excitedly. Sara rounded on Emrys. "How dare you!" she spat at him. "To come in here like this and think you can order us around!"

"As long as you're squatting here, I have every right to order you around, Miss Jones. Don't forget—I happen to own this place." The man's calm was infuriating.

"You don't! I'm sure of that." Sara took a deep breath and tried to control herself. "That may be my father's signature, but I'm sure there's something amiss here." She opened the deed again and looked at it. The signature hadn't changed. It was still her father's carefully rounded penmanship. "Clayton Jones," she read slowly aloud. "It just can't be. He always planned to come back here to live. He wouldn't sell it. I know he wouldn't do such a thing without telling us."

"He did." Emrys reached over and plucked the deed from her fingers, then held out his hand for the map. Garfield handed him the map of the boundary lines and frowned, but Emrys ignored him. "So, Miss Jones, I'm afraid you'll have to admit defeat." He smoothed the map, folded the papers, worked the black ribbon back over the packet, and glanced up at the sky then back at the children. "Very well, I'm not an unreasonable man, whatever you may think, and, since it's late today, I will allow you another night here. However, I insist you be gone tomorrow. I'll bring the magistrate with me when I come to burn the place." He looked at her, his eyes hard again. "Do you understand?"

Sara stared right back at him. "I understand that I'm not going anywhere until I'm forced to do so. My father didn't sell this house, I'm sure of it. I don't know what kind of chicanery you employed, Lord Emrys, but I don't intend to let you take our property."

He turned to mount his horse as the beagle sniffed at his boots. Emrys nudged it out of the way and turned to look back at Sara as the dog sat down in front of her. "There's nothing you can do except leave, Miss Jones. My deed is good." He struck his palm with the packet of papers, making a sharp sound. The dog jumped straight up and threw itself against Emrys, knocking him back into his horse. The horse shied and danced away, rearing in the air. It took Emrys a good five minutes to catch and calm him. When he finally had the horse under control, he turned back to Sara, and she was extraordinarily pleased to see Emrys was sweating and his cravat was rumpled. "Damned devil dog," Emrys snapped. "You can take that thing with you when you go or I'll take care of it myself. I've had enough of it." Catching his tone, the beagle cowered beside Sara and stuck its nose under the hem of her gown.

"We, too, have had enough, Lord Emrys," Sara said, trying to keep from smiling at Emrys' appearance. "Not of the dog, however, but of your tricks. I don't know what deception you used to claim this land, but I intend to find out." She reached down and patted the dog. "There, there, Lucifer," she murmured, scratching him behind his ear. "Ignore him. I'll take care of you."

Emrys mounted his horse and looked down at her, his eyes almost molten. "There's no chicanery on my part,

Miss Jones. I bought the place and paid for it." He glared
at her. "Tomorrow, Miss Jones. I'll be here with the magistrate and my men, and I expect to find an empty house."
Without waiting for her reply, he turned and urged his
horse to a gallop. In just a few seconds, he was out of sight.

Sara finally let herself go and sagged against the weedy
side of the house. "Now what?" she said aloud, her voice
breaking.

"God helps those who helps themselves," Garfield said
with a shrug. "Mayhap we need to see the local parson."
He looked at Sara. "Mayhap we need to find our deed or
at least a letter to see if the signatures match, although
Mr. Chiswick seemed certain of it." He shook his head.
"I don't know letters, but it looked the same to me."

"I'm almost certain of it," Sara said sadly, "and I can't
understand it at all."

"There's a man in London who could copy the Prince's
signature if he wanted to. Some of them are that good,
missy."

"Do you think so? How could we prove a forgery?"

Garfield shrugged. "I don't know how we could do it,
but I do think something's amiss," Garfield said, holding
out his rough hand to her. "Come on, missy, put a smile
on. We've got to go inside and figure out a way to stay
here."

Sara took his callused hand and smiled. "Garfield, you're
wonderful."

"I know." He stood aside so Sara could go in the door. "I
also don't wish to make that muddy trip back to London."

Inside, Mrs. Jones sat in her chair, pale and moaning. Mr.
Chiswick fanned her vigorously, and the odor of burned
feathers filled the room. "Don't worry, Mama," Sara said,
patting her mother's shoulder. "We're going to stay until
he forces us off."

"That may be tomorrow." Chiswick looked worried. "Emrys gets what he wants around here."

"That seems to include Saint's Haven," Sara said with a touch of bitterness. "Mama, do you have a letter from Papa somewhere that we could use? When Emrys comes back tomorrow, I want to compare the signatures." She paused. "It might be a forgery. If it is, there should be some sort of tiny difference. We just have to find it." She looked around. "In the meantime, let's clean up in here and try to set the place to rights. I don't know about the rest of you, but I vote to stay if we possibly can. I think wherever he is, Papa wants us to be here." She paused a second. "It may be easier to argue our case with the magistrate if we don't look like a bunch of vagabonds."

Jack looked around and nodded. "Home," he said simply. Sara could have hugged him, but she'd had to stop that when he was twelve. He had whispered to her that it embarrassed him. Jack sensed her mood and moved, reaching over and putting his arm around the dog.

"His name's Lucifer," Sara said. "I think we should keep him, don't you? He doesn't seem to get along with Emrys any better than we do."

Jack smiled up at her and scratched the beagle. Lucifer, as though he knew what they were saying, wagged his tail and barked, then lapped the side of Jack's face until Jack rolled on the floor.

Chiswick looked around the room and walked over to the doorway to see the back rooms. "It's going to take more than some women and children to clean this up," he said. He paused, then sighed. "I don't want to get on the bad side of Emrys, but you do need help. I have a man I've hired recently, and I'll bring him over this afternoon."

"You don't need to do that, Roger, but I thank you for it." Mrs. Jones looked at him with gentle eyes.

"I do need to." He looked back at her with an unreadable expression. "Clayton and I were friends, and you and I. . . . Just say that I feel obligated as a friend." He turned to Sara. "The man's name is Edward Moore, and perhaps you might consider keeping him for a short while. He's been with me for a fortnight now. He's an excellent worker, but I. . . . He was in the army, and he was wounded and doesn't remember very much; but he's a willing worker." He paused. "I ordinarily wouldn't have hired someone who just came by looking for work; but Gwendolyn's been very . . . ill, and I needed an extra hand. He's given me no cause for regret, but I can't keep him on." He looked apologetic. "Gwendolyn's taken him into dislike for some reason, so I'm going to have to let him go. As an old army man myself, I'd like to see another army man find a post, though, if I could."

"I don't think we should." Sara hesitated. "We can't pay him," she finally blurted out.

Chiswick shook his head. "I don't think that's necessary. The man told me he wanted to work for just room and board until he got on his feet. I give him enough for spending money, but it doesn't add up to much of a wage." He glanced back at the doors and windows in disrepair. "I know you're reluctant, but if he wants a small wage, I'll be glad to take care of it for a fortnight or so." He held his hand up as Sara started to protest. "Just look at the condition of the house. Even if you just stay here the night, you need help with this."

Sara looked at her mother and Aunt Zell, but they said nothing. Sara sighed and thought about their finances. Her father had always been adamant that it was better to give than receive, but this seemed to be the exception. "Thank you so much for your offer," she said to Chiswick. "It's very kind of you. We'll certainly consider it."

True to his word, Chiswick returned with Edward Moore, and the two of them set to work, cleaning up broken panes of glass and bits of wood. By unspoken agreement, no one wanted to replace the glass or make any permanent repairs. That would have to wait until they saw what Emrys would do.

Edward Moore seemed, as Chiswick had said, a willing worker. He was fairly young, younger than Sara had expected. He appeared to be in his late twenties and had dark brown hair and brown eyes. His hair wasn't cut fashionably, and had a touch of curl to it. His eyes were warm, and he smiled often at something the boys or Chiswick said to him. His smile was as warm as his eyes, but there was more—a hint of recklessness or even of danger. Sara thought that perhaps the army had bred that into him.

By evening, the place had been put to some semblance of order inside, and Garfield and Jack had even cleaned some of the weeds from the yard. "Another six months and this place might be presentable," Sara said to Briget as the two of them stood and watched Mary and Matthew play. "This is a wonderful place for all of you. Yes, you included," she said, looking down at the dog. Lucifer—a misnomer if there ever was one, she thought—had settled right in. In one short afternoon, he had become a part of the family.

"Do you think Lord Emrys will make us leave?" Briget sounded truly worried. "Where will we go?"

"Don't you worry." Sara reached over and gave her a hug.

"I can't help it, Sara. Aunt Zell says that God will provide, but I'm not so sure. Is that blasphemy?"

Sara laughed. "I don't think so. And let's do hope that God will provide. Let's go inside now and see if there's anything to eat." She tried to sound lighthearted, but her mind was asking the same questions Briget had asked: what would Emrys do and, if he made them leave, where would they go? In spite of her smile, there were no answers.

The next morning, Emrys was there as promised. He had several men with him, two or three of them carrying unlit torches. There was another man with him who was about the age of Roger Chiswick. This man, however, had a hard look about him, much like a man who had never laughed. "This is Squire Sherman," Emrys said, dismounting in front of the house. "He's the magistrate."

Squire Sherman dismounted and stood beside Emrys. "I understand you dispute the deed Lord Emrys has in his possession." It was a statement, not a question.

"That's right." Sara lifted her chin, hoping no one would see her fingers tremble. Lucifer sat down beside her and didn't move. "I don't know how Lord Emrys came by that deed, but I don't believe my father would sell the house from under us."

"It's been done before." Squire Sherman turned toward Emrys. "Do you have the contested document with you?"

Emrys produced the deed from the pocket of his waistcoat. He was all dressed in black again, his waistcoat embroidered in gray. As he untied the deed and pulled it from the packet, he happened to see Mary and Matthew playing in the yard, making flower chains. His eyes softened into amber for a moment; then, as if he caught himself, he forced his expression to become blank, and his eyes once again turned cold and yellow. "You'll see that everything is in order," he said, handing the deed to Squire Sherman.

"Is this your father's signature?" Squire Sherman frowned and pointed to the name.

"It looks like it, but I'm not sure. I have a letter of my father's to use for comparison." She handed Sherman the letter and watched anxiously as he opened it. He held the deed and letter side by side. Sara felt her hopes crash as she looked and saw that the signatures looked the same.

"It can't be." Sara shook her head. "I refuse to believe it."

"It's true, Miss Jones," Sherman said. "You're going to have to vacate. This deed proves that Clayton Jones sold this property to Lord Emrys in January."

Sara's head snapped up so abruptly that her curls fell into her eyes. She pushed them back quickly, heedless of how she looked. "January? Let me see that!" She reached for the deed, but Emrys was faster. He took the paper from Sherman. "Don't think you're going to be tearing this up, Miss Jones," he said.

"I'm not going to tear anything up. You may even hold it if you like. All I want to see is my father's signature and the date."

Emrys held the deed up so she could see it, and Sara broke into a broad smile. "Mama, Garfield." She stepped to the door and called inside. "Come here, please."

Mrs. Jones tottered out of the house. "Is it over, Sara? Are we to stay or go?" Her voice was weak.

"I think we may be staying, Mama. Come here." She motioned to her mother. "Mama, tell Squire Sherman and Lord Emrys when Papa died."

Mrs. Jones put a hand to her head. "Don't make me dredge up sorrowful memories, Sara. You know how it distresses me."

"Mama." Sara was firm and put her hand on her mother's arm. "Tell them when Papa died. It wouldn't hurt to tell them where he died and from what."

"You know how trying this is for me." Mrs. Jones put her handkerchief to her eyes and dabbed. "Clayton died of fever while we were in Africa as missionaries. I'll never forget the date—he died June 6, 1803." She put her hand over her eyes. "You know all of this, Sara. Why do you ask?"

Sara looked at Emrys as the significance of the date sunk

in. "Yes, Lord Emrys, you've been taken. I'm sure you get whatever you want around the village of St. Claire, but even Lord Emrys can't purchase land from a man who's been dead for almost eleven years. Exactly what are you trying to do? Forgery is against the law."

Emrys paled, then turned the full force of his cold yellow gaze on her. "I'm well aware of that, Miss Jones, and I assure you that I've never done anything dishonest in my life. I purchased the land from Mr. Bekins, and I bought it in good faith. If he was acting in some way as the agent for your father's estate, then the land is still mine."

"No." Sara hoped her voice was as cold as his. "It belongs to us until you can prove otherwise. You'll just have to get your money back from Mr. Bekins."

"He's been gone for months," Squire Sherman said, annoyance vying with distaste in his voice. "I can't let you take possession until this is clear," he said to Emrys. "We'll have to find Bekins and discover his authorization to sell the property."

"I realize that." Emrys' lips were compressed into a tight line. "This isn't over, Miss Jones. I've wanted this property for years, and I intend to have it."

"Is that a threat, Lord Emrys?" Sara asked, more lightly than she felt.

"No." He looked down at her. "I'm merely suggesting that you don't get too comfortable here. You may have to leave at any moment." He motioned for his men to ride away and waited until Squire Sherman was mounted. "This is no place for unprotected women and children, Miss Jones. As you may have heard, while I was in London this winter, Ned Perkin and his gang stayed here and plagued the countryside. Ned, so I hear, promised to come back for some loot he left buried here somewhere. What will you do then?"

"The Lord will provide," Aunt Zell said cheerfully, stepping up and scooping Mary up from the yard. She brushed the dirt from Mary's pinafore and put her back down. "That's what we always say."

"I only hope He does. Don't count on assistance from me." Emrys mounted his horse, gave them a last cold look, and rode away.

Garfield looked at Emrys' retreating back as he rode away, his black horse gleaming in the morning sun. "That's a man that's not used to being crossed," Garfield said. "We'll hear from him all right."

"No matter." Sara couldn't keep the glee from her voice. "What can he do?"

"Don't get too cocky there, missy," Garfield said. "There's ways."

Sara ignored Garfield's gloom as the family stood in the yard and watched in silence while Emrys rounded the bend in the road. The second he was out of sight, they turned to each other, hugging each other and whooping for joy. Even Jack joined in and Lucifer jumped on him. In a few moments, Sara, all the children, and the dog were jumbled up in a pile, hugging each other.

"Do you know," Jack said to Sara as they all stood back up and looked at what they now regarded as their house, "the next time I see that snooty lord, I think I'll just plant him a facer."

"Don't you dare." Sara laughed and squeezed his shoulder. "Although I confess I'd like to do it myself." They all laughed as they went inside to plan their day's work.

Garfield touched Sara's shoulder as they let the others pass. "Edward Moore's coming back today," he said thoughtfully. "Do you want to go ahead and offer him a place here for a while? I think it might be a good idea as he said he'd work here for room and board until he gets back on his feet. He said yesterday that he can't stay any longer at Chiswick's. It seems Mrs. Chiswick's touched in the head and has decided Moore is Napoleon or some such.''

"The poor woman." Sara frowned. "We can't pay him, Garfield, and in spite of Mr. Chiswick's kind offer, I don't want to take his charity.''

"I know that. Your mother told Chiswick that we couldn't accept that." He frowned slightly, obviously disapproving. "At any rate, Moore has to leave Chiswick's since he and Chiswick's missus don't get along, and right now, he doesn't have a place to go. I think it would be a good idea to talk to the man since he said he'd stay for just board and a place to sleep. He says he's going back to his family before long—as soon as he remembers them, at any rate.'' Garfield looked around at the weeds and disrepair. "Jack, James, and John are help; but another man would make a difference, and we do need to get the place fixed up. It doesn't seem so now, but winter will be here before we know it.''

"All right, Garfield. You talk to him." Sara's gaze followed his. "Another man on the place might not be a bad idea." She bit her lower lip and frowned as she thought.

"What's wrong, missy? Are you thinking about the highwayman—Perkin?''

Sara sighed. "I don't think he'll bother us. We don't have anything, and I'm sure all that story about hidden loot is just another village tale.'' She paused as she thought. "No, Garfield, I'm worried that our troubles will come in another form." She looked down the empty road. "In spite of what I said in front of Mama and the others, I'm afraid we haven't heard the last of Lord Emrys.''

Chapter 6

Garfield wasted no time in informing Edward Moore that everyone would be delighted to have him at Saint's Haven, and asking him if he wished to stay there. By nightfall, the man was bedded down in a room at the side of the stables that had been untouched by the fire. Garfield seemed relieved to have him around. "The poor man," Sara had said when Garfield discussed with her that Edward Moore didn't know where his family was or really didn't even remember much about his past. All he could remember, Moore told her, was his name and a vague recollection that he had been in St. Claire before. He hoped to recover his memory enough to find his family. If he didn't answer her sometimes when she called his name, he explained, it was because he couldn't remember. "Then, too," he added, almost as an afterthought, "the noise of the cannon firing did something to my ears. Sometimes I don't hear things as I should."

"I do believe he's of good birth," Aunt Zell said to Mrs. Jones as they sat sorting out their knitting yarns in the late afternoon. Lucifer had received a suitable chastising for snarling the yarn, and Sara had to sit and help untangle it. Lucifer draped himself across her feet and didn't seem at all penitent.

"Do you mean Mr. Moore—that is, Edward? He asked that we call him Edward rather than Mr. Moore. The poor man said he wanted to feel a part of the family." Mrs. Jones gave up on a knot and snipped the thread with her scissors.

Aunt Zell nodded. "Yes, of course. He is a member of our family now. He told me he was a captain in the army and was wounded. The poor boy." She paused. "I think he'll fit in nicely here. It will be good for the children to see how someone with no family makes the best of things."

"He does seem a fine young man," Mrs. Jones agreed. Lucifer stretched, rolled over on Mrs. Jones's feet and sighed contentedly. Mrs. Jones wrinkled her nose as Lucifer jumped, then sat up and began scratching furiously. "Sara, I do believe your dog needs a bath. Perhaps you should leave the yarn to us and do it now. I'm not sure I can sleep another night with that hound smell in the house."

Sara looked down at the tangled yarn and then at Lucifer. A few minutes with a wet dog was preferable to spending the rest of the afternoon sitting inside untangling skeins of yarn, so she dropped her yarn and whistled for Lucifer to follow her out the back door. She got some soap and headed for the pond, passing Edward and Garfield working hard clearing weeds in the back. Sara waved to them as she went by. Garfield grunted her way, but Edward gave her his rakish smile and a wave. Sara didn't look back, but she felt his gaze on her back as she walked away.

At the pond, Lucifer thought he was in for another swim and waited patiently for Sara to take off her dress. "Not this time," she told him, grabbing him by the paws and dunking him. Lucifer spluttered and promptly drenched

Sara with pond water as she lost her grip on him. She grabbed him again and began lathering him with the soap. "This is French milled, you unappreciative dog," she muttered, trying her best to hang on to the slippery animal. "You're going to smell like lavender when I'm finished." The beagle didn't seem impressed.

Finally Sara rinsed him completely and pulled Lucifer from the water. He seemed smaller and more ragged-looking, so she quickly toweled him off. He shook hard and splattered the few dry spots left on her clothing. She turned to say something to the dog and saw Emrys leaning against a nearby tree trunk, watching her. His black horse was nibbling grass contentedly beside him.

"Well, Miss Jones," he said, walking toward her, "have you managed to tame the devil's own cur?"

Sara lifted her chin. "Of course. Meet Lucifer, our new dog."

"Lucifer, is it then?" Emrys laughed as he looked at the drenched beagle. His gaze shifted from the dog to Sara's soaked dress. "It seems your Lucifer gave as well as got," he said with a grin. Sara glanced down at her dress and was mortified. The sopping cloth clung to every curve and hollow of her body. She pulled her dress away from her skin as much as she could and wracked her brain for something to say that would divert Emrys. Those amber eyes seemed to see right through the soaked cloth.

"And what brings you here?" she finally asked, edging as close to a bush as she dared. Lucifer, drat him, was frisking around as he dried off, nipping at her heels, running off, and then dashing back.

"Several things," Emrys said. "First, I wished to talk to your mother—or to you, if you prefer. I regret that our acquaintance began with such a contretemps." He paused, but Sara didn't say anything. She realized a similar comment was called for—just one of those polite murmurings others were so good at saying—but she had never been very good at hiding her feelings under a polite veneer. Still, she was cudgeling her brain for something to say when Emrys continued. "At any rate, I want to do the right thing, of course."

"I don't see that there is anything else you can do," Sara said. "The date on the deed is clearly wrong. Saint's Haven belongs to us."

Emrys looked at her, a swift flash of irritation crossing his face. However, he erased it quickly and smiled at her. Sara noted that his eyes had changed from amber to yellow ice again, despite the smile on his face. "I don't relinquish my claim to Saint's Haven, Miss Jones. After all, I bought it and paid for it in good faith, believing that Bekins was an agent for your father as his father had been before him. My contention is that in selling me the property, he was acting on instructions your father had at one time given to him or to the elder Mr. Bekins. I am, however, willing to allow you to stay at Saint's Haven until the matter is resolved in the courts."

"The courts?" Sara's voice was faint. Wherever would they get the money to fight Emrys in the courts? she wondered.

Emrys nodded. "I think perhaps we could have this settled within a month or two. In the meantime, I realize you and your . . . your family have no other accommodations, so I'm agreeable to you staying at Saint's Haven." There was another pause, but Sara said nothing. Something didn't ring true with what Emrys was saying, but she couldn't put a name to whatever was bothering her.

Emrys waited for a moment, then continued. "I realize the place is in disrepair—as I told you, I plan to burn it as soon as possible—so if you wish to move on, just let me know and I'll assist you in any way I can."

Sara finally realized what had struck her as peculiar

about his speech. It sounded just like that—a speech. It was as though he had deliberated about what to say and was now saying it. The man, she thought to herself, must already think himself in court. Worse, he probably didn't mean a word of what he was saying.

"Thank you, Lord Emrys," she said coolly. "Your concern is appreciated, but I don't think you need to worry about disposing of the place. Since Saint's Haven does belong to us, we plan to stay."

He gave her just a flash of a grin, and this time the smile touched his eyes as they turned to warm amber. "Somehow, Miss Jones, I thought you might say that."

"Yes." There didn't seem to be anything else to say. "Good day, Lord Emrys. I really must get back. I'll tell my mother what you've said, but I doubt we'll have time to discuss this with you. We understood that everything was settled, and, as you may imagine, there's a great deal to do—not only the repairs, but making all the children feel at home and providing for them."

Emrys picked up his horse's reins, and Sara thought he would mount and ride away; but instead he began walking beside her toward Saint's Haven. "There's more than a great deal to do regarding the repairs, Miss Jones. The place is falling apart. I don't know what the house looked like before, but I was in there when we searched for Ned Perkin and his bunch. They had been there for weeks, and the place was a shambles."

"Ned Perkin? I've been here only two days and already I've heard a dozen stories about the infamous Mr. Perkin. I don't really believe the man could have done everything attributed to him unless he'd spent many years doing it. He'd have to be seventy, at least." She looked right into Emrys' eyes. "I'm not afraid of Ned Perkin—from what I hear, he's just another country outlaw."

Emrys nodded. "That's putting it mildly."

Sara tossed her damp hair back from her face. "I assure you, Lord Emrys, that we certainly aren't afraid of any local outlaw. You forget that we've been living in London, where evil abounds. Pickpockets, cutpurses, murderers, what have you. If there ever was a place for learning about outlaws, it's that city." Sara picked her way across the field. Her brogans had gotten wet, and now mud was sticking to them.

"I agree with you about London," he said, pausing as she scraped her shoes against a rock. "However, Ned Perkin is not to be termed a petty outlaw. Furthermore, he's hardly a country bumpkin," Emrys said, amused at her attempts to knock the mud from her shoes. "He primarily did his thievery elsewhere and hid out here, I understand. Rumor has it that he's done worse than thievery—some even saying he's committed murder." He reached out quickly and steadied Sara's elbow as she tottered on one foot. She glanced at him, startled. He caught her look, and a touch of embarrassment crossed his face. He quickly moved his hand as soon as she steadied herself, then put his hands behind his back as he walked with her. "As for Perkin, I know the Bow Street Runners were after him, but couldn't catch him. They ran him to earth near here, but got no farther." His voice was sounding strange again, almost that same rehearsed tone, Sara thought.

"And?" she prompted as he paused.

Emrys shrugged. "It seems he had some relatives here who helped him. Bold as brass, he's always been. This last time he came through, he set himself up at Saint's Haven as though he owned the place."

"I believe someone said Perkin had hidden part of his loot here," Sara said. "I don't see how. There's nothing left—no place at all." She glanced over at the partially burned tables. "Is Perkin the one who burned the stable?"

Emrys reddened slightly under his olive complexion. "No, I'm afraid I did that. Not on purpose, of course."

"Of course." She gave him a frankly skeptical look.

"I would never burn something on purpose." He seemed offended.

"Didn't you say you intended to burn Saint's Haven?"

There was a pause. "Touché, Miss Jones. What I meant is that I would never burn a useful building on purpose." He turned to look down at her. "Don't say what I know you're going to." He chuckled, and Sara was surprised— it was the first time she had heard him laugh. "Back to the burning of the stables—we were this close to catching Perkin—" he held up two fingers close together—"and Chiswick said he thought the man was in the stable. We were running to the stable, and I thought I saw a man darting inside the door. I fired my pistol."

"And?" Sara prompted as he paused.

Emrys frowned. "I don't know what could have happened, but I finally decided that the ball must have ignited the wood. After all, the stable was an old building and dry as tinder." He sighed. "At any rate, in just a few moments, the entire end of the building was burning heavily."

"And you just let it burn? You didn't try to save it?"

He looked at her, offended. "Of course not. As I said, I would never allow a building to burn if it wasn't necessary. We tried to save it, as you can see. We contained the fire in this end and saved the rest. And it wasn't easy to get water, considering the shape the well was in."

They stood in silence while Sara thought about the fire. "Could Ned Perkin have set it?" she asked.

"That's what I thought at first, because in the confusion, if he ever was there, Ned Perkin escaped. I finally decided that he didn't have time to start the fire."

"Perhaps it was already burning and you just hadn't seen it yet."

He raised an eyebrow. "A good point. I didn't think the flames could spread that fast either. Some weeks later, when Chiswick and I were discussing it, Chiswick's man Moore told me that he had seen such a phenomenon when he was in the army." He glanced at the stable. "The worst thing was that Perkin escaped. I hoped to catch him and kept a guard on the property for a while, only removing it during the past week." He grimaced slightly.

"I take it that you wish you had left the guard in place so he could have prevented us from moving in?" Sara couldn't resist.

"Of course not," he said hastily. His protest was cut short as the beagle shot by them, knocking Emrys to the side. Lucifer ran straight to the kitchen garbage and began rolling over and over in it.

"Lucifer! Stop that!" Sara dashed over to the beagle. She was too late. Lucifer was covered with kitchen waste, and the odor was terrible.

Behind her, she heard Emrys laugh. "I'm afraid, Miss Jones, that you've set yourself an impossible task. No one I know has ever been able to teach parlor manners to a beagle."

Sara glanced down at the lavender soap in her hand and back to the dog who was now shaking himself off. Lucifer ran to her and tried to rub himself against her dress. The smell was revolting, but Lucifer seemed quite happy. Emrys and Sara watched him dash off to roll in the dirt.

"In answer to your question, Miss Jones . . . ," Emrys began.

"Question?"

"Yes. You wanted to know if I wished I had kept the guard posted." He looked at her, his eyes a strange yellow color. "Yes and no. I had removed the guard in hopes of tempting Ned Perkin back here. I thought he would return if the guard was removed; then we could nab him. He's a thoroughly bad sort. However"—he looked at her and grinned—"I seriously doubt that a guard would have made any difference to you and your family. I dare say you would have smiled politely, insisted that this was your home, and then proceeded with your moving in, just as you intended."

Sara found herself smiling back. "I think you're quite right."

"Still, I do worry." Emrys was frowning again. "Ned Perkin is a rogue and a murderer from all accounts. I worry about you and your family staying here. If the story about hidden loot is correct—and I believe it is—then I think Perkin will return. He's killed before for baubles; a trove such as the one he's supposed to have buried here would cause him to go to any lengths."

"I think we can protect ourselves from Mr. Perkin or anyone else," Sara said coolly. "After all, we have Garfield, while Jack, James, and John are almost grown. Then there's Mr. Moore."

"Moore is here?"

Sara nodded toward the side of the house where Garfield and Edward Moore were working. "Mr. Chiswick sent him to us. I think he's going to be a great help."

Emrys frowned. "Do you think it wise to keep him here? All we have is the man's recollection—dim as it is most of the time—that he is who he says he is."

"Mr. Chiswick seems quite sure of him," Sara said. "As to what I know of him, he seems to be a gentleman."

A surprised expression crossed Emrys' face; then he smiled. "I suppose he must be a paragon if you think him a gentleman. That, however, does not address my point, Miss Jones. Let me sum this up: for protection from a known murderer, you have one broken army captain, one old man, and three boys. It seems to me, Miss Jones, that you still need to think of your safety." He held up a hand as Sara started to reply. "Hear me out. I repeat—think of your safety, and if you're not worried about yourself, think of the older women and the children here. It might be dangerous for all of you to stay here. Anything could happen."

Sara drew herself up to her full height which, unfortunately, just came to his broad shoulders. "Is that a threat, Lord Emrys? If so, you've selected the wrong people to intimidate. We do not move. My father braved more adventures in Africa than you've ever seen or even dreamed of, I'm sure, and my mother and I are of the same character. We're going to stay here and that's all there is to it."

Emrys looked surprised at her outburst, then angry. "That was no threat, Miss Jones, merely a statement of fact. What you choose to do with it is your own business. In the meantime, as I told you, I intend to pursue my claim." He appeared calm now, his eyes like golden ice once again as he pulled his horse to him and mounted, looking down at her. "For the first thing, I intend to locate Mr. Bekins and get to the bottom of this. However, we are neighbors, even if it's for only a short time. Therefore, please let me know if you need assistance." He nodded his head curtly. "I'll be in touch, Miss Jones. Good day." Without waiting for an answer, he rode off at a canter across the ploughed field.

Lucifer rubbed up against Sara's hem, bringing her mind back to reality. "Good Lord, what a smell!" She reached down and grabbed the dog, holding him out as far as possible. "It's back to the pond for you, and this time there'll be no gentle scrubbing."

The mud on Sara's dress had turned to muck by the time she had rewashed Lucifer and returned to the house. Chiswick was there, talking with her mother and Aunt Zell.

"Whatever has happened to you, Sara?" Her mother gasped and wrinkled her nose.

Aunt Zell looked her up and down again. "Cleanliness is next to godliness, young lady."

"Tell that to Lucifer," Sara said briefly. The dog had followed her inside, smelling of sweet lavender and dancing around, licking every hand he could reach. His tail was wagging so fast it was a blur.

Sara left them and went upstairs to change. She had chosen the small bedchamber at the end of the house, one that overlooked the grounds. She went in and quickly washed herself from the bowl and pitcher. The boys had brought up her boxes and had simply dumped them on her bed. She rummaged quickly through her things, rejecting most of her London clothes. She finally found a serviceable gray gown and quickly put it on as Lucifer knocked the door open and wandered inside. He nosed her soiled dress on the floor, and she quickly scooped the garment up before Lucifer got dirty again. The dress—and her whole room—smelled of kitchen garbage, so she wadded the dress up, wondering what to do with it. The stench was unimaginable, so she hurried to the window and tossed it out. She would retrieve it later and try to wash it, but suspected it was beyond help. "You're turning into an expensive animal," she said to Lucifer as he flopped to the floor and looked at her with expressive, brown eyes. "I can't afford a new gown right now." Lucifer wagged his tail and tried to lick her hand, then rubbed against her ankles. "Indeed, you're the cause of all this," she said severely. Lucifer wagged his tail again and rolled his eyes as though he were fully aware that he was the culprit, but was too fetching to scold.

When Sara went back down the stairs, Chiswick was almost ready to leave. "Stay a moment, Mr. Chiswick," Sara said, motioning him back inside the front room they were using as a parlor. "I'd like for you to hear what Lord Emrys just told me."

Quickly she informed everyone that Emrys was not relinquishing his claim and intended to go to court, if necessary. "The man even tried to warn me away as he left," she concluded. "I wouldn't have thought it of him."

Chiswick frowned. "That doesn't sound like Emrys at all. We know his father was often cruel and unfair, but Emrys has gone the extra mile to get along with everyone. He makes sure that help is available to anyone in the village who needs it. He even gets along with his father-in-law, and I'd say he's the only one in the county who does."

"His father-in-law?" To her surprise, Sara felt a tug of disappointment.

Chiswick nodded absently and glanced at Mrs. Jones. "Simpson Brook. You remember him, don't you, Sophie? The stingiest, greediest man alive, I'd say."

Mrs. Jones nodded. "I remember him well. He must not have changed at all."

"Not a bit." Chiswick chuckled. "Everyone thought it was a feather in his cap when he managed to marry his Elizabeth off to old Lord Emrys' son." He frowned. "Although he's not a man to cross, threatening you doesn't sound at all like the Emrys I know. Are you sure he threatened you?"

"He said it might be dangerous for us here," Sara said. "He mentioned Ned Perkin and said something might happen to us if we stayed here."

"Well, I don't think he meant it as a threat. Emrys was probably trying to warn you about Perkin because he was truly worried that you might come to harm." Chiswick spoke slowly as he thought. "Perkin's a bad one indeed. I was hoping he was gone to the Continent or to Hades, but he's been blamed for some stagecoach robberies close by. He's wanted for murder, you know."

"I don't think he'll bother us," Mrs. Jones said. "What

on earth could he want with us? We've a house full of children and no possessions.''

"Men like Perkin don't have to have a reason, but unfortunately, Perkin does. According to the gossip, he's supposed to have a fortune buried somewhere at Saint's Haven. That's why all the holes are in the yard—everyone in the village dug the place up hunting for Perkin's treasure when he fled.''

"If they didn't find it, then it isn't here," Mrs. Jones said firmly, "so we have nothing to worry about."

Chiswick frowned. "I don't know about that, Sophie. It may just be gossip or the treasure may well be here. If it is, I guarantee Perkin will come back for it, and men like Perkin are always a worry. I think he'd do anything he had to in order to survive."

Much later, Sara was to remember those words with rue.

Chapter 7

Aunt Zell spent the day washing sheets, and Sara finally took the time to give her little room a thorough cleaning and even made a fluffy, clean bed for Lucifer just outside the back door. Lucifer spent the evening watching her clean, and she took him down to his bed just before bedtime. He walked around it and looked at it, then at her. Finally, he lay down across the step and looked at the bed, his nose on his paws. Sara left him there, then went back to check on him just before she went to bed. There was no beagle to be found.

She looked for Lucifer for almost a quarter of an hour, but couldn't find him anywhere. "He must," she commented to Jack as they locked and barred the doors from the inside, "have gone hunting. At least I can get a night's sleep without being bothered by that dog. Emrys' description of that thing as a devil is true."

Sara went into her room, put the candle down on the table, and luxuriated in the feeling of having her own space, and a clean space at that. She picked up the small picture of her father and smiled. "We're going to make Saint's Haven a home again, Papa," she said with a smile. She blew out the candle and looked at the moonlight flooding the room, outlining everything in it. The bed was lower than most, although higher than a trundle. She suspected that this had once been her father's room when he was a boy, and it gave her a good feeling to be here. She was tired, and her body ached all over; but it was good. For the first time since her father died, she felt completely at peace and productive. She slipped into her nightgown and crawled between her clean sheets, stretching and enjoying the feeling of being in her own bed in her own house.

Just as Sara was dozing off, she heard a scuffling sound under her bed. She sat bolt upright and grabbed for the candlestick to use as a weapon. In just a second, she heard panting and whining. "You!" she said in disgust, putting the candlestick back on the table and leaning over the bed. Lucifer poked his head from under the bed and snuffled. He crawled out on his belly, wagging his tail all the while. Then, before Sara could stop him, he hopped up on the bed and snuggled down beside her.

"Oh, no, you don't," Sara said firmly, putting the dog back onto the floor. "Just for tonight, I might let you stay on the floor beside the bed if you behave, but you're *not* getting on the bed." Sara could have sworn Lucifer grinned at her as he trotted to the foot of the bed and hopped up again, curling up on top of her feet.

Sara sat up and put Lucifer back down on the floor, trying to be firm. This time, Lucifer managed to stay there until Sara was almost asleep. Then he hopped up on her feet again. Sara put him back down, but when she woke up in the middle of the night, Lucifer was curled up against her back, snoring and snuffling. With a defeated sigh, Sara shoved him to the edge of the bed and went back to sleep. She would deal with the pesky beagle tomorrow.

The next morning at daylight, Lucifer crawled up and licked her ear. Sara jumped up, disoriented from lack of sleep. Lucifer hopped to the floor and looked at her expectantly, waiting for her to take him outside. Sara was wide awake now, so she dressed and went out. "I can't believe I'm letting an animal dictate my whole life," she grumbled to no one in particular as she went down the stairs.

"Seems to go that way, missy," Garfield said as he lit the morning fire in the kitchen. "You're up early."

"No thanks to that thing." Sara waved toward Lucifer, who dashed out the door into the backyard. "Why are you up so early, Garfield?"

"Much to do today, missy. Yesterday, we worked on the inside of the house, but there's more to do outside. We've got to get ready if we're going to get in any crops this year."

"I'll help you, Garfield. We'll get most of it today, I'm sure." She smiled as she let Lucifer back inside.

By midmorning, Sara realized she hadn't even had a vague idea of how much there was to do. Garfield had been right—everything had to be cleaned up outside. She had taken a break from her work and was standing, arching her back to relieve the muscles there, when she saw several men riding up in a wagon. The driver stopped the wagon, and he and three other men jumped down. Quickly the three men began to unload various tools from the back of the wagon while the driver came up to Sara. He tugged his forelock and smiled at her. He was very big, very strong, and fairly young. "Lord Emrys sent us to help," the driver said, still smiling. "He said you needed to have some work done. What do you want us to do first?"

Garfield came to stand beside Sara.

"You may return to Brookwood and tell Lord Emrys that his help isn't necessary," Sara said. "We'll manage."

The young worker looked doubtful. "I dasn't dare. He said to come here and work, and that's what we have to do." He motioned to the men by the wagon, and they came to stand behind him. "What do you want us to do first?"

"It simply isn't necessary . . . ," Sara began, but Garfield took her by the elbow. "A word, missy," he muttered, drawing her away.

Sara glared at him. "Garfield, if you're even going to suggest that we take charity from Emrys . . ." Her voice trailed off.

"Now, missy," Garfield said, looking back at the four strong men standing there with their tools. "I don't reckon as I'd term it charity. Neighborliness may be more like it."

"Not Emrys. He's trying to get us to leave. This must be part of some plan he has."

Garfield looked around. "Think a moment, missy. If he wanted us to leave right quick, would he send men to help us fix the place up? That wouldn't make sense." Garfield's voice took on a persuasive tone. "Maybe he's talked to his solicitor and seen that it's hopeless, and this is his way of making up for yesterday."

"Maybe giraffes crawl through mouse holes," Sara retorted. "Garfield, these men must return to Brookwood."

"And so they will, missy, but why don't we get what we can out of them while they're here? 'Twon't hurt a thing, and we'll be ready twice as fast." He looked around again. "Four times as fast."

"Garfield . . ."

"Now think, missy. Here it is late spring and we're behind with the planting already. Edward Moore and I just can't do everything that needs to be done. With even a day of these four to help us, we could be ready to plant in no time at all.''

"Garfield . . .''

"We have to have crops to get us through the winter. Then, there's the orchard to prune and clean, a chicken house to build, the stables to repair . . .'' He paused and looked at her. "Edward and I could work in the orchard while these four repaired the stables and cleaned up the back here.''

Sara felt her aching back again and looked at Jack and James tugging ineffectually at a large piece of a fallen tree. "All right, Garfield. I suppose there's no harm, but I worry about Emrys attaching strings to this. I don't believe he's the kind of man to give a gift without expecting something in return.''

"Maybe he's just being a good neighbor.'' Garfield loped off to assign the men to work without waiting for Sara's reply. "A good neighbor?'' Sara said to no one. "Not Emrys!''

By late afternoon, Sara had to admit that the men had worked wonders. The back garden had been cleared, and she could see outlines of the lovely garden it had once been. Garfield and the boys had cleared the orchard, and now the limbs were piled in a large heap, waiting to be burned. The trees looked clear, and the beginning buds gave promise of a great deal of fruit in the fall. Even the stables looked better. Sara watched the four men carefully put their tools in the wagon and get ready to drive back to Brookwood.

She approached the driver, who was talking to Garfield. "Thank you for your help,'' she said with a smile.

He touched his forelock again. " 'Twas nothing. I believe the master'll send us back tomorrow. We'll make some show then.''

"Thank you, but that really won't be necessary.''

Garfield started to protest, but a voice came from behind Sara first. "Unnecessary? Really, Miss Jones, do you plan on doing all this rebuilding by yourself?"

Sara spun to face Emrys, a retort on her lips. However, she stopped herself and remembered her manners. "I believe we can manage, Lord Emrys. However, I wish to thank you for your help. These men have done a wonderful job."

"I expected no less." He nodded toward the men. "Jenkins, you may go on. Well done."

The men mounted the wagon and drove off. "I'll be glad to send them over tomorrow. I believe you can use them, and they certainly don't have that much to do at Brookwood."

"Thank you, but I really don't—"

Emrys held up a hand. "Please, Miss Jones. Allow me to improve my property."

"Your property?"

Emrys nodded. "I haven't relinquished my claim to the property, after all. I've decided not to burn it, but to improve it instead. Perhaps we can work out a rental agreement in the future." The trace of a smile played around his mouth.

Sara drew herself up to her full five feet, three inches. "I think not, Lord Emrys. The property is ours, and there's no question about it."

Emrys turned and untied his horse, then mounted. "Oh, I do believe there's a question, Miss Jones. In fact, I've already begun a search for the younger Mr. Bekins to try to discover the truth of the deed I hold. In the meantime"—he turned and smiled at her—"I'll send Jenkins and the others over. Just let me know if I need to purchase anything. Jenkins is authorized to get what he needs." He touched his hat. "Good day, Miss Jones."

Sara watched him ride around the corner of the house

and move into the road. "Of all the nerve!" she muttered. "The man is impossible!"

"That he is," Garfield said, "but neighborly." He glanced at the sun. "It's about supper time. I told Moore that we'd try to fire the dead branches in the orchard, but I think I'll wait a day or two. Mayhap we can work a little on the tool shed." He gestured to the one building that didn't need too many repairs. "Just the roof and the door and that building will be right as rain. We need the shed to hold the tools."

"Whatever you want," Sara said absently as she went inside to help with supper.

It seemed to take forever to get the children to bed after supper, and Sara was exhausted when she finally went to her room. She had not seen Lucifer, and took the precaution of looking under her bed, then carefully shutting the door so the dog wouldn't attempt sleeping with her. When she tugged at the covers so she could crawl into bed, Lucifer stuck his head out from under the pillow, and Sara could have sworn the beagle grinned at her. "No, you don't," she said, pulling the dog to the edge of the bed. "I'd wager my clean bedcoverings already smell of beagle." She wrinkled her nose and put Lucifer on the floor. Lucifer lay down and looked up at her, pleading, tail wagging. Sara was firm. She opened the door and pointed. "Out you go. You will not sleep in here tonight."

Lucifer whined and edged forward on his belly, grinning again. Then he bounced up and scuttled under the bed. All Sara could see was the gleam of his eyes. "All right," she said, relenting and standing up, "tonight only. I'm just too tired to go chasing all over the room trying to get you out. But not on the bed." She heard an answering thump as Lucifer's tail hit the floor.

Sara crawled into bed and blew out her candle. She was asleep in minutes. Lucifer crawled out, whimpered a little, hopped up on Sara's footstool, then jumped on the bed. In just a minute, he was curled up firmly against Sara's back and was snoring gently.

In the middle of the night, Sara roused, dreaming about the noise of a cannon. It took her a few moments, but she groggily realized that the cannon in her dream was, in reality, Lucifer barking excitedly. The dog was on her bed, dancing around, looking out the window into the orchard and barking nonstop. Sara threw a pillow at him, but Lucifer kept barking. He ran to the side of the bed next to the window and put his paws on the glass, barking and barking. Sara put her head under the covers, but it didn't help. Lucifer kept barking. Wearily, Sara crawled down the bed and put her hands on Lucifer's back. "Will you be quiet!" she muttered. "You're going to wake up the entire household." She tried to pick Lucifer up, but the beagle slipped from her grasp and stood with his front paws against the window. As Sara reached to grab him again, she stopped as something in the orchard caught her eye.

Outside, in the orchard, there was a white form floating in the moonlight. Her heart almost stopped beating, and she shook herself. "There's no such thing as a ghost," she said aloud. She jumped from the bed and put on her dressing gown. "Come on," she said to Lucifer, "we'll go see what that is."

As she started down the stairs, Jack came running from his room. "What is it?" he said.

"Shhhh." Sara put her finger to her lips. "Nothing. I saw something from my window and thought I'd go check."

"The white thing?"

"You saw it, too?"

Jack nodded. "Lucifer's barking woke me up, and I glanced out my window. It looked like a woman in white walking in the orchard." His eyes were wide. "Do you think it's a ghost?"

"It wasn't a ghost," Sara said firmly. "Let's go see."

They didn't go into the orchard. They went outside and looked around, but saw nothing in the moonlight. The orchard was empty, and Lucifer sat down next to Sara's hem. He didn't make a sound.

"Look, is that it?" Jack pointed to a shape that was barely visible in the distance.

Sara peered into the bluish light cast by the moon. "Yes, that's it. What's it doing?"

They both looked intently at the white wisp at the edge of the orchard, near the pond. "Whatever it is, it's leaving," Jack said. "It *must* be a ghost, Sara. What else could it be?"

"I don't know what it could be, Jack, but I do know that there's no such thing as a ghost." Sara drew her dressing gown tightly around her body. The spring night was chilly. "It's gone, so let's go inside." She paused and put her hand on Jack's shoulder. "This is just between us. Don't tell anyone, not James or John or even Garfield."

"But . . ."

Sara shook her head. "No buts. This is probably only some kind of low trick Emrys is trying to play on us to make us leave. There are no ghosts—that was only someone in disguise. Emrys thinks we'll be nothing except a hysterical bunch of women and children and will leave." She chuckled. "We'll beat him at his game, Jack. We won't say a word, and then we'll unmask this so-called ghost."

"I don't know." Jack sounded doubtful. "It might be real. There *could* be ghosts."

"Nonsense. It's just another of Emrys' ploys. Let's go to bed and we'll go into the orchard tomorrow. I'll prove that there are no such things as ghosts. I'll wager that we'll find footprints where this very real 'ghost' walked through the orchard."

In spite of her brave words, Sara checked all the locks before she went back to bed. Then she couldn't go to sleep. Lucifer jumped up beside her again and was soon snoring. This time, Sara let him be—his warmth and gentle snoring somehow reassuring.

The next day, Jack and Sara glanced at each other over breakfast and nodded. Neither of them looked as if they had slept the rest of the night. They said nothing to any of the others, but met outside just after the dew had dried off the grass. "Did you figure out what it was?" Jack asked, absently scratching Lucifer.

Sara shook her head. "I thought we should go out there and try to find some sign. I don't know what it was, but I'm sure it wasn't a ghost."

"Could have been." Jack straightened as Lucifer began to rub against his legs, tail wagging.

"No, Jack." Sara was firm. "There has to be a reasonable explanation. Stop that." This last was for Lucifer, who had given up on Jack and had started nuzzling Sara's leg. Sara looked around. "No one's out yet, so let's look now."

"Edward is. I saw him near the stables."

"Mr. Moore," Sara corrected absently. "You should always address your elders properly. Of course he's at the stables—his room is there." She glanced around. "I think we're safe. If anyone asks, we can say we were discussing what we could do to the orchard, because we'll do that, too."

Jack sighed as he fell into step beside Sara. "Garfield already told me what we're going to have to do to the orchard. It involves a great deal of sawing, chopping, and hard work."

"It won't hurt you at all," Sara said with a smile.

There was nothing in the orchard except some bent grass. "I think Garfield is right," Sara said, looking at an apple tree that had been split by lightning. "This is going to take some hard work."

"On our part, not yours," Jack said with a groan. "I

don't see a thing here except jobs to do. We might as well go back."

"You're right." Sara whistled for Lucifer, and they started toward the house. They had almost reached the edge of the orchard when something caught Sara's eye. "Look, Jack," she said, pointing. "Right there on that limb on the ground." They went over to look.

A limb had fallen and was partially hidden in the grass. There, on a broken branch that stuck up sharply, was a shred of white cloth. Sara grabbed it and turned it over in her palm. It was white and hadn't weathered at all in the recent rain. "This proves there was no ghost, Jack," she said with a triumphant grin. "Ghosts don't wear white muslin, and this looks fairly new." She held the scrap up. "Look, the edges are still fresh."

Jack turned the scrap in his fingers, then handed it back. "All right, it appears you're correct. But if it wasn't a ghost, what was it? Who was it?"

"I told you—it was Emrys trying another ploy to get us to leave." Lucifer dashed around Sara's ankles and bounded toward the shed after a bird.

Jack frowned and shook his head. "But, Sara, if Emrys was trying to do that, wouldn't it stand to reason that he'd do something that we'd be sure to see? If Lucifer hadn't been barking, neither of us would have seen the ghost."

"Don't get complicated, Jack. I'm telling you—it was Emrys' doing." She looked at the shed as Lucifer dashed around to the back of it, barking furiously. "Whatever is that devil's spawn up to now?"

Jack chuckled. "Perhaps we'd better check. He's liable to have anything cornered from a bird to a stray elephant."

"Don't be dramatic, Jack," Sara said, laughing as they went around the corner of the shed. "I doubt it's anything more than a mouse."

They turned the corner and stopped suddenly. Lucifer

was facing the rough wood of the shed, barking, the hair on his back standing up straight. He was staring at a small depression at the base of the shed wall where a pile of rags was heaped. "What is it, Lucifer?" Sara asked, stooping to put her hand on the dog. She got slightly off balance and put her hand out to steady herself. She missed the side of the shed and instead clutched at the pile of rags. She felt something very hard and cold and looked again at the pile, this time carefully. That was when she realized that the rags weren't just tossed away debris—there was someone inside them, and that someone was quite dead.

Chapter 8

By the time Jack arrived back at Saint's Haven with the magistrate, Sara had managed to stop shaking. Mrs. Jones and Aunt Zell hovered over her, plying her with tea. "It wasn't the body so much as it was the sheer surprise," she told Garfield when he came back into the kitchen after he had gone to the shed to check. "Do you know who it might be?"

Garfield shook his head. "No idea. Looks like some scum-of-the-earth thief. I've seen a million of them in the London stews."

"I can't imagine one of those being here in St. Claire." Sara shook her head and took another sip of Aunt Zell's strong, sweet tea. "Perhaps the man was seeking shelter and just got weary and died there. It's happened."

Garfield raised a skeptical eyebrow. "It has. However, in this case, I'd say not. His skull was neatly split with an axe. Just like a piece of green wood." He stopped and looked curiously as Mrs. Jones grabbed her throat and daintily fainted across the table. Sara swooped her teacup out of the way just in time.

"Look what you've gone and done!" Aunt Zell was angry. "You know her constitution happens to be delicate. Just you take her up to her room right now!" She glanced at Sara. "Will you be all right alone? I've made the children wait in the front."

After assuring Aunt Zell that she was fine, Sara gulped down the rest of the tea and then leaned back in her chair. She closed her eyes and relived that awful moment when she had realized her hand was clutching a body. She hadn't seen the blood or the split skull—all she had seen when she jerked one of the rags away was the face, bloodless and twisted in horror, the mouth open in a scream that never came. That was when she had tried to be brave for Jack's sake. "Go to the village and get the magistrate," she had said faintly. "Hurry."

Jack had taken one look at her face, then another at the body, and dashed off. Sara had put the rag back over the man's face and tottered around to the side of the shed where she had propped against the wall for a few moments, trying not to retch. She had made her way blindly to the kitchen without even remembering it.

There was a commotion out front now, and Sara heard Aunt Zell fussing. As Sara rose to see what was happening, Squire Sherman strode into the tiny kitchen. "I understand you've found the body of a vagrant," he snapped, obviously annoyed to have his day disturbed. "I assume he died of natural causes."

"Someone just naturally split his skull with an axe," Garfield said, stepping to stand beside Sara. She looked at him gratefully.

Sherman's eyebrows rose. "Someone here? And do you know the deceased?"

"Never saw 'im before, but I've seen the type," Garfield said. "Would you like to see 'im?"

"Certainly." Squire Sherman nodded briskly, still annoyed that someone would die and interrupt his afternoon game of cards. "Let's try to get this over with." He glanced at Sara. "I'll be back in to get the particulars from you."

Sara sank back into her chair and picked up her empty cup. She jumped straight up again as the kitchen door burst open and slammed against the wall. "What's happened here?" Emrys asked, his dark presence filling the room. "What's this about a body here. Who died?"

"I have no idea." Sara made herself look up at him. "And of what interest is this to you, Lord Emrys?" All the terror and frustration she felt came welling up. "Furthermore, what right do you have coming in here? I thought we established that Saint's Haven belongs to us, and you certainly have no right to think you can run tame here." Sara stood, getting angrier by the moment. She wasn't angry with Emrys—it was just that he was there. "Is this part of your nefarious scheme to terrify us? It would be just like you to—" Sara stopped as she finally saw the expression on his face.

"I can't believe you would say that, Miss Jones. I would never stoop so low." His face was a mask that couldn't hide his feelings, and his eyes were ice chips. "I was in the village and heard the story. In a place this small, every move is remarked, and the story was in every house before Sherman even left his card game. I came because I was worried that someone here had come to harm."

Sara sat back down and put her hand over her eyes. "I do apologize, Lord Emrys. The events of the day—and last night—have interfered with my judgment."

To Sara's surprise, Emrys touched her shoulder. "I understand, Miss Jones. If you don't mind, I'd like to go see what Sherman's doing outside. The children told me the body is behind the shed.''

Sara nodded and heard Emrys leave by the back door. How could she have accused him of such a thing? she wondered. Emrys might want them to leave, and might even try every legal means, but Sara couldn't believe that he would stoop to murder. *Murder.* She shuddered as the impact of the word hit her.

Squire Sherman returned in a short while and listened to Sara retell her story. "And you have no idea of this man's identity?" he asked.

"None. I've never seen him before."

Sherman turned to Garfield, who leaned against the door beside Emrys. "And you? You said you knew the type."

Garfield nodded. "Don't know him—never seen him before. But I do know the type. Every London stew has dozens of him. You can look at him and see it. He was either a pimp or a thief—maybe both."

"Now, Garfield, you don't know that," Sara said. "He might have been a lost traveler."

Garfield laughed shortly. "You always believe the best. I'm telling you that I've seen men like him all my life. I'd recognize the type anywhere." Garfield looked at Sherman. "Any clue as to who he is? I saw you going through his pockets."

Sherman shook his head. "Not a thing, not even a scrap. Right now, I'm going to list this as 'Murder by person or persons unknown' and let him be buried. I'll have to take the axe."

Garfield made a face. "We don't have another."

"I'll be glad to loan you an axe until that one's returned," Emrys said.

Sara stood up. "We don't want it back, Squire Sherman. I don't want that axe on the place again, ever. I'm sure we can buy another." She glanced around. "Will that be all?"

Jack and John went with Sherman to take the body into the village. The bloody axe was a wonder to the both of them, much to Sara's dismay. Emrys finally wrapped the axe in a rag and bound it. He accompanied Sherman, Jack, and John to the village, pausing only long enough to tell Sara he wanted to return to talk to her. She told him it wasn't necessary as she had nothing else to add to her story.

When the house was finally quiet, Sara went back outside, Lucifer at her heels. Garfield and Edward Moore were there, cleaning up around the shed. There was no trace left now. The shed looked like just any other outbuilding and better than most at Saint's Haven. Edward smiled at her as she came toward them. "Quite a shock you've had," he said. "I told Garfield we should clean this up. No point in leaving unpleasant reminders."

Sara smiled back at him, grateful. In the short while she had known Edward Moore, she had noticed that he always had a ready smile and was considerate. She had seen him with John and James, showing them how to handle a hammer. The boys had been fascinated.

"Some people come to a bad end and we don't know why," Edward said, tossing a short board on a pile to be burned. "That's probably what happened here. You didn't see anything to make you think otherwise, did you?"

Sara shook her head. "The poor man. I hope he didn't suffer."

"He didn't," Garfield said briefly.

"His expression was . . ." Sara stopped and shook her head, trying to get the horror on the man's face out of her memory. She turned and looked out to the orchard. "I wonder if his death has anything to do with the ghost we saw last night."

"Ghost?" Edward looked at her curiously. "What ghost?"

Sara laughed a little at herself as she told him about the white wraith she and Jack had seen. "It was probably a wisp of fog," she said, finishing her tale. She realized suddenly that she hadn't mentioned the ghost to Sherman nor had she told him about the scrap of white muslin she and Jack had found. She should have done that.

"Is there more?" Edward asked, scrutinizing her face.

Sara shook her head. She needed to tell Sherman before she said much else. Perhaps she could go see him in the morning.

The night was uneventful, but Sara couldn't sleep. She spent part of the night tossing Lucifer off her bed and the other part gazing out the window to see if the ghost reappeared. As daylight was breaking, she finally dozed off and woke up when the sun was high in the sky. She dressed hurriedly and ran down the stairs. "Mama, why did you let me sleep so long?" she asked, taking the cup of tea her mother had ready.

"I knew you were exhausted, my dear. I said as much to Roger this morning."

Sara raised an eyebrow. "Mr. Chiswick was here this morning? Isn't it a trifle early to be visiting?"

"He hadn't been to bed yet. He was on his way to the doctor for some laudanum drops. Poor Gwendolyn had a very bad night, he told me." Mrs. Jones turned and gazed out the window. "We must go visit them soon. Perhaps I can help Gwendolyn in some way."

"Perhaps." Sara nibbled on some toast. "Mama, I've got to walk into the village to see Squire Sherman." She hesitated. She certainly didn't want to lie to her mother, but on the other hand, she didn't want her mother to be terrified of a nonexistent ghost. "I wanted to see if he's made any progress in discovering the identity of our . . . our intruder." That was true as far as it went.

"Wonderful, dear, although I do wish you'd take one of the boys with you."

"I'll be fine, Mama, I really will. It isn't far and there are houses all around. Besides"—she gave her mother a quick hug—"I could use a walk in the sunshine and a little time to myself."

The day was balmy, the sun warm, and the gardens along the roadway just beginning to grow. Sara stopped and admired several flower gardens and tried to guess what flowers would be blooming later. Lucifer, who had elected to accompany her, skipped along in the lead.

To Sara's dismay, when she was admitted to Sherman's heavily decorated house, Emrys was conferring with the squire. Mrs. Sherman was as heavily decorated as her house and insisted that Sara wait and have tea in the overheated parlor. The squire didn't come into the parlor for the better part of an hour, and by the time he arrived, Sara had a crashing headache. She hesitated to divulge her information about the ghost, remembering Emrys' comment about how everyone in the village knew everything. She was sure the squire's wife would spread the word far and wide. "In the excitement," she told Squire Sherman as soon as he sat down across from her, "I neglected to tell you something." To her annoyance, Emrys had come into the parlor with the squire and had accepted a cup of tea from Mrs. Sherman. The woman positively fawned over Emrys.

Sara made herself not look at Emrys as she told Sherman about the white wraith and the scrap of muslin. Halfway through her recitation, she realized that the squire thought she was making things up. He was looking at her strangely. "And you saw nothing else? Found nothing else?" Squire Sherman asked.

Sara shook her head. "Nothing. No one. But there was the scrap." She took it from her pocket and handed it to him.

Squire Sherman looked at it and passed it to Emrys. "This could have come from anything. Any woman walking in the orchard might have caught a hem and left this." He nodded his head toward Emrys and dismissed Sara's tale with a wave of his hand. "Probably doesn't relate." He looked at her kindly. "You do need to get some rest, Miss Jones. I know this has been quite a shock to your system." His wife nodded assent and patted Sara on the arm.

"I'm perfectly fine." Sara sat straight up and frowned. Neither Sherman noticed.

"Of course you are." The squire's tone was soothing. "I'm sure you think you saw a ghost."

"What about the muslin? That's real."

Squire Sherman nodded and raised his eyebrow at Emrys. "Of course, the muslin. As I said, it could have come from anywhere. I'll be sure to ask if anyone's been in the orchard lately. That could have even been there for months."

"It's almost new. Look at it." Sara heard a note of desperation in her voice.

"Of course. As I said, I'll make the proper inquiries." He nodded toward his wife and rose. "You'll be fine, I'm sure."

"Of course you will, dear." Mrs. Sherman patted the back of Sara's hand. "Don't you worry about a thing, my dear."

"So right." Squire Sherman moved toward the door. "Right now, I'm of the opinion that this was a vagrant done in during the heat of the moment—probably an argument among thieves. Nothing for you to concern yourself about." He picked up a deck of cards on a small table by the door and fingered them. He was obviously in a hurry to get to his daily card game. "Is that all?" he asked.

Sara stood. "It is. I would appreciate it if you would keep us informed." She gave the Shermans and Emrys a stiff goodbye and left, wondering just how fast Mrs. Sherman would dress and make the rounds in the village to tell this newest tale.

Lucifer was sitting on the steps waiting for her, wagging his tail. Another beagle was there, sniffing Lucifer's nose with interest. "Come, Lucifer, let's leave. We've done all we can do." She was really annoyed. She could see that her story had been discounted entirely, and worse, Squire Sherman had treated it as mere delusion. She glanced down at Lucifer. The other dog was trotting along beside them. "Go back," she said, leaning down and trying to turn the other beagle around. "Go home."

She stopped in the roadway as Emrys shouted behind her. "Wait a moment, Miss Jones. I wanted to talk to you." Emrys ran to catch up with her. "Shall we sit here under the tree? I don't want you to worry about your complexion in the sun."

"We shouldn't be here that long, Lord Emrys." Sara was still angry. Emrys must have dismissed her story in the same way as Squire Sherman or he would have said something. "I need to get home."

"In that case, let me walk you there. I wanted to ask further about what you saw." He fell into step beside her and offered his arm. Sara ignored it.

"You heard what I told Squire Sherman. That's all I saw."

"Yes, I heard, but there's a difference between Sherman and me. I happen to believe you. I've seen something in that orchard myself, but by the time I get there, it has always disappeared."

Sara stopped and stared at him. "You believe me?"

Emrys smiled. "I certainly do. However, I don't know if the . . . the, shall we call it a 'specter'—if the specter is related to the brutal murder at Saint's Haven. Splitting a skull with an axe isn't usually considered a feminine way to murder."

"I was unaware there were distinctions." Sara's tone was tart.

Emrys chuckled. "Oh, anyone is capable of doing any heinous act, but usually women resort to pistols, poison, or such." He stopped laughing and caught Sara by the arm. "I don't mean to discount the seriousness of this, Miss Jones. I'm convinced that this murder is somehow related to Perkin and could have repercussions for your family."

Sara stared right back at him. "Are you telling us again in your so subtle way that we should pack up and leave? If so, Lord Emrys, it won't work. I've told you before that we have no intentions of going."

"I understand that." He paused as they began walking again and came into sight of Saint's Haven. "I merely want you to be on your guard. If Perkin is responsible for this crime, I don't think he'd hesitate to commit another."

"Thank you for your warning." Sara stopped in front of the house. "Thank you as well for walking me here." She turned to go into the house, but stumbled over Lucifer, who was playing with the other beagle. "Go back home, you!" she said to the other dog. "Go back to where you belong."

"He belongs with me," Emrys said. "Although I believe it will be difficult for me to get him away. I'll probably have to carry him with me, unless you can loan me a rope to tie him."

"Well, you should take him. He's certainly annoying and won't let Lucifer alone. Your dog has been chasing him since the village."

"Him? Are you speaking of your dog? Lucifer, I believe you said."

Sara started off around the side of the house. "I have a piece of rope in the shed that I saw this morning. I'll get it for you." She glanced behind her to see Emrys following her, laughing. "I fail to see anything humorous in this. I'm sure poor Lucifer doesn't care to have your dog bedeviling him constantly."

"What a choice of words, Miss Jones." Emrys couldn't keep the mirth out of his voice and, to Sara's annoyance, began laughing uproariously and collapsed against the side of the house, convulsed with laughter.

"As I said, I fail to see the humor here." Sara glared at him when he finally stopped laughing.

"You are a city girl, aren't you?" Emrys said, mopping at his eyes. "I know from experience just how much of a plague that particular beagle can be, Miss Jones, and to keep you from having a worse experience, perhaps I should tell you that the name you've given that dog is incorrect."

"Incorrect?"

Emrys nodded, trying to keep a straight face. "I do believe you should have named it Lucy, not Lucifer. You see, that's a female beagle and is, um, as we say, in season. That's why my male dog is chasing her."

Sara felt her face flame and turned away quickly so Emrys wouldn't see her mortification. "I'll get you a piece of rope, Lord Emrys." She almost ran toward the shed.

Emrys caught up with her easily. "Perhaps you should consider putting Lucifer—or Lucy—in the shed for a week or two. Just until she's ready to mix in polite company again, of course." His voice bubbled with repressed laughter.

"Thank you." Sara was icy. "I'll do that right now. Here's your piece of rope." She tossed him a short length of rope and snatched Lucy up just as Emrys' beagle made a mad dash for her. She shoved Lucy into the shed and slammed the door, dropping the bar that kept it closed.

"In the nick of time," Emrys murmured as Sara tried to concentrate on a nearby bush and keep from blushing. She wasn't successful.

Emrys made a noose and slipped it over his beagle's head. "Here, Sir William, it's time to leave off amorous pursuits." Emrys tugged at the rope, and the dog followed him, turning back to gaze longingly at the shed. "William may be back if I can't tie him. He prefers the company of women."

Sara glanced down at the dog. "Oh, does he belong to your wife?"

Emrys stopped suddenly and looked at her, his eyes once again yellow ice. "My wife?" His whole body stiffened. "I do not discuss my wife, Miss Jones."

"Why should . . . ?" Sara stopped. She had meant to ask why she would want to discuss Lady Emrys, but one glance at his face convinced her to try another tack. "I'm sure your wife would—"

Emrys interrupted her, his voice as icy as his eyes. "I'm amazed you would listen to salacious gossip, Miss Jones. I hadn't expected it of you." He turned and jerked on Sir William's rope. "Good day, Miss Jones." He went around the side of the house without another word, Sir William running to keep up with him.

"Salacious gossip, indeed," Sara said to no one. "The nerve of the man." Behind her, in the shed, Lucy began to howl piteously.

Just before bedtime that night, Jack came to Sara. "I think we should stay up and watch," he said. "I watched last night, but nothing came to the orchard."

"I'm not sure it's necessary," Sara said, glancing around to see if anyone had heard them. "Squire Sherman may be right—that scrap could have been left there any time."

"And what about the thing we saw?"

Sara had no answer for that, so agreed to take watch part of the night. She and Jack enlisted James, and they each stayed up for two hours. Sara was ashamed to admit that she fell asleep during her watch, so the ghost might have come by then. Nothing at all happened during the watches Jack and James took. They were sorely disappointed. The only thing to mar the quiet of the night was Lucy's occasional pathetic howling. Evidently, the shed wasn't nearly as comfortable as Sara's bed.

The next day, Sara and James were weeding the front garden when Roger Chiswick came by. He nodded at them, went inside, and stayed for the better part of an hour. "Do you think he's still in love with Aunt Sophie?" James whispered.

"In love?" Sara turned on him, newly sprouted grass in her hand. "Just what do you mean by that? The man happens to be married."

"Oh. I didn't know that. Any fool can see that he's sweet on Aunt Sophie. Jack tells me they used to know each other."

"They did." Sara spoke firmly. "Now don't you go starting tales and imagining things. None of you. And you can tell Jack the same thing. Mr. Chiswick is an old friend of Mama's and of Papa's, too. He's just here to make sure we're doing fine."

"Shhh," James mumbled as Chiswick came outside, Mrs. Jones walking with him.

"You shouldn't do that kind of work, my dear," Mrs. Jones said as Sara tossed a hunk of dead grass over the fence. "You should be resting. I heard you up wandering around last night. Couldn't you sleep?"

Sara was about to concoct some story to cover the noise she, Jack, and James had made during their night on watch, but was interrupted by James. "That was the three of us, Aunt Sophie. We were just watching for the ghost."

"Ghost! Sara, whatever is he speaking of?"

Sara was forced to recount the tale of the white wraith and the shred of muslin. She had thought Chiswick would act much as Squire Sherman, but instead, he questioned her carefully about the time and the place. When Sara finally gave him all the information she had, he seemed disturbed.

"I'm sure you saw something, but I'm also sure there's a logical explanation," he said quickly, patting her hand. "Don't worry a bit about it. I don't think it's at all connected to the tragedy here." He turned back to Mrs. Jones. "I must be going, Sophie, but as always, if you need anything, just let me know." James gave Sara a nudge with his elbow as Mrs. Jones walked Chiswick to the hole in the fence where the gate was supposed to be. "Told you," James whispered. Sara ignored him.

By dusk, Sara was nodding in her chair. She didn't want to move and had to make herself go outside to check on Lucy. Everything was quiet as she went up to the shed. She put the dish of food she had brought down on the ground and raised the bar. Lucy leaped right into her arms, almost knocking her down. "Bad dog," Sara muttered, holding the wriggling beagle with one hand and grabbing for the food dish with the other.

"I believe you could use a little help. Allow me." Edward Moore smiled at her as he lifted Lucy and held her tightly. "She's wanting out."

Sara nodded. "Emrys said she should stay in here for about two weeks." She put the food dish on the floor and checked to see that Lucy had plenty of water. Lucy had been digging all around the dirt floor and scratching at the pile of debris stacked inside the shed. Sara scooped the tumbled mess together and pushed it against the wall, then fluffed the pile of rags she had brought for Lucy's bed.

"Two weeks?" Edward looked down at the panting dog. "Probably a week would do it. No point in keeping her inside any longer than you have to." He put Lucy back on the floor, and they edged backward out the door.

Sara smiled at him as she rebarred the door. "I hope you're right. I hate to think of her being locked up in there. She loves to run outside."

He smiled back at her. "I'll keep a close eye on her. I think a week will be enough." He began walking with Sara back to the house. "Have you seen any more of your ghost?"

Feeling foolish, Sara grinned ruefully. "Squire Sherman thinks it was nothing. And no, I haven't seen anything else. No doubt it was a wisp of fog."

"Probably so." They had stopped at the back door, and Edward looked down at her in the rising moonlight. For a minute, Sara knew that he was thinking of trying to kiss her.

"I really must go inside, Mr. Moore."

"Edward, if you please. I thought we were agreed that we're all family here. If so, we certainly can't stand on formality."

"Edward." She smiled at him. "Good night."

"Good night," he said with a wistful smile, realizing the moment had passed. Sara slipped up to her room and watched him as he went into his room in the stables.

She was just getting ready for bed when Jack and James tapped softly at her door. "We thought we should watch again tonight," they said. They were excited at this new game.

Sara shook her head. "Absolutely not. We saw nothing last night, and I'm convinced that whatever we saw had no bearing on what happened. I want both of you to go

to bed and get a good night's sleep. We need you rested
to help with all the work around here." She glared at them
sternly. "Do you understand?"

After they left, she went to bed, pausing before she
snuffed out her candle, long enough to pick up the painting of her father and smile at it. "We're doing it, Papa."
She thought she could almost detect a touch of knowing
in her father's smile. She drifted off to sleep, content for
the first time in several nights.

The moon was streaming into her window when she
woke up. Someone was shaking her all over. She sat bolt
upright and cracked her head on something hard.
"Ouch!" Jack muttered. "You've almost broken my chin."
He rubbed his chin and grabbed Sara's hand. "Come on,
Sara. James and I decided to watch anyway, and the ghost
is back!"

By the time Sara scrambled into her dressing gown,
grabbed her shoes, then ran down the stairs in her bare
feet, James was running up to fetch them. "It went out of
sight in the trees next to the pond," he whispered, his
voice shaking. "I lost sight of it."

"I told you not to lose it." Jack was exasperated. "Why
didn't you follow?"

James's eyes widened in the pale light. "Do you think
I'm going out to the pond in the dark to chase a ghost all
by myself? I'm not that stupid."

"Quiet, or you'll wake the others," Sara hissed. "Come
on, we may see it again. Are you sure it was the ghost?"
She slipped on her shoes and headed for the back door.

"We're sure." James and Jack got on either side of her,
and together they approached the orchard and pond. As
they passed the shed, they heard Lucy whimpering, and
Sara paused. Jack pulled her hand. "Let's go."

They walked out into the orchard and saw nothing. They
even went toward the pond, but still saw nothing. "There's

no point in trying to look in the dark," Sara finally said. "Let's keep watch for the rest of the night and we'll come out first thing and look for something that will give us a clue." She looked at the boys. "You two go to bed and I'll watch. I've been sleeping and you haven't."

Jack grinned at her. "And you think we can sleep after all this?"

Sara laughed softly as they went back inside. All three of them sat up, looking out the back through different windows, but they saw nothing. The next morning, they slipped out before breakfast, while the dew was still heavy on the grass, covering everything with a coat of white shimmer. They went over the orchard but saw nothing, not even a track. It was only around the pond that they found something. "Look," Sara said, pointing, "tracks. It looks as if one person—the one with the small foot—was on the ground, but two were on horseback." She walked around the edge of the pond. "There are no more footprints on the ground, but the horses' tracks continue."

"Then there could have been two people and two horses, or three people—two on horseback and one on the ground. If that's the case . . ." Jack stopped and thought.

"If that's the case," James finished, "then the person on the ground was carried away on one of the horses."

"The horses go this way," Jack said, pointing.

"Toward Brookwood." Sara stared in the general direction of Emrys' estate. "That means our 'ghost' is a real person, and has been sent to scare us. I know I first thought Emrys might have been a part of this, but I had convinced myself that he was above it." She remembered his laughing and the warmth of his eyes, but then she chilled as she remembered as well the shift of his mood to hard and cold when she asked about his wife. At that moment, she could have well believed Emrys capable of doing something nefarious—his eyes were that cold and bleak. Her mouth set in a grim line. "We'll show Lord Emrys that this ploy isn't going to work. Let's get back to the house. We have work to do on Saint's Haven."

Jack looked doubtful. "I think you're wrong, Sara. I don't think he'd do that. Lord Emrys may want Saint's Haven, but this doesn't seem something he would do."

Sara turned, remembering Emrys' cold, hard eyes. "Don't let him fool you. Emrys would do whatever he had to, Jack. Don't ever forget it."

Chapter 9

Later that day Roger Chiswick rode by and brought some jams and jellies for the children. He asked if Sara had seen anything else, and after hesitating a moment, she told him about seeing the ghost again and her suspicions of Emrys.

"I'm sure it isn't Emrys," he said thoughtfully.

"Who else could it be?" Sara sipped at her tea as she thought. "No one else in St. Claire would like to see us leave."

"Perhaps the ghost isn't trying to frighten you away," Chiswick said with a smile. "There have been friendly ghosts, you know." He shook his head. "If, as you say, it isn't a ghost at all but a person, then there must be an explanation. Someone may just like walking in the moonlight."

"You'd have to be crazy to do that," James said, "but some people are."

Chiswick winced slightly and sipped his tea. He said nothing for a moment. "True," he finally said. He appeared as if he planned to say something else, but he didn't.

Jack shrugged. "Just for my opinion, I don't think it's Lord Emrys either. If he really wanted to get rid of us, I think he'd find some other way."

"Good thinking, lad." Chiswick smiled and put down his cup. "I've got some business to see to, but I'll return to check on you later this evening." He looked up, and a smile lit up his face as Mrs. Jones walked into the room. "Sophie." He rolled the name around, almost savoring it. "How are you today?" Mrs. Jones sat, and they all had another cup of tea, Chiswick's business postponed. When the clock struck the hour, he jumped up, amazed that the time had passed so quickly. Mrs. Jones walked him to the door, then turned and asked him if it would be all right for them to visit Gwendolyn.

"I think she'd love a visit, but not right now. She's not at her best." Chiswick's voice held something more than a note of regret. Sara couldn't quite place it. "Would you mind waiting a week or so until she's feeling better?" Chiswick asked.

"Of course not, Roger." Mrs. Jones picked up a jar of jam. "We should be sending her restoratives instead of her sending us this. I'm sorry I didn't think of it."

Chiswick shook his head. "Nothing helps a great deal except quiet and time. I do thank you for thinking of her, and I'll tell her you asked about her." He gave them all a short smile and left.

That night, James, Jack, and Sara kept watch once again, but observed nothing unusual. After two nights of staying up, Sara declared that the ghost had disappeared and she, for one, was going to get a good night's sleep. It was bad enough having to listen to Lucy howl and scratch on the shed door.

The next few nights were quiet and the days productive.

Every day, Sara opened the shed door and gave Lucy food and water. Lucy always thought Sara was going to let her out and was incensed when Sara shut the door once again. Worse, every time Lucy heard Sara outside, she began howling piteously. This created quite a problem as Sara spent most of every day outside, supervising Edward and Garfield with the garden and the outbuildings. Rather, she thought to herself more than once, they let her appear to be supervising to keep her busy—they knew exactly what needed doing. Edward, in particular, was becoming a necessary part of their family. He was always there with a smile, always ready to help. Sara found herself liking him more and more. He said very little about his family, but his manners and his intelligence marked him as well-born, no matter his station now. Perhaps, she mused to herself, he would someday discover his family and would be reinstated in some grand house. For now, however, he seemed quite content to be around Saint's Haven, digging in the garden and doing repairs in the house.

Sara hadn't seen Emrys for almost a week and had reached the point that she didn't think about him more than four or five times a day. She should have been glad that he wasn't there plaguing them, but now she worried that he was up to no good. Since he wasn't around, she decided, he had to be in London, trying to find some way to move them off of Saint's Haven. Drat the man, anyway, she thought to herself. He worried her when he was around and he worried her when he wasn't. She really hoped his wife made his life miserable.

Sara and the twins were in the orchard one warm afternoon, working in the drift of fragrant apple blossoms, picking up dead branches and piling them up. Sara had stopped a moment to pick up a spray of pink blossoms that had accidentally been knocked from the tree. She closed her eyes and inhaled the sweet spice fragrance of the flowers. When she opened her eyes, she caught the trace of another scent right behind her. She wheeled and took a step, almost colliding with Emrys. He had evidently ridden over from Brookwood and then dismounted and walked up to them. Sara hadn't heard him coming and almost ran right into his chest.

"Good afternoon, Miss Jones," he said, smiling.

"What are you doing here?" Sara dropped the spray of blossoms and reached up to pat her hair. She had caught her curls a dozen times in branches, and her hair was sticking out everywhere. Her dress was dirty, and she was wearing her old brogans. Emrys couldn't have picked a worse time to visit.

Emrys raised an eyebrow, then bent and picked up the spray of apple blossoms. "You'll have no apples, Miss Jones, if you pick the flowers." He smiled. "As to your other question—I'm merely making a friendly visit."

Sara blushed and took the spray. "I do apologize. You startled me and I forgot my manners. It's good to see you again."

He looked at her strangely, his topaz eyes seeing right through her. "Is that true? I thought you would have wished me off to the demons of hell with good riddance." He smiled. "I'm glad you're relenting. I'm not a bad sort, you know."

Sara was saved from answering by Mary running up to them. "Found a flower," she said proudly, holding up the remains of a small, yellow blossom. Mary suddenly turned to Emrys and held it out to him. "For you," she said with a shy grin, giving him the flower and then running away. Sara turned to Emrys to make a joking remark, but was stopped by the expression on his face. It was a mixture of terrible sadness and longing, touched with bitterness. For a second, Sara thought she saw his eyes glassy with unshed tears, but then he dropped a blank expression over his face like a mask. When he turned to look at Sara, he was as always. "Thank her for me," he said carefully, tucking the battered yellow blossom into the buttonhole of his waistcoat.

"Do you have children?" Sara asked impulsively. To her horror, his eyes turned to yellow ice again and his expression hardened. "I'm sorry," she said, turning to watch the twins pull a limb across the new spring grass. "I didn't mean to pry into your private life."

"In a small town, nothing is private," Emrys said. "I thought you would have heard by now, but evidently, you're too new here to have heard all the gossip. Perhaps I should tell you myself."

Sara looked at him. His eyes were no longer hard, but were tinged with sorrow. "You don't have to tell me anything," she said. "You and Lady Emrys are entitled to keep your lives private."

He smiled, that twisted, faintly bitter smile she had seen before. "There is no Lady Emrys."

Sara paused, confused not knowing what to say. "I'm sorry. I must have misunderstood. I thought you were married."

There was a pause. "I was. My wife died a little over a year ago."

"Oh." Sara groped for words of sympathy and finally resorted to the basic. "I'm sorry." Emrys said nothing. As the silence lengthened, Sara felt she had to say something else but couldn't think of a thing.

"Have you had the children long?" Emrys asked, still looking at Mary and Matthew as they tugged at the limb. They were laughing at themselves, their high, childish laughter filling the orchard.

"We've had those two since they were born. Their mother was . . . was unable to take care of them and left them in a basket on a street corner, so we took them in.

We've had most of the children for years. Briget's parents brought her to us because they couldn't keep her. We haven't seen them since. Parson Grimm rescued the other boys from the streets and brought them to us."

Emrys looked at her. "That's admirable."

Sara shook her head. "There's nothing admirable about it. Papa always said it was our Christian duty to do whatever we could for others. Some are called to build churches, some to preach. This was just what we were supposed to do to help."

Emrys stood silent so long that Sara wondered. "Do you need help at Saint's Haven to make it livable?" he asked suddenly. "Financially, I mean. Perhaps . . ." He left the sentence unfinished.

Sara pretended to misunderstand. "We're doing fine. Edward . . . Mr. Moore has been invaluable. The damage wasn't as much structural as it was cosmetic. Garfield seems to think that he, Mr. Moore, and the boys will have everything in shape shortly."

"All right." Emrys took one last look at Mary and Matthew and untethered his horse from a tree. "Call on me if you need anything." He mounted and looked down at her. "Anything at all."

Sara stood and looked at him in amazement as he rode away. What was the man trying to do? She talked to Garfield about it as they were standing in the front yard later that evening.

"Mayhap the man's sincere." Garfield shrugged. "Mayhap he's given up."

Sara shook her head. "I don't think so. I just can't decide what he's about."

Garfield looked at her shrewdly. "Mayhap he's not about a thing. He may just be looking for a way to make things up to us. He's been trying to be friendly, I'd say."

Sara worried her lower lip with her teeth as she thought.

"I don't know. I just can't read the man." She sat down on the garden bench and looked at the moon. "This is a lovely place, isn't it, Garfield?"

He leaned against a large beech growing there and glanced around. "Will be. Right now, there's plenty to do."

Sara laughed. "There's always plenty to do, Garfield. Sit down and look at the moon. It's a perfect night—warm with the smell of grass."

Garfield scratched his head. "I had Jack trim the grass. It's growing like anything now in this warm weather. We've got to get some flowers in here and get the walk fixed. Those stones are going to trip someone." He stretched. "I'd better get to bed. I'll get started on that tomorrow. Good night." He ambled off toward the stables, and Sara knew he was going to make plans for tomorrow with Edward. She smiled to herself and leaned back, looking at the moon and breathing in the heady scent of the freshly cut grass tinged with the spice of the apple orchard. *Home,* she thought to herself, *this is really home.*

The sound of a horse interrupted her reverie. In a moment, she recognized Emrys riding alone down the road toward her. He was almost by the house when she called out to him, wishing him good evening. He dismounted and tethered his horse to the garden post, then came toward her, smiling. "It feels more like midsummer tonight, doesn't it?" He sat down on the bench beside her. "Are you planning your flower garden, Miss Jones?"

Sara smiled back. "I'm afraid I don't know much about flowers, Lord Emrys. I know what I like, but have no idea when to plant what."

"Would you like to borrow my gardener for a few hours to assist?"

Sara started to refuse, but remembered Garfield's words. "Thank you. That would certainly be a help to us."

He smiled broadly. "Done. Expect him within a few days." He turned and looked back at the house. "You haven't seen anything else . . . unexpected, have you?"

All her doubts came back in a rush. "No, why do you ask?"

"I was just worrying about Ned Perkin. I asked about the man, but he seems to have gone to earth somewhere. From what I know of him, I don't like the idea of him loose in the country with all of you undefended here." He turned to her, frowning. "Promise me you'll send one of the boys to get me if you hear or see anything at all unusual."

Sara laughed. "I don't believe those stories at all. Ned Perkin has probably gone to Paris with all his loot and is gambling the night away."

Emrys shook his head. "I hope you're right."

"From what you know of Perkin, you said. Just what do you know of the man? I've heard story after story. He seems to be either the devil incarnate or Robin Hood, depending on who's telling the story." She chuckled. "What's your story about Perkin?" To her surprise, she felt Emrys stiffen beside her. He let his breath out in a long, measured exhalation and seemed to will himself to relax. "I'm sorry," Sara said quickly, "I didn't mean to ask. As I said this afternoon, you certainly don't have to say anything."

"Quite all right, Miss Jones. As I told you, nothing in a small town is private. I'm sure that someone in the village will tell you all the details sooner or later, so I've decided that I'd rather tell you myself." There was a pause. "My wife was in love with Ned Perkin."

The words hung in the air for a long minute. "I'm sorry, Lord Emrys." Sara's voice was soft. "I didn't mean to pry."

"There's more." he tried unsuccessfully to keep the bitterness from his tone. "I might as well tell you all of it." He turned and looked at her, his eyes gold in the moonlight. "No, it's all right, Miss Jones. I want you to hear my side of this." Sara nodded her head, and Emrys went on. "Elizabeth and I had an arranged marriage. I didn't know her at all, even though her father and mine had planned on our marriage for years. Neither of us was ever consulted—our fathers just arranged it all. I saw her a few times when she was a child, but then I went off to Italy and was gone for a while. She grew up while I was gone, and I didn't see her at all until a week before the wedding. I didn't know that she had met someone else and fallen in love during the time I was gone."

"Ned Perkin?" Sara murmured.

Emrys nodded. "I didn't know it at the time, but she threatened to kill herself if her father made her marry me. She intended to run away and meet Perkin on the Continent. Then, three months before our wedding date, she received word that Perkin had been in a duel in Paris and had been killed. Our wedding went on as planned, and I had no idea that all this had happened." He hesitated, sorting through his memories. "We had been married over a year—not particularly happily, although not unhappily either—when she got a letter from Perkin. He hadn't been killed, but had been in a French prison somewhere. He had escaped and was in England."

The silence was heavy. "And she wanted to join him?" Sara asked.

"Yes. He visited her while I was in Brussels on business, and they planned to leave together. Perkin had some things to do first, however. He left, telling her he would be back in a month." He paused, and Sara sensed how much effort the story was costing him. "He didn't try to reach her until several months later." He stopped to take a deep breath, then took up the story again. "Perkin sent for her to come to him. There was a complication, however." He stiffened, and bitterness flooded his voice. "Elizabeth was expecting a child, but she tried to leave anyway. The housekeeper discovered her plans and told me, so I was able to prevent her leaving." He shook his head. "She tried more than once. Finally . . ." He stopped, then began again. "Finally, she rode away one night to meet Perkin. She tried to jump a ditch in the dark, the horse didn't clear it, and she broke her neck."

Emrys looked at her, his eyes hollow and shadowed. Sara had to fight off the urge to put her hand on his and offer comfort. "I'm sorry," she said softly. "The baby died?"

"Yes. There was an inquiry, of course, and many who knew that we were unhappy whispered that I had killed her, but that was proven untrue. I tried to keep her relationship with Perkin a secret, but her maid blurted it out when the magistrates questioned her."

"You must hate Ned Perkin very much."

"In one way, maybe I do. Elizabeth would be alive today if it hadn't been for Ned Perkin. I don't know how he felt about Elizabeth. Perhaps he loved her; perhaps he was only using her. I don't know."

"Did you ever ask him or speak of it when he was here?"

Emrys shook his head. "I've never seen the man. I knew he was here, but I didn't want to talk to him. It was . . . it was too . . ." His voice trailed off.

"I understand." To her surprise, Sara did understand exactly.

Emrys looked at her gratefully. "Thank you. So many people have . . . have . . ." He groped for words.

Sara smiled back at him. "Yes, I do understand. It must have been very difficult for you to come here to evict him. I'm sure you had to do what you felt right in spite of what people said."

"You're very perceptive, Miss Jones. I knew many would say that I was simply trying to get revenge on Ned Perkin. As you said, some regard him as a renegade while others see him as Robin Hood. He is, as I have heard, well-mannered and personable when he wishes to be." He paused for a beat. "I think he would have to be charming as well. Elizabeth loved charming men who flattered her." The implication was clear—Emrys would be unable to flatter unless he meant it sincerely. No more than she knew him, Sara sensed that much about the man.

"He's probably gone now."

"I don't think so, Miss Jones. I've been told by several who should know that Perkin loved Elizabeth and blames me for her death. One of the reasons he was here, I've been told, was to see that Elizabeth's death was avenged." Sara gasped, and Emrys went on. "After she died, I went back to Italy to get away. I needed to sort things out in my mind and begin again. When I returned, I learned Perkin was here. So, not because he had been involved with my dead wife, but because I truly thought him a murderer and a menace, I took steps to capture him."

"And that was when he slipped away."

"Yes." Emrys looked at her, and his hand touched her arm briefly. "And that's the story, Miss Jones."

"Thank you for telling me, Lord Emrys. I do believe you, but I don't think Perkin would harm any of us. He's probably gone by now."

"I fervently hope so." Emrys stood up and looked down at her. "Thank you for listening to me, Miss Jones. I . . . we . . ." He stopped and started again. "We seem to have gotten off on the wrong foot, Miss Jones. I do apologize for that." He backed up and untethered his horse. "I'll have my gardener here as soon as possible. He has a good selection of plants he's been growing in the hothouse. Just tell him if you need anything, Miss Jones." He gave her a strange look, then smiled at her. "Good night, Miss Jones." Before Sara could do more than murmur good night in return, he was gone. Sara sat on the bench listening to the sound of his horse's hooves fading in the distance. Finally, she got up and went around the house to the shed to make sure Lucy was all right. She opened the shed door and petted the beagle. "The poor man," she said, hugging Lucy.

"Is anything wrong?" Edward Moore came up to the shed door and looked in.

"No." Sara gave Lucy one last pat and shut the door, fastening it firmly. "I was just checking on the dog." She looked around. "I didn't know you were still up, Edward. Is anything wrong with you?"

He smiled at her. "Just making sure my family is safe." He touched her shoulder. "I consider all of you my family since I don't have one. I hope you don't mind." He fell into step beside her and walked her to the back door.

"We consider you family as well, Edward." Sara paused and glanced up at him. He was looking at her strangely, and before she could think, he bent and brushed her forehead with his lips. "Good night, Miss Jones," he said and quickly walked away.

Sara touched her forehead and looked at the empty yard. She could barely see Edward going into the stables to sleep. She looked at her fingertips as though she could see his kiss there. "Good night, Edward," she whispered.

Chapter 10

The next morning, when Sara went to feed Lucy, she took one look at the shed, stopped, and cried out. In seconds, all the children were standing beside her, looking at the shed. The shed door was open and Lucy was gone. All of the children denied letting the beagle out and joined Sara in searching for her. Even Edward, who had been working on the corner of the stables, joined them, but there was no sign of Lucy.

"She could be anywhere," Edward said. "I suppose it's my fault. I went in the shed to get a saw and some boards, and I was sure I shut the door behind me. I must have been careless with the latch." He gave her a rueful smile. "I'm sorry. I'll finish what I'm doing and spend the rest of the day looking. I'll find her for you."

"She'll be back." Jack was confident. "Where else could she get such treatment?"

Sara raised an eyebrow. "You heard her howling. Do you really think she liked being cooped up in the shed for such a time? Hardly what I'd call wonderful treatment, Jack."

Jack looked around, crestfallen. "You're right—we may never see her again."

"Don't you worry." Edward smiled. "I'll find her one way or the other." He glanced over at the stables. "I need to get back to help Garfield. I'll look this afternoon."

"Thank you." Sara met his eyes, and what she saw there made her blush. Disconcerted, she gathered up the children and hurried back to the house. There she found Mrs. Jones and Aunt Zell getting ready for a trip to the village to buy some material for new curtains. As usual, they were disagreeing about what was needed. "Muslin," Aunt Zell said firmly as they went out the door. "Just the thing for summer."

"Brocade," Mrs. Jones said, nodding her head. "It will look excellent all year and give us just the touch we want for the house. Perhaps a nice green."

Sara laughed and closed the door behind them. They would probably come home with something entirely different, as they usually did. Or even, as they had done occasionally, come home with nothing at all. While they were in the village, they were planning to do some visiting and leave some cards, so shopping might be delayed.

Garfield came in, mopping sweat from his forehead. "I can't believe it's this hot in the spring. The weather's gone crazy." He wiped his face with an already wet handkerchief. "Do we have any lemons for lemonade?" He looked positively wistful.

Sara laughed and went to the kitchen to make lemonade. She took a glassful to Garfield, and he downed it and another before he went back out to the stables to finish the work there. It was a good hour before Sara thought that Edward might want a glass of refreshment as well. She pondered sending the lemonade out by Jack, then decided that was cowardly. She poured it herself and carried it out to the stables. There were no hammers, no saws. Just Edward Moore standing there in the hot sunshine. Edward Moore without his shirt, his back shiny with sweat, the muscles rippling as he pulled at a nail with his hammer.

Sara tried to speak, but her mouth was suddenly dry. She tried his name again, but it sounded strange. Edward whirled around, the hammer raised, and Sara shrank back, almost dropping the glass of lemonade. For just the fraction of a second, she saw something in his eyes—something she couldn't name. It wasn't the same look she had seen before. This was something else entirely, something raw and wild. Before she could identify the look or even make sure she had seen it, it was gone. Edward smiled at her and then looked down at his bare, sweaty chest. His shirt was draped over a board behind her. He reached to get it, and his scent filled her nostrils. It wasn't unpleasant, and did strange things to her.

In just a moment he had his shirt on and tied. "I apologize," he said with a smile. "I wasn't expecting such company." He glanced at the glass of lemonade in her hand. "For me? What a nice thought."

Sara gathered her wits and handed him the glass, but had trouble meeting his eyes. That was worse because then she wound up looking at his chest which was indeed sweaty. His shirt was beginning to cling in quite a few places, all of them muscular. She looked back at his eyes and found him smiling. He seemed to know the effect he was having on her. "Would you like to come into my parlor, Miss Jones?" he asked, a laughing edge to his voice. He gestured to the dim recesses of the stable.

"N-no." Sara took a step backward. "I just thought you might want . . . I thought some lemonade would be nice."

"And it is." He drained his glass and put it down beside him. "Thank you."

"You're welcome." Sara snatched up the glass and scurried to the house. She thought she heard Edward chuckling behind her, but she didn't dare look back to see. When she went into the kitchen, she felt quite warm herself, but a glass of lemonade didn't seem to help. All she could think of was the way Edward looked in that damp shirt. It was, she reminded herself firmly, time to think of something else—time to do something that would take her mind off that . . . that body.

One sure way to stop thinking of that shirt and what was in it was to get away from the house. Every time Sara glanced out the window, she saw Edward working outside, whistling sometimes, humming sometimes. With each glance, she was more and more aware of him as a man. Finally she could stand no more. She gathered up Mary and Matthew and set off for the pond to see if she could find a trace of Lucy.

The ground under the willows was cool, and Sara took off the twins' shoes and watched them wade in the shallow water. It looked so inviting that she took off her own shoes and dangled her feet in the water, swishing them back and forth as she edged her gown higher and higher to keep from getting it wet. The water felt really good, and she felt totally decadent, knowing that she should be back at Saint's Haven, working. Instead, she leaned back and closed her eyes, turning her face upward and taking a deep, satisfied breath.

"From that smile, I'd say the water was just right." The voice held more than a touch of amusement, and Sara didn't even have to turn to recognize it. Hastily she sat up and shoved her dress down below her knees. She stood and waded farther out into the pond to get Mary and Matthew. They had other ideas, however, and splashed past her toward firm ground. They had been splattering each other for the better part of the hour and were soaked all over.

"Urchins," Emrys said, smiling down at them. "Let me help you." He held his arm out and the twins grabbed him, heedless of the water dripping on his exquisite tailoring. He laughed as he swung each of them up out of the water and onto one of the flat rocks at the edge. "By August, the two of you will be swimming like fish," he said, laughing. "And what about you, Miss Jones?" he asked, turning to Sara. "Will you be doing the same?"

"Hardly." Sara glanced down at her bare legs in the water. She was having to hold her dress up almost to her knees to keep from getting it wet. Clearly, she was at a disadvantage, and Emrys knew it. In fact, he seemed to be enjoying it immensely. He held out a hand. "Assistance, Miss Jones?"

"Thank you." Even to her own ears, Sara sounded prim. She took Emrys' hand and steadied herself as she waded out of the water and onto the rock. Emrys was trying not to smile as she hastily smoothed her gown and tried to make sure it covered her ankles and bare feet. He wasn't successful—the dimple at the edge of his mouth was twitching. "And what brings you for a visit, Lord Emrys?" Sara asked, sitting down on the rock with as much dignity as she could muster.

"I'm returning something." This time Emrys laughed aloud. He went back toward his horse, Mary and Matthew close on his heels. Sara heard the twins squealing with excitement, and then Matthew was right in her lap. "Just look!" He pointed.

"It's impolite to point," Sara said automatically as she turned. She was caught unawares as a brown, black, and white streak of fur landed in her lap, and she would have fallen right into the pond if Emrys hadn't caught her arm and shoulder. Lucy was back.

Sara caught her breath and turned to look at him. For an instant, he had a strange, faraway look in his eyes. Then he turned her loose, and his face became blank and expressionless with only a polite smile.

"You found her? You're returning Lucy?" Sara longed to see again the warmth that had been in those amber eyes.

Matthew tugged at Emrys' sleeve again. "Can we wade again?"

"May we," Sara corrected automatically.

Emrys grinned at her, the warm smile this time. "You're dodging the question with a technicality, Miss Jones." He sat down beside her and stretched his long legs until his shiny boots almost touched the water.

"*May* we wade again?" Mary stuck her toes in the water.

"For a few minutes." Sara laughed as Lucy's wagging tail brushed across her nose and back, and she shifted to move the beagle. "Thank you, Lord Emrys, for bringing her back. We were worried."

Emrys put a hand on Lucy, and she stopped wriggling. "I'm afraid I have a confession to make, Miss Jones." The dimple at the side of his mouth was twitching again. "I'm afraid I haven't returned exactly the same animal to you." He chuckled at Sara's surprised look. "Oh, it's your demon beagle, all right, but I must tell you that she, ah, she. . . . Miss Jones, when I came upon your Lucy, she was, shall we say, engaged in amorous pursuits with my beagle."

Sara felt herself turn red, and it had nothing to do with the heat. "Oh."

Emrys' voice was bubbling with suppressed laughter. "Yes, Miss Jones, unless I miss my guess, you'll have several beagles here at Saint's Haven. Beagle puppies. The children should be ecstatic." He shook with laughter. "I don't know about you, of course. Some delicate females don't care to have puppies underfoot."

"Puppies?" Matthew had heard the word and came splashing over. "Can I have one? I want a puppy. I've never had one and I've *always* wanted a puppy."

"May I," Sara corrected.

"Oh, good! Thank you!" Matthew threw his arms around her and hugged her. "I've always wanted a puppy."

Mary burst into tears. "I want one, too," she wailed. "Why can't I have a puppy, too?" She splashed water at Matthew, although most of it landed on Sara. "You get everything!"

"That's enough!" Sara's voice was stern, and the twins looked at her in surprise. "Out of the water, right now." She pointed to the rock and started to stand. Lucy wriggled and twisted to put her paws around Sara's neck and threw her off balance. With a tremendous splash, Sara fell into the pond. When she managed to stand up, water running from her nose, mouth, and the sleeves of her dress, she couldn't see a thing for the hair across her face. She could hear, however, and all she could hear was Emrys roaring with laughter. She slapped her hair back from her face and glared at him. He was laughing so hard he was bent over. Lucy was sitting beside him, quite dry and wagging her tail. Sara could have sworn that Lucy was grinning.

"I fail to see the humor here," Sara said, swishing through the water to the rock.

"That's because you can't see yourself, Miss Jones." Emrys gasped from laughing so hard and bent over again. He ducked his head, his shoulders shaking. Before she thought, Sara reached up, grabbed his arm, and pulled. Emrys went into the water head first.

"Oh, my heavens!" Sara was horrified at what she had done. The surface of the pond stilled, and she didn't see Emrys. Good Lord, had she drowned the man? She waded toward the place he had fallen in and felt around with her hands. Then her arms were caught, and she was pulled under again, choking and gasping. When she was finally able to stand up and catch her breath, she heard Emrys laughing again. He was up on the rock with Mary and Matthew, all three of them soaked to the skin, and all three of them laughing. Sara glared at Emrys and searched for something appropriately mean to say, but then thought of how she must look. She began to giggle; then she was laughing with the others. Emrys held out a hand to help her onto the rock, and she hesitated.

"No tricks this time, Miss Jones." He pulled her to the rock and looked at her, his eyes warm. "I should apologize, and I do. I couldn't resist."

"Nor could I, Lord Emrys." She looked at his dripping clothing. "I suspect your valet will have some words to say about your attire."

He glanced down at his soaked waistcoat, then wrung some water out of his cuff. "No doubt." He grinned at her wickedly. "I must say, Miss Jones, that I didn't expect that of you. I suspect something of the devil dog has rubbed off on you."

Sara looked at Lucy, who was wagging her tail in excitement. "No doubt." She tried to think of a delicate way to ask a question. "I've had little experience with, ah, amorous beagles. Should I put her back inside her shed? Or is it any use now?"

"I believe I'd put her up for another few days," Emrys said, looking thoughtfully at Lucy. "Although I do believe she'll probably be a mother."

Sara sighed. "Just what we need."

"I'm sure you'll manage to adopt every single puppy," Emrys said, chuckling as he picked Lucy up and tucked her under his arm. He offered his other arm to Sara. "Allow me," he said. Sara took his arm, and he turned to Mary and Matthew. "Come along, urchins," he said. "I have no more arms, so you'll have to walk beside me.

You can help me make sure this devil dog doesn't escape again."

Mary held her arms up. "Carry me." She sounded wistful.

Emrys gave Sara a look of regret. "Other duty calls, Miss Jones." Sara moved from his side and gathered up their shoes as he scooped Mary up to his shoulder, and they went off across the field. Sara followed them, laughing at the sight of Emrys from behind. Mary's head was bobbing above his shoulder, Lucy's rump was sticking out from the crook of his other elbow, and he was dripping water everywhere. *He's really quite a family man,* she thought to herself. With a chill, she remembered what he had told her of his life. Emrys had no family, for Ned Perkin had wrecked the one chance Emrys had had at happiness. Sara was beginning to see Emrys in a new way and realized that the ice in his eyes was only part of a wall he had built to insulate himself from the world. She resolved to ask him over to play with the children more often. It would do him good.

Lucy was unceremoniously dumped back inside the shed, and she gave Sara a beagle glare as she settled herself onto her bed at the back of the building. Sara glanced around as soon as she had shut the door. Emrys had put Mary down and was looking around at the work done on Saint's Haven. In particular, he was looking at Edward Moore, who had once again removed his shirt and was working on the outside of the stable, the sweat glistening on his tanned body.

"Hardly a sight for an orphanage," Emrys said with a raised eyebrow as Sara walked up to him.

"I see nothing wrong with it."

Emrys glanced at her, then back at Edward. "I doubt you would, Miss Jones." The ice was back in his eyes and voice. "I need to be getting back to Brookwood. Good afternoon." He nodded politely and was off across the field toward the pond where he had left his horse.

Sara glanced again at Edward, who was working with his back to her. Sara had the distinct feeling that Edward was doing this on purpose—he knew exactly the effect his behavior was creating. Worse, as she looked at him, she felt herself blush, and there was a strange feeling in her stomach. She turned and hurried into the house with the twins. To her dismay, her mother and Aunt Zell were there, having a cup of tea with Roger Chiswick. At first glance, it struck Sara that her mother looked different. Her color was higher, and she was smiling broadly at Chiswick. The smile faded and turned to horror as she saw Sara. "Whatever happened to you?" she gasped.

The story was too much to tell. "I fell in the pond." It wasn't exactly the truth, but it wasn't exactly a lie either. "Mary and Matthew are wet, too."

"You could have drowned!"

"I'm fine, Mama. I'll get the twins changed." She herded Mary and Matthew in front of her and hurried out of the room. "Evan is fun, isn't he?" Mary asked, running up the stairs.

"Evan?" Sara was at a loss.

"She means Emrys," Matthew said. "He told us his first name was Evan."

Sara hustled them into the room Matthew shared with the other boys. "Surely he didn't tell you to call him that, did he?"

"No." Matthew ran to the window and looked out, oblivious to the water he was dripping on the floor. "But I know he wouldn't mind."

Sara turned him around and handed him dry clothes. "You are not to address him by his first name. I don't want you to call him anything except Lord Emrys. Children do not address their elders by first names." Her voice was firm. Before she took Mary with her to find some dry clothes, she asked, "Do you understand?"

"Yes," Matthew sighed. "Could we call him Papa?"

Sara stared at him and gasped. "Certainly not, Matthew. He isn't your father."

"I know that. I'd just like to have a father." His mouth turned down in a pout. "You just take all the fun out of everything, Sara."

"That's why I'm here." She winked at him and shut the door.

Sara spent the next day working in the yard with Edward and Garfield. They and the boys did wonders with both the front and the back. By nightfall when they went in to supper, the debris had all been cleared away, the flower beds dug up and planted with some plants Mrs. Jones and Aunt Zell had bought in the village, and the hedges trimmed. Sara was tired, sore, and very pleased with her day's work. Just before bedtime, she wandered out to the front yard and sat down on the small garden bench to admire her handiwork in the moonlight. It was almost like day outside, and the heat had given way to a smooth balminess that required no more than a light shawl. Sara sat with her back to the road, looking at Saint's Haven. It was going to be a beautiful place, she thought. No wonder her father had loved it. He would be proud of the way they were all working together to make it a home.

Edward came around the corner of the house and stopped in surprise. "I had no idea you were here," he said. "I hope I'm not interrupting."

Sara shook her head. "No, I was just thinking about Papa and the house. I think he'd be happy to know we were here."

Edward sat down beside her and looked at the house and garden. "I think he probably knows."

"I hope so." Sara gave him a grateful smile. Edward

always seemed to understand how she felt. "Thank you for doing so much today."

"I was glad to." He smiled back at her, darkly handsome in the moonlight. He looked at her a moment. "You're a beautiful woman, Sara." His voice was soft as the breeze. Before Sara could think of anything to say, Edward had cupped her face in his hands and was kissing her. The touch of his lips on hers was unlike anything Sara had ever known, and she felt dizzy even though she was sitting down. Edward deepened the kiss, and Sara caught her breath, making a little sobbing sound in her throat. She was unable to think, unable to reason. There was only the soft breeze, the moonlight, and the feelings Edward was arousing in her. "Edward," she murmured as he put his hands on her arms and slid them up to her shoulders. She felt the coolness of the breeze as her shawl slipped from her shoulders, but then she couldn't feel anything except his lips and the touch of his fingertips as he teased the nape of her neck and her jaw. She was getting goose bumps all over, even though there was a heat rising from somewhere in the middle of her body. Sara felt her reason and control slipping and knew she had to move away. "Edward," she murmured again.

"Sara," he whispered against her cheek, "Sara, you're beautiful. Please . . ." His fingers slipped to the buttons on the front of her dress. Sara grabbed his hand and jerked back.

"No, please, Edward." She jumped to her feet, breathing heavily.

"Sara . . ." Edward stood and reached for her, but Sara stepped backward. "I . . . I've got to go inside," she stammered. She turned and ran into the darkened house and shut the door behind her, breathing heavily. The warmth was still inside her body, and she felt hot all over, even though there were goose bumps on her arms. She had never experienced such sensations. "Is this what love could be?" she whispered to herself, rubbing her arms. She went to the window and looked out at the garden bench, but there was no one there. Edward had gone. The only thing there was her shawl, on the ground where it had fallen.

Sara opened the door cautiously and looked outside. No one was there. She was relieved, because she knew in her heart that it would be difficult to resist Edward Moore if he kissed her again. She hurried to the bench and bent over to retrieve her shawl.

"An interesting scene, Miss Jones," Emrys drawled, looking down at her from atop his black horse. Emrys was all dressed in black, as usual, and Sara hadn't even seen him in the shadows of the trees at the edge of the property. He flicked the reins, and his horse moved out into the clear road in front of the house. "I know that wasn't overly improper for a London miss—some of them, anyway— but here in Saint Claire, your reputation will be in shreds if anyone else ever saw such a scene." He crossed his arms on the saddle horn and looked down at her.

Sara felt her face flame. "Perhaps others in Saint Claire don't wish to spend their evenings spying on others." She tried to make her voice as cold as she felt inside.

Emrys' laugh was short. "On the contrary, Miss Jones, everyone in a small village spies on everyone else. There isn't anything else to do to pass the time." He straightened in the saddle. Sara couldn't see his expression—she couldn't see anything except his looming black silhouette against the moonlight. "Even so, Lord Emrys, there's no excuse for you spying on others."

"Spying?" he asked smoothly, turning his horse. "Hardly that, Miss Jones. I was merely out for a ride at night and what should I see when I rounded the bend in the road but you and Mr. Moore becoming acquainted. Quite well acquainted, I should say.''

''Well, I should say that what I do is none of your business,'' Sara said, her voice trembling from either rage or mortification, she couldn't distinguish which. She groped for something else to say that would put the man in his place and thought of nothing. She flung her shawl around her shoulders. ''Good night, Lord Emrys,'' she said, marching to the door.

Before she got the door closed behind her, she could hear him urge his horse on down the road. Worse, she could hear him chuckling softly to himself.

Chapter 11

Sara was accustomed to rising early. This morning, the sun was just beginning to stream into the kitchen windows when she picked up the dish containing Lucy's breakfast. Jack came in, rubbing his eyes, and began to scavenge for breakfast. "I thought I saw the ghost in white again last night," he said around mouthfuls of bread, "but it might have been a dream. I didn't wake up." He paused. "At least, I don't think I did."

"It was probably a dream. Don't talk with your mouth full." Sara tucked the dish under one arm and picked up a pitcher of water for Lucy.

"When are you going to let her out? That poor dog's been in there forever." Jack bit into a hunk of cheese and spread some jam on another piece of bread.

"I think I may let her out tomorrow," Sara said. "She's been in the shed long enough." She thought about Lucy's foray to Brookwood. "I'm not sure this is doing any good. It's so much trouble, and Emrys thinks she may become a mother anyway."

"I heard." Jack got up and took the pitcher from her. "Here, I'll help you." He reached for the door latch and pulled the kitchen door open. Lucy bounded inside, wagging her tail. She was covered with mud and had obviously been out for hours.

"How do you suppose she got out? Dug her way under the shed wall?" Jack put the pitcher down on a small table near the door and peered out. "Sara, the shed door is open."

Sara put Lucy's food beside the pitcher and followed Jack out the door, Lucy whining behind her. "It's been opened from the outside by someone," Jack said, looking at the latch. Sara looked down at the ground in front of the shed and saw some tracks. "Look at this." She put a hand on the wriggling Lucy to keep her back and knelt by the tracks. "These footprints are so small. One of the children must have heard her whining and let her out."

"In the middle of the night?" Jack knelt and looked at the prints.

Sara stood and walked backward a few steps. "Jack," she said in a strained voice, "those footprints are going that way." She pointed toward the pond—or to Brookwood—and began following the small tracks. "It has to be a child," she said.

"Or a very small woman." Jack looked closely at one of the tracks. "I think it's a woman's shoe. The heel is small."

Sara was puzzled. "But who? I certainly don't know anyone who would come set Lucy free."

"Our ghost?"

Sara caught her breath. "Don't be silly, Jack. We've already established that there is no ghost." She stopped and looked at him. "I'm sorry. You're probably right and you must have seen something—or someone—last night. We know that the wraith in white is a real person and these are real tracks."

"*Were* real," Jack said with a sigh. "They disappear into the tall grass right here, and I can't find any more." He looked straight ahead. "If the ghost or whoever it was went in a straight line, where would she be?"

Sara looked straight ahead. "Brookwood," she said quietly. "Do you think Emrys could have anything to do with this?"

Jack shook his head. "I can't see a trick like this from him, but I really don't know him." He turned to Sara. "We're going to have to stay up for a night or two and watch again."

"I know." Sara sighed. "This is just between us, Jack. I don't want Mama or Aunt Zell or the children to know about this. We'll watch on our own."

"I'll have to tell James." Jack whistled for Lucy, and they began walking back to Saint's Haven.

Sara smiled. "All right, but only James—none of the other children. Are we agreed?" Lucy rubbed up against her leg and then scampered on ahead, headed for the kitchen door. "I may tell Garfield, but I'll see." Sara paused and looked back toward Brookwood. "The thing I can't understand, Jack, is Lucy. Why would the ghost—or person—let her out. Why that? Why not start a fire or break windows or whatever if this is designed to frighten us. It doesn't make sense."

"No, it doesn't." Jack stopped to latch the shed door. "You're right, Sara, about one thing, though. If Emrys wanted us out, the ghost would be doing something to harm us. Maybe he doesn't have anything to do with this."

"I hope he doesn't, Jack." To her surprise, she found she really hoped Emrys was innocent.

Roger Chiswick came by shortly before noon. He brought them some flower plants for the garden and the backyard, as well as a few young apple trees. Sara took him to the orchard so he could show her where to plant the trees. He suggested cutting down some old ones that had been damaged by weather and age, and replacing them. "I'll bring you some others tomorrow to fill in over there," he said as Lucy ran up to them. Chiswick glanced down. "I see you've let your beagle out."

"She got out—not once, but twice—and I just decided to leave her out."

"Dug out?" Chiswick grunted. "Beagles hate to be confined. They'll get out of almost anywhere. They're not going anywhere; they're just independent." He chuckled. "They just don't want you telling them what to do."

Sara thought a moment, then decided Chiswick might be able to help her. "Someone let her out," she said slowly. "Jack and I think it's the ghost."

Chiswick stopped short in his walk back to the house. "The ghost? You've seen it again?"

Sara shook her head. "No, not seen it, or at least not for sure. Jack thought he saw it last night. This morning, there were tracks outside the shed, and Jack and I think the person dressed in white might have been the one to free Lucy." She looked right into Chiswick's eyes. "We lost the tracks in the grass, but if the person followed a straight path, she'd end up at Brookwood. Do you think Emrys would do such a thing? What would it benefit him?"

"He wouldn't." Chiswick dropped his eyes. "She? Why do you say 'she'?"

"The tracks are small. We at first thought they were the tracks of a child, but Jack suggested it might be a small woman. Who—?"

Chiswick interrupted her. "Would you show me the tracks?" He headed for the shed, and Sara was hard put to keep up. At the shed, the tracks had almost been obliterated, but Sara found some right before they disappeared in the grass. Chiswick fell to his knees and looked at them carefully. He stood and brushed at his clothing. "You may be right in thinking your specter is a small woman, Miss Jones. I'll make some discreet inquiries. However, I doubt you'll be bothered again." He smiled at her, although his eyes weren't smiling. "I've got an errand to run or I'd stay and help you look further. I'll return tomorrow or the next day." He patted her hand. "In the meantime, I don't think you'll be bothered." He smiled at her again, took his leave, and hurried away. Puzzled, Sara frowned after him and sighed as Lucy rolled in the dirt at her feet, trying to look appealing. "I see you, you lazy animal." Sara skirted the dog and headed into the house. "You stay outside and practice being a watchdog. I think we need one."

That afternoon, just to get away for a while, Sara took Mary, Matthew, and Briget to the village. They browsed in the few little shops and even bought Briget a new pink hair ribbon. The color didn't suit at all; but Briget loved it, so Sara gave way. As they were leaving, Sara saw a bit of lace that would fit perfectly at the bodice of her green dress and had to have it. It wasn't expensive, but even a little seemed an extravagance when she could be spending on things for the house. The shopkeeper, Mrs. Abney, a plump, cheerful woman who seemed to know everyone and everything in St. Claire, nodded as Sara tried to make up her mind. "Nothing like lace to spruce up a dress, I always say. Try it with this ribbon."

Mrs. Abney was right—the ribbon and lace were just what Sara had envisioned to renew the dress. Actually, she was saving by not buying a new dress, Sara rationalized as

she paid Mrs. Abney. "Do come back and show me what
you've done," Mrs. Abney said, walking them to the door.
"I always like to pass on ideas to the women in the village."
As they came out of the shop, Emrys was riding down the
street on his huge, black horse. "Poor man," Mrs. Abney
said, clicking her tongue against her teeth, "always alone,
always dressed like a funeral. What he needs is a good
woman." She leaned toward Sara. "I heard half of the
females in London are after him, but he's sworn off women.
Figures."

Sara was torn between wanting to find out more and
not wanting to be caught gossiping. Mrs. Abney had no
such scruples. In just a few moments, Sara was given the
story of Emrys' sad marriage. "Beautiful girl, that Elizabeth," Mrs. Abney said, looking at Emrys riding slowly out
of town, "but not the marrying kind. Not that one." She
shook her head, and her voice dropped to a whisper. "A
rounder, you know."

Sara didn't know, but gathered that Mrs. Abney thought
Elizabeth wasn't quite a pattern card of propriety. Mrs.
Abney clicked her tongue against her teeth again. "Why,
once I heard that—" She stopped as a customer
approached, then smiled and introduced Sara to Mrs. Jor-
dan and her daughter. The daughter looked older than
Mrs. Jordan. "I was just telling Miss Jones about Lord
Emrys," Mrs. Abney said.

"Poor man." Mrs. Jordan looked at her daughter in a
significant way. "What he needs is a good wife." The
women nodded. Sara made hasty farewells and left. She
certainly didn't want to hear any more about Emrys. He
had been right—everything was known and discussed in
the village.

Back at Saint's Haven, Sara hurried up to her room to
see if the lace and ribbon matched the green of the dress.
She shoved open the door to her room, went inside without

looking, and ran right into Edward Moore. Startled, she stared up at him and was surprised at the look in his eyes. For just a moment, his eyes were windows into a cold, unfeeling soul. Then the look disappeared, and Sara thought she must have been mistaken. "A thousand pardons, Miss Jones," he said, waving a hammer. "I thought I heard you say there was a loose board here, and I came up to repair it. If you'll show me where it is, I'll fix it right now."

"A loose board?" Sara was blank.

"No matter, I'll see to it later." Edward walked to the door. "Do you have anything else that needs repairing?"

Sara put her purchases down on the bed. "The kitchen table," she said, frowning. "It wobbles, and I'm afraid it will fall while we're eating."

"Are you sure? I hadn't noticed it."

Sara put her lace and ribbon down on her bed. "Let me show you." She smiled at him as he held the door for her.

In the kitchen, she showed him a cracked leg on the table and made a pot of tea while he repaired it. Edward was quick and deft, and he had the table ready about the same time that she had the tea tray ready. "I certainly appreciate this," he said with a smile as he held her chair for her. "It isn't often that I get to sit down to tea with such a lovely companion."

Sara laughed and thanked him for the compliment. She had the impression that in his past, Edward Moore had been quite an accomplished flirt. Just looking at him, the sparkling, roguish eyes, the devil-may-care smile, and the slightly rakish expression, Sara could see that the man could easily play havoc with hearts. Since she had never been a flirt, Sara changed the subject and began talking about the gardens and repairs. Edward sensed her mood and outlined several good suggestions. Still, as Sara stood up to move the tea things, Edward reached over and took her hand. "You're a beautiful woman, Sara," he said with an odd note in his voice. "No, don't blush and don't thank me. I mean it." He stood beside her and touched her arms lightly with the flat of his palms. "I know you don't know much about my past, and I still have gaps in it, but I don't want you to think I'm not worthy of you. I've remembered some things: I know that I'm from Cornwall and my family is a good one. I remembered a name and a village, and I've written there to inquire. I do recall that my family is prosperous, so I could . . ." He paused and looked at her softly. "I could give you a comfortable life, Sara, if you could find it in your heart to consider me."

"I . . . I . . ." Sara stammered. "I don't . . ."

Edward put his fingertip on her lips to silence her. "Don't. Don't say anything just yet. Please just think about what I've said. That's all I ask. I'll leave things as they are for a while as I want to hear from my inquiry, but I do want you to think about it."

Sara looked up at him. His fingertip on her lips felt like a feather touch, but yet held her fast. "I will," she whispered. "I'll think about it."

He smiled. "That's all I ask of you." He moved his finger and, before Sara could catch her breath, kissed her softly on the lips. "Thank you." He moved away and backed right into Matthew. The twins were standing there, watching, their eyes huge. Sara put her hands over her face as Edward laughed and herded the twins out the door.

Sara didn't see the twins until supper, and they didn't mention what they had seen. She thought perhaps they had forgotten it. Edward was nowhere to be seen either— Garfield said he had gone into the village to see a friend. Sara wandered around the house after supper and then decided to heat enough water to give the twins a sponge bath. When she had the water on, she went to search for the twins. They weren't in the house, so she went outside to call for them. "Over here," Matthew called back. Sara found them in the front garden. Emrys was sitting on the garden bench with a twin perched on each knee. The children had sticky faces. "Sweets?" Sara said severely, looking down at them.

"A little won't hurt them," Emrys said. Sara looked at him and saw a smear of candy across his immaculate waistcoat front.

"It appears they've had more than a little." Sara tried to sound stern, but it didn't work. Emrys offered her a bonbon and smiled at her, a little sheepishly, she thought. He scooted over and made room for Sara on the bench. She sat down and ate the bonbon. It was delicious, and she looked at her chocolate-covered fingers. "Go ahead," Emrys said. "Everyone else has."

Sara laughed and licked the chocolate from her fingers. "Thank you, Lord Emrys. I appreciate your lack of formality. That was wonderful." She licked her lips.

"You look like you did today in the kitchen," Matthew said.

"When you were kissing Edward." Mary nodded in agreement.

Sara felt her face flame with embarrassment, and waited for Emrys' comment. He merely raised an eyebrow at her and began talking about taking the children to Brookwood to ride a pony he had there. Mary and Matthew were ready to go at that moment, but Sara told them they had to go take a bath. "Cleanliness first," Emrys said, swinging them onto the ground. "I'll be back another day, and we'll go have a pony ride." He looked at Sara and raised his eyebrow again. "That is, if Miss Jones isn't busy with—um— other things."

It was dark enough for Emrys to miss her blush. "The

children would be delighted. I'm sure we can find the proper time, Lord Emrys."

"I wonder." He laughed, ruffled Mary's hair, and left them. He was laughing to himself as he mounted his horse and went around the bend.

Jack came knocking on Sara's door around midnight, and they went to the window to keep watch on the shed, but saw nothing. Finally, as the clock struck four, Sara suggested that they try to get some sleep. She fell into the bed, Lucy snoring gently beside her on the floor, and went to sleep immediately. The sun was shining full into her bedroom when something awakened her. Lucy was growling and had jumped up on the bed. She was sitting right on Sara's stomach. Sara followed Lucy's gaze. Her bedroom door was being opened very slowly, almost as though someone didn't want to be seen or heard. In just a moment, Edward came into the room, his hammer and saw in his hands, and stealthily closed the door behind him. Sara sat straight up, tumbling Lucy off her lap onto the bedcovers. "What is this?" she asked, pulling the covers up under her chin.

Edward looked astonished. "I'm sorry, I didn't realize you were in here." He reached behind him and opened the door, then stepped backward into the hall. "I apologize."

"What are you doing?" Sara still had the feeling that Edward was in her room for a reason.

He waved his hammer in the direction of her bed. "I'm still looking for that loose board that's in here. I heard one squeak yesterday and remembered last night that I hadn't checked it. I thought I'd find it and fix it." He smiled that devil-may-care smile at her. "I apologize, although I can't really say I'm sorry." He turned and glanced down the hall. "I'd better be going. Let me know when it will be all right for me to fix that board." He smiled at her again and pulled the door shut. Sara heard him walking down the hall.

Although Sara was tired that night, Jack convinced her to watch with him. They sat together, looking out the window at the back grounds lit by the bright moonlight. After Sara had dozed off for perhaps the fourth or fifth time, she stood and drew her shawl around her. "This is no night for a ghost, Jack. It's too light. I'm going to bed."

"I suppose you're right." Jack sighed and stood. "I just wish—" He grabbed Sara's arm. "Look, right there," he hissed, pointing. Sara looked and saw a flash of white just going around the willows at the edge of the pond. It was too far away to distinguish anything except the touch of white. "Let's go," Jack whispered, already at the door.

Sara trailed after him, stumbling once over Lucy, who insisted on following along. At the back door, Lucy darted around her and ran off across the yard, stopping to sniff at the shed. Sara and Jack went by the shed and on toward the pond, and Lucy trotted by them, racing ahead and out of sight.

When Sara and Jack reached the willows, they saw nothing except Lucy standing there, wagging her tail and whining. She began to run around excitedly and bark at the base of one of the willow trees. Sara walked toward her. "What is it, Lucy? What do you see?"

"Just me, I'm afraid." Edward came from the murky darkness of the willows. "I heard a noise out by the shed and thought I saw something. Whatever it was came this way, so I followed." He looked around. "I've searched all along the marge, and can't find a thing." He looked at the two of them. "Did you hear something as well?"

"We . . . no, we didn't hear anything. Jack and I thought we saw something." She looked into the darkness under the trees. "Are you sure there's nothing there?"

"I'm positive. Would you like me to go with you while you look?"

Sara sighed and shook her head. "I suppose whatever it was has gone. We might as well go back."

"I'll walk you back." Edward looked up at the moon. "It'll be daylight before long, and we all need to get some sleep. We certainly have enough to do tomorrow." He laughed. "I suppose that's today instead of tomorrow."

"It is." Sara stifled a yawn and called for Lucy. The beagle kept dancing round the willow, then ran into the darkness, barking. Sara whistled for her, and she came, running around Sara's feet. All the way back to the house, Lucy ran back in the direction of the pond, barking, then came back when Sara called her. At the shed, she stopped and ran around it twice, barking. "Hush, Lucy," Sara said, stooping to pick her up. "You'll wake everyone on the place."

"Would you like for me to put her in the shed?" Edward asked.

Sara shook her head. "No, then she *would* howl. I'll just take her inside with me." She cast one last look toward the willows, but things looked just as they always did. "Good night, Edward."

Edward's fingers lingered on her arm. "Good night." He glanced at Jack, then returned to the stables as Sara and Jack went into the house. Upstairs, they looked once again at the pond and the willows. "I know I saw something," Jack said.

"We both did." Sara leaned wearily against the window. "We both know there was something there, but, just as it did before, it disappeared. We'll just have to try to find out, Jack."

His eyes shone with excitement. "We can stay up every night."

"Oh, my Lord." Sara sagged with fatigue and went into

her room. "Good night, Jack," she said firmly, closing the door behind her before he had any more suggestions. She was almost asleep before she fell into her bed, and the last thing she remembered was Lucy jumping up on the bed and curling up against her back.

Chapter 12

Sara worked in the back garden most of the next morning. She probably could have finished the whole thing, she thought wearily, if she wasn't so tired. She had glimpsed herself in the mirror this morning and had hardly recognized the creature who stared back at her. Her skin was pale, and there were dark smudges under her eyes. Her eyes were gritty from lack of sleep. Tonight, she had promised herself, she would go to bed early and ignore Jack. He had already mentioned standing watch again. Staying up all night didn't seem to bother him.

It didn't bother Lucy either. She was so glad to have the run of the yard that she rolled and tumbled with the twins, dug in the dirt Sara troweled up, and scampered off in every direction with whoever seemed to be moving. Some time in midmorning, she ran to her water dish, saw that it was empty, and loped off toward the pond.

"She should have waited for me," Sara muttered to Jack. "I could have used a break from this digging."

"Just train Lucy to do it for you," Jack said with a laugh

as he forked weeds into a wheelbarrow. "You could, for instance, line a trench with moles and set her loose."

"Oh, really? And why have her dig them up if I have to dig the trench in the first place?"

Jack looked at her and grinned as he picked up the wheelbarrow handles. "You do have a fancy for that dog, don't you?"

"Almost as much as I have for you." Sara grinned as Jack made a face at her as he went toward the stable to dump the weeds.

Lucy came running back, her paws wet, and squirmed under Sara's gown, whimpering. "Get out of there," Sara said, trying to step aside. Lucy stuck her long nose out and looked up at Sara, rolling her eyes. Sara stepped aside and bent to move the beagle. "You've got to learn to stay out of the way," Sara said firmly. Lucy ran over to the back door and scratched on it. When no one opened the door, she ran back to the shed and sniffed. Then she ran back to Sara, nudged her, and began whining.

"Are you still thirsty? I thought you had visited the pond to get a drink. Go away."

Lucy ran toward the pond, then back, then toward the pond again. Sara stood and put her hands to the small of her back. "All right, you reprobate. I'll walk with you. A break from these weeds would be welcome." She put her gloves and trowel beside the shed. "Come on." She whistled softly and walked toward the pond. Lucy hesitated, then ran up beside her and almost caused Sara to fall by getting under her feet. Sara sidestepped nimbly; but Lucy darted right back under her feet again, and Sara staggered as her feet and the beagle tangled. She stopped to fuss at Lucy, but the beagle paid no attention. Instead, Lucy began barking and running around and around a bush at the edge of the pond.

"A mouse or a rabbit?" Sara asked, walking away. "Leave

it alone, Lucy. Come on, let's sit over here and enjoy the sunshine.''

Instead of coming to her, Lucy continued to run under the bush and out again, whining. Sara was determined to ignore her, but finally gave up. ''All right, I'll look, but there had better be nothing bigger than a rabbit under there. Then we're going back home.'' She parted the low limbs of the bush and glanced on the ground. There was something white there, and she looked again, carefully this time. What she saw froze her, and she couldn't even make a sound. There was a body under the bush—the body of a woman clothed all in white.

Shaken, Sara leaned back on her heels, holding on to Lucy. ''I'm sorry I doubted you, Lucy,'' she whispered, glancing back at the bush which looked as it usually did. Nothing, not even a thread of white, showed. ''Maybe she's still alive,'' Sara whispered to herself as much as to Lucy. ''We have to find out.''

Shaking, she made herself look under the branches again. The bush hung over the edge of the pond, and the woman was caught in the branches that dipped into the water. Her hair was floating, and part of her was submerged. As soon as Sara took a good look, she knew the woman was dead. She had to be absolutely certain, however, and forced herself to touch the body. It was cold, and when Sara touched it, the woman's head turned toward her, the eyes wide and unseeing. Sara jumped back, rolling onto the warm spring grass, and caught her breath. Before she could think, she leaped to her feet and began running. She was halfway across the orchard before she was able to calm herself. Lucy was right beside her. Sara made herself take three deep breaths and then began walking toward Saint's Haven. Jack and Edward were in the back garden, digging in the dirt, and the twins were helping pull the weeds. It looked like any other day.

Jack glanced up as Sara walked up to them. "Well, Sara, much as I hate to tell you, you look terrible. You look as if you'd seen a ghost." He chuckled at his own joke.

Sara grabbed his arm. "I did, Jack." She stopped and tried to form her words. "Matthew, Mary, will you go inside and get me a drink of water?"

"Mary can go." Matthew was busy trying to find the end of a long root.

"No, I want both of you to go." Sara's voice sounded strange enough to cause Matthew to look up at her in surprise. He shrugged and motioned to Mary. It seemed an eternity before they were out of earshot. Jack didn't wait, however. "Whatever's the matter, Sara? You haven't looked this sick since we found . . ." He paused. "Good God, you didn't find another one, did you?"

Sara nodded. "At the pond. I think it's our ghost, Jack. It's a woman, all dressed in white, and I think she's drowned."

"Wait here and I'll go look." Jack put his hands on her arms and plopped her unceremoniously against the side of the shed. "I'll be back in a minute."

Edward glanced at her, then at Jack. "I'll go as well." He looked at Sara. "Will you be all right until we get back?"

"Yes." Sara nodded and watched as the two ran to the pond. After a few minutes, Matthew and Mary brought her a glass of water. "You look really sick," Matthew said. "Do you want me to tell Aunt Zell?"

Sara knelt beside him. "No, don't say a word. I'll be fine." She drank the water and made herself smile at them. "There, see. All I needed was a glass of water. Now show me what you've been doing."

"Picking up worms," Mary said, proudly showing her a jar of wriggling worms. "We're going to try to catch some birds."

"Good." Sara saw Edward and Jack coming back. "You've been so good that I have a treat for you. I want you to go up in my room and look in the little cabinet by my bed. There are some peppermint candies for you there." They left before she finished speaking. "Just take one each!"

Jack and Edward looked grim. "You were right," Edward said. "We need to get the magistrate here immediately."

"I'll go get him." Jack glanced from Sara to Edward. "If you want me to, that is."

Edward nodded. "That will be a good idea, I think. Someone should watch over the body until the magistrate gets here, so I'll go do that." He looked at Sara. "And you need to go inside and have a cup of tea. You're almost in shock from this." He put his hand on Sara's arm and led her to the back door. "Jack, you go ahead now. I'll be at the pond, and you can just bring Sherman there." He helped Sara inside and explained to Mrs. Jones and Aunt Zell what had happened, then left to wait at the pond.

Aunt Zell put a cup of steaming tea in front of Sara. "Lots of sugar in it to brace you."

Sara sipped at the tea. It was almost like syrup, but it was just what she needed. "Do you know who it was, Sara?" Mrs. Jones asked, sipping her own tea. "Surely it wasn't one of those gypsies."

"I don't think so, Mama." Sara jumped as she heard a noise.

"It's only the door," Aunt Zell said briskly. "Mr. Chiswick was going to stop by with some apples he had left over from last fall. They'll do us until our trees come in." She bustled out of the room, and in just a moment, Chiswick came in behind her.

"Oh, Roger, you'll never guess what Sara found."

Chiswick looked at Sara vaguely. "Something exciting, I dare say." He turned back to Mrs. Jones. "I'm sorry I didn't have time to get the apples for you, but something has come up. I can't stay today, but I promise I'll bring them as soon as I can.'' He backed toward the door and ran right into Briget.

"Did you hear?'' Briget's eyes were huge and round. "Sara found a body at the pond.''

"A woman this time,'' James said, coming in behind Briget. He was clearly annoyed at missing the excitement. "Why couldn't you have called me?''

"I didn't . . .'' Sara stopped as Roger Chiswick grabbed both her hands and looked right into her eyes. "A woman,'' he whispered in a hoarse voice. "Would you describe her?''

"Roger . . . ,'' Mrs. Jones began, but Aunt Zell put a hand on her shoulder and stopped her.

"Please.'' Chiswick's voice was ragged and about to break.

Sara spoke firmly. "She was dead, drowned in the pond, I think. She had long hair that was floating in the water. I couldn't tell what color it was because it was all wet.'' Sara paused as Chiswick's grip tightened on her hands. "She was all dressed in white.''

Chiswick let her loose, put his hands over his face, and made an inarticulate sound, rather like a hurt animal. Aunt Zell came over to him and put her hands on his shoulders. "Sit down,'' she said gently, helping him into a chair.

"Do you know who this is?'' Sara asked.

Chiswick moved his hands, and his face had aged five years in less than a minute. "Gwendolyn.''

Mrs. Jones caught her breath. "Are you sure? Roger, are you really sure?''

Chiswick nodded. "Almost. She's missing and has been gone since last night. She always . . . she always wears white.'' He looked at Sara. "I knew from the first moment you mentioned your ghost in white that you'd seen Gwendolyn, but I couldn't say anything. Gwendolyn isn't . . .

wasn't mentally . . ." His words trailed off. He stood up wearily. "At the pond, did you say? I'd better go there."

"Edward's there," Sara said gently. She stood and looked at Mrs. Jones. "Perhaps Aunt Zell and I should go along, Mama."

"Yes." Mrs. Jones's voice was a whisper. "I'm so sorry, Roger."

He shook his head. "Something was going to happen, I knew. I'm just sorry that it had to be this way."

"It may not be Gwendolyn," Mrs. Jones whispered.

"I think it will be." He picked up his hat and headed for the door, dazed. Sara and Aunt Zell followed him out just as Jack rounded the corner with Squire Sherman. The squire was quite put out at having his midday meal interrupted. Then he saw Chiswick.

"You're here, too, Roger?" Squire Sherman asked. "Doesn't anyone stop to eat around here?" He fell into step beside Chiswick. "What do we have out here? Another one of those gypsies?"

Aunt Zell stepped in front of him and pinned him with a glare. "Mr. Chiswick is afraid the lady at the pond is his wife, Gwendolyn."

Squire Sherman stopped and stared, openmouthed. "Oh, I say. Sorry, Chiswick, I never thought of Gwendolyn. Have you made a positive identification?"

Chiswick shook his head, and they all walked in silence to the pond. There, Edward was sitting on the rock in the sun, waiting. Chiswick waded into the water and looked at the body. There was no need for him to say anything— they could tell from his expression that it was Gwendolyn. "Is it all right to move her?" he asked Sherman, and, at Sherman's nod, gently put his arms under the body and carried it out. He carefully put Gwendolyn on the grass and closed her eyes and mouth, his fingers lingering on her face for a moment. Then he patted her dripping hair in place and removed some leaves and twigs from it.

"I knew something like this was coming," he said, looking down at Gwendolyn's waxen face. "She hadn't been with me in a long time." He looked at them, his eyes hollow. "Gwendolyn really died years ago, and this was only a shell. When she lost her mind, she didn't know what she was doing, and she was always rambling off. It's been worse lately." He paused and shut his eyes, then began again. "Last night, I thought she was in her room, but she wandered off. When I discovered she was gone, I looked all night for her. I usually found her before she wandered too far, but last night was different. I came over here in the dark"—he looked at Sara and Jack—"and the two of you almost saw me. I must have just missed her." He looked up at Squire Sherman. "She must have slipped and fallen into the pond. Gwendolyn couldn't swim."

"Then," Squire Sherman said, "what we have here is a case of accidental drowning, I'd say." He sent James and Jack to Brookwood to get a wagon to carry the body. "My condolences, Chiswick. I'm going to rule this an accident." He looked down at Gwendolyn's body. "Perhaps this is a case of the less said, the better." Squire Sherman paused, then with the air of a man doing his duty, forged on. "But, still, it is my duty to inquire. I do need to talk to you about the many trips you've made to Saint's Haven. There's been a deal of talk, you know."

Sara gasped as the implication of Squire Sherman's comment hit her. Before she could say anything, Chiswick made a strange noise. He had been touching Gwendolyn's hair again, and this time he looked at his fingers. He turned her head and looked down. "You need to see this," he said in a strangled voice.

"See what, man?" Squire Sherman was clearly ready to return to his dinner. He leaned over to see what Chiswick

had found. "Good God, that looks as if—" He stopped
and dropped to his knees, looking and probing with his
fingers. "This side of her head's been bashed in." He
peered closely. "I'd say with a rock, from the looks of it."
He stood up and glared at all of them. "In that case, it's
murder by person or persons unknown. Everyone's suspect
until we determine what happened."

"She could have fallen in and hit her head on a rock,"
Edward said, peering over Chiswick's shoulder. "I've seen
men fall in battle and hit their heads on rocks. It looked
just like that."

"We'll see." Squire Sherman looked around at each one
of them.

It took the better part of an hour before the wagon
arrived from Brookwood. In the meantime, Sara had gone
back to Saint's Haven and gotten a quilt to cover Mrs.
Chiswick and tell her mother what had happened. Mrs.
Jones wanted to return to the pond with Sara. "I should
go," Mrs. Jones said. "Roger will need a friend."

"I don't believe it would be a good idea, Mama." Sara
wasn't about to tell her of Sherman's suspicions. "Why
don't you make tea for everyone? I think Squire Sherman
is planning to come back here and ask some questions.
Tea will certainly be welcome."

"Why should he ask questions here?" Mrs. Jones turned
as the back door opened.

"Because he's got a damned low-life mind," Roger Chiswick said, shutting the door behind him. He leaned back
against it and took a deep breath. "The stupid fool thinks
that you and I . . ." He looked at Mrs. Jones and his voice
was ragged as he spoke. "He seems to think that you and
I are more than friends and that we hatched some kind
of plot to get rid of Gwendolyn."

Mrs. Jones gasped, paled visibly, and sank to the floor. Chiswick bounded across the kitchen to try to catch her, but she collapsed onto the tiles. "We need to get her to bed," Sara said, kneeling.

"Let me help." Chiswick put his arm under Mrs. Jones's shoulders. "I shouldn't have been so brutal. I know how sensitive Sophie is, but I wasn't thinking. Sherman's intimations were so . . . so . . ."

"I know." Sara gave him a brief smile. "I know my mother is beyond reproach, and I have every confidence in you, Mr. Chiswick." She stood. "Now, if you'll just help me get Mama upstairs . . ."

Chiswick stood, holding the unconscious Mrs. Jones, her head cradled against his shoulder. "A very pretty scene," Squire Sherman said from the door. "Tell me, Chiswick, does this happen often?"

Sara rounded on him. "No, it does not happen often, Squire Sherman. In fact, it has never happened before. Furthermore, I would appreciate it if you would knock before you enter this house. As for this scene—my mother has fainted and Mr. Chiswick—at my request—has offered to help me get her upstairs to her bed, so if you'll excuse us, we'll tend to her."

Sherman raised an eyebrow, but didn't seem at all embarrassed. In fact, he sat down and looked at the teapot on the table. "I'll wait here until you get her settled. I believe we need the answers to some questions." He paused and raised his eyebrow again. "From both of you."

Sara nudged Chiswick through the door and up the stairs before he could say anything. "He wants you to say something that could be misconstrued," she whispered as they went up the stairs. "Don't talk to him until you're completely calm."

Chiswick nodded and followed Sara to Mrs. Jones's room. There he put her down and left, promising Sara that he would go out the front door and go back to the pond. "You're right," he said as he left, "if I go through the kitchen and Sherman says one word, I may plant him a facer right there. I know I'd regret that." He shook his head. "The stupid fool. To think that Sophie would do anything at all untoward. She didn't even know the true nature of Gwendolyn's condition." He looked bleakly at Sara. "If you think it wouldn't cause too much talk, I'd like to return tonight or tomorrow and explain things to her. Since there's talk, she has a right to know."

Sara glanced back at the bed and her mother. "All right. I'm sure there will be talk if you so much as knock on the door, but as long as we know what's right, I don't care. I'm sure Mama would want to talk to you."

It took two pots of sweet tea for Mrs. Jones to recover. In the meantime, Squire Sherman found himself on the receiving end of Aunt Zell's sharp tongue. When he discovered that Chiswick had gone back outside, he was annoyed, and accused Sara and her mother of plotting to muddy the legal investigation. Aunt Zell told him in quite certain terms what she thought of him and his investigation. For good measure, she told him what she thought of his cock-eyed theories about Roger Chiswick and Mrs. Jones. Squire Sherman left before she had finished.

"Good riddance," Aunt Zell muttered to Sara as the door closed behind the man. Sara had recognized Aunt Zell's tone and had come downstairs to see what the commotion was all about. She had had to make her way through all the children, who were standing in the doorway, round-eyed. Aunt Zell was truly full of righteous fury.

"The squire didn't stand a chance," Jack whispered to Sara later. "You should have seen her."

Sara chuckled. "I saw enough." She only wished she had been able to capture Squire Sherman's expression on paper. It would be a long while before he dared cross Aunt Zell's path again.

True to his word, Chiswick came by after dark. The family had gathered around the kitchen table. It seemed closer, somehow, than the dining room. Matthew, Mary, John, and Briget had gone to bed, but James, Jack, Sara, Aunt Zell, and Mrs. Jones were in the kitchen drinking tea when Chiswick knocked at the back door. "I saw you in here and came in this way," he explained when he stepped into the kitchen. "I walked in from the orchard." He looked back over his shoulder. "I can't tell you the times I've found Gwendolyn there." He sat down at the table and gratefully accepted a cup of tea from Aunt Zell.

"Did the questioning go well?" Sara asked.

Chiswick nodded. "Fine. I simply told the truth and then refuted all of Sherman's suspicions. Emrys came by late and had some things to say to Sherman."

Sara felt her heart stop. "Such as?"

"Such as this conspiracy theory was nothing but a lot of claptrap. Emrys is of the opinion that the same person who killed the man at the shed also killed Gwendolyn."

"Then it's certain that she was killed?" Mrs. Jones said faintly. "Sara said that Edward thought she might have hit her head on a rock."

"They're certain she was killed." Chiswick shook his head. "Poor Gwendolyn. Long ago, she was so full of life, so happy. She knew I . . . I . . ." He stopped and looked down into his cup as though there was an answer there. "I promised I would tell you the full story, and I want to do that." He glanced around at them. "It's not a pretty story."

Mrs. Jones poured him another cup of tea, and he smiled gratefully at her and began. It seemed that Chiswick had married Gwendolyn after Mrs. Jones had married and gone off to Africa. Gwendolyn was penniless, and Chiswick had been frank that while he admired her greatly, his heart, as he had said delicately, belonged to another. He didn't look at Mrs. Jones as he said this, but everyone knew. Gwendolyn accepted his feelings. She was happy to have a husband and a home.

At first, he and Gwendolyn were happy. He was in the army, and she stayed at home, waiting for him. She loved taking long walks and picking wildflowers. Sometimes she came over to Saint's Haven to pick up apples. One day, while Chiswick was in the Peninsula, as Gwendolyn was in the orchard at Saint's Haven picking up some apples, one of Ned Perkin's gang had attacked her. Once when she was lucid, she had told Chiswick that more than one of the gang had been involved, even naming Perkin himself.

Chiswick stopped, finding the story difficult. Then he swallowed hard and continued. When Perkin's gang finished with Gwendolyn, they took her outside and threw her aside like so much garbage. She managed to crawl back home, but her mind was gone forever. She blocked out everything, including her life in the village and her marriage to Chiswick. She was like a simple, helpless child.

Chiswick left the army and came home to care for her. He tried to watch her himself, but that was almost impossible. He had to spend a certain amount of time seeing to his property and his farm. The one thing Gwendolyn remembered was how much she had liked to walk around the countryside. She was always slipping away and wandering the fields and orchards, usually in her white nightgown. About a year ago, Chiswick thought that she was getting better; but then something happened, and Gwendolyn's condition got much worse. Chiswick wasn't able to figure out why until he heard the stories that Ned Perkin and his men were in the vicinity. Then he knew that Gwendolyn was in real danger.

Because of the stories about Perkin being near the village and Saint's Haven, Chiswick began keeping Gwendolyn locked in the house and even hired some village girls to stay with her and try to keep her in. It didn't work—she still managed to slip out. He was terrified that she would return to Saint's Haven and be attacked again. If that happened, he knew, it would kill Gwendolyn.

It didn't happen; but what progress Gwendolyn had made was lost, and her mind got even worse. The village girls didn't like to stay there, and then Edward Moore appeared. Chiswick was delighted as Edward seemed to be the only one who could manage her. When Edward was around, Gwendolyn would be calm and quiet. Still, she kept telling Chiswick that Perkin was after her. Often, she would scream that Perkin had her, and it would take both Chiswick and Edward to restrain her. At these times, she became incoherent and terrified, crouching in the corner of her room like a frightened animal. Then, suddenly, she seemed to improve slightly, but began slipping out to walk again. "The moment I heard about your ghost, I knew it was Gwendolyn," Chiswick said. "I wanted to tell you then, but I hated to. I thought I could keep her inside and no one would know." He looked around at them brokenly. "I couldn't have her put away—I just couldn't. If I had done that, she might still be alive."

Mrs. Jones patted his arm. "You did the right thing, Roger. The poor woman wouldn't have lasted in an asylum. Those places are horrible. As it was, you did the very best you could."

"I tried." Chiswick's pain was evident. "I had hoped Edward was right and that she had merely fallen into the pond and the end was quick. Sherman says she was killed by being hit with a rock." He put his hand over his eyes. "I hope she didn't suffer. I hope she wasn't afraid."

There was nothing to say. Mrs. Jones patted his hand again, and Chiswick covered hers with his own. "I'd better be leaving." He stood and picked up his hat. "I hope I haven't added to the talk by coming here, but I wanted you to know."

Mrs. Jones stood. "Thank you for sharing this with us, Roger. I know it must be very painful for you."

He nodded, and it seemed that he wanted to say something else; but he didn't. Instead, he opened the back door and disappeared into the night. Mrs. Jones sat back down and looked all around at the others. The kitchen was heavy with silence. "The poor man," Sara finally said.

Aunt Zell nodded. "Let us hope that God helps us find the answer." On that note, they all went to bed. Sara took one last look out the window before she went to sleep. "Rest in peace, Gwendolyn," she whispered, and fervently hoped that it would be true.

Sara didn't want to work in the back the next day. It was too easy to look at the pond and remember the way Gwendolyn's hair had floated around her head like a cloud. Instead, she went to the front of the house and began working on cutting the tangled vines at the front and side walls. Edward cut the vines while she stood back and told him which ones to trim. Before long, there was a pile of vines.

Edward was on a ladder, trimming around the upstairs window, when Emrys rode up on his big black. Emrys rode into the yard, but didn't dismount. His face was grim. "I understand you found Gwendolyn Chiswick," he said to Sara without preamble.

"Yes." She barely glanced at him, then looked back at

Edward. "The tendril over there, I think," she said, pointing. "Cut that one."

"Did you see anything yesterday, Moore?" Emrys asked, his voice quiet but carrying. Edward looked down at him, then back at Sara. He left the vine uncut and descended the ladder, coming to stand beside Emrys' horse. He looked much smaller standing beside the huge black. "No, nothing then."

"But you've seen something before?"

Edward shrugged and looked up at Emrys. "There was a stranger standing under that tree day before yesterday." He hesitated. "I didn't want to say anything because I didn't want to scare the family. He was probably just a traveler resting a moment."

"But he could have been Gwendolyn's killer," Sara exclaimed. "You should have told us, Edward."

Emrys raised an eyebrow at her use of Edward's first name, but he made no comment. "I didn't want to frighten you," Edward said. "I shouldn't have even mentioned it. The man was probably just a traveler."

"He might have been Ned Perkin." Emrys' voice was harsh. "I talked to someone who should know, and he told me that Perkin is around here."

"I'm sure I'd know Perkin if I saw him," Edward said. "After all, the man's a known criminal, and the man I saw certainly didn't look like a criminal. He looked . . . ," he paused as he thought, "he looked more like a vicar."

Emrys shook his head. "He could have been Perkin. Hell!" He hit his thigh with his palm. "Excuse me, Miss Jones. No one here knows what Perkin looks like. He could look like a vicar or Prince George—we just don't know. At any rate, watch for strangers."

"I hardly think that's necessary." Sara kept her voice frigid.

Edward smiled at her and touched her arm. Emrys raised

his eyebrow again. "He's right, Sara," Edward said. "That man could have been anyone." He looked back at Emrys. "Thank you for reminding me. I'll keep a close watch from now on."

"Good," Emrys grunted, turning the black. He tipped his hat briefly. "Good day, Miss Jones, Mr. Moore. I'll be in touch." With that, he wheeled the horse around and rode out the gate and down the road.

The nerve of the man, Sara thought. Just to ride in and think he could tell everyone what to do. She turned back to the vines. "The tendril at the side of the window, I think, Edward." Edward grinned at her and climbed back up the ladder.

That evening, Sara sat on the garden bench with Mary and Matthew, admiring her day's handiwork. The side of the house looked very nice, she thought, and the windows gleamed in the sunset. Saint's Haven was turning into a real home. She turned as she heard a horse behind her and saw Emrys ride up to the gate. This time he dismounted and walked up to the bench, sitting down beside her. Matthew and Mary came running up. "Did you bring us something?" Mary asked, hopping onto Emrys' knee.

"Rascal," Emrys said with a grin. "You're just going to have to search my pocket and see for yourself." With a laugh, both Matthew and Mary stuck their hands in his pocket and found a wrapped piece of candy for each of them. "Now off with you. That's all you get for now. I don't want you having too many sweets." He shooed them off and watched them go back to the grass to play with a ball. "They're wonderful children," he said unexpectedly.

"Yes." Sara was too surprised to say much else.

"I want you to watch them. I wouldn't put it past Perkin to try to do something to the children." He turned to look at her. "I don't want to alarm you, Miss Jones, but this man, Perkin, will stop at nothing to get what he wants."

"And what does he want, Lord Emrys?"

Emrys sighed. "That's the question. I know he has no love for me, but why he would torment you is beyond me. The only answer I have is that story about Perkin leaving loot here at Saint's Haven. It may be true, or it may be just another story, I don't know." He paused, but Sara said nothing, so he went on. "I hope you don't mind, but I'd like to come by and check on you and the children until I deem it safe." He caught her gaze. His eyes were warm topaz and concerned. "As I told you this morning, I've heard from a reliable source that Perkin is in the neighborhood. I wish I knew what he looked like, but since I don't, I worry about every stranger." He paused. "Don't laugh at my worry, Miss Jones. I've discovered something else."

"And that is . . . ," she prompted.

"The man found dead at your shed was called Black Tom. According to a man who had had a brush with him, Black Tom got in his cups over at the Boar and Briar and boasted about being a member of Perkin's gang. He said he knew things on Perkin that would get the man hanged. Then he said Perkin was around here and he was going to meet him." He hesitated. "That was the last time anyone saw Tom alive. I suspect that Perkin heard of his boast and killed him."

Sara gasped. "But why here? Why not out in a secluded place?"

Emrys shook his head. "I don't know. Perhaps they agreed to meet here at some time in the past, before everyone knew that your family had settled again in Saint's Haven." Emrys looked back at the children laughing as Lucy went chasing their ball. "I'd hate to think of anything happening to them. To anyone here." He turned back to Sara. "I don't want to alarm you, but I want you to be on your guard. I think . . ." He paused. "It's merely a personal feeling and I have no basis for it, but I feel perhaps Perkin is responsible in some way for Gwendolyn's death as well."

Sara was speechless. "But why?"

"I don't know. Call it a feeling, for lack of a better term." He ran his hand through his hair, ruffling it. "I know Roger Chiswick, and I know he certainly had nothing to do with it. He never truly loved Gwendolyn, but he did his best to make her happy and care for her. He's devoted his whole life to taking care of her since . . ." His voice trailed off.

"He told us."

Emrys sighed. "Another life wasted by Perkin." He shook his head as if to get rid of the thought. "Let's change the subject, Miss Jones. I like what you've done to the house. It's looking like a house again."

"Thank you." They sat in silence for a moment, casting around for something to say. "Thank you for sending a wagon from Brookwood," she said, unable to think of anything else. "I've been meaning to come look at the place. Mr. Chiswick once told me it is a lovely place."

"It is." He sounded sad. "My father loved the place. I'm sorry to say that it doesn't have the same happy memories for me. My father always hoped that my children would live there, but that isn't likely to happen." He was unsuccessful at keeping the bitterness from his voice.

"What will happen to it?"

Emrys hesitated. "If I die without an heir, the whole estate and title will pass to a distant cousin who lives in Cornwall. My cousin, Edmund." He gave a short, harsh laugh. "I haven't heard from him or seen him since we were three or four years old. I didn't care for him then, so I doubt much has changed."

"Perhaps he's a much different person now."

"Perhaps." Emrys didn't sound convinced.

"Perhaps you'll marry and have an heir." As soon as

the words were out, Sara could have bitten off her tongue, but it was too late.

"I think not, Miss Jones." There was a pause. "I always wanted children." He looked at Mary and Matthew, and there was a profound sadness in his voice. He shook his head and stood. "That time is past for me, Miss Jones." He picked up his hat and waved to the children. "As I said, I'll be by every evening just to check that things are all right. I hope you don't mind if I bring a sweet for the children? They seem to expect it of me." He stepped over Lucy and walked toward the gate. Lucy kept rubbing up against his boots. "Perhaps this reprobate expects a bone, but I don't think I can manage that." He stepped over Lucy one last time and mounted his black horse. With a polite good night, he disappeared into the dusky evening.

Sara stared after him for an instant. She had never realized the depth of Emrys' sadness. It had touched her deeply. Despite the fact that he had possessions and a title and houses scattered all over, he really had nothing that mattered to him. Lucy nudged her ankle, searching for the twins' ball that had rolled under her feet. Sara knelt and hugged Lucy and Matthew and Mary all at once. "I love you all," she said fervently, wishing that Emrys could feel the same happiness that she felt at this moment.

Chapter 13

The morning sun was up and breaking through the clouds that had threatened when the gardener from Brookwood rolled up in a cart. He brought an assortment of shrubs, herbs, perennials, and tender annuals. He doffed his cap and proudly showed Sara the thriving plants. "Lord Emrys said as I was to bring these to you since he'd seen you didn't have any." He picked up a delicate-looking plant. "He said to bring all these herbs because you'd need them. This here's sweet woodruff, and over there I brought some rue, and here's lavender. There's balm, dill, basil, and pennyroyal." He glanced down at Lucy cavorting and rolling on the ground. "Lord Emrys was most particular that I should bring enough tansy, so I did. Just the thing for fleas, you know."

Sara glanced down at the beagle, who was busy scratching her ear. "I think with summer, we're going to need it."

"That's what Lord Emrys said." The gardener looked

around. "Do you want me to plant them for you, or had you rather do it? Lord Emrys told me to ask."

Sara smiled at him. "Thank you so much, but I'll do it myself. That way, I'll arrange everything just the way I want it." Sara ran inside to get some paper and had the gardener give her the name of each plant as he unloaded it. She made careful notes and then, when the gardener had gone back to Brookwood, sat on the garden bench, surrounded by herbs on one side, annuals and perennials on the other. Raspberry plants were propped against the side of the house. Sara looked from plant to plant and made a careful plan detailing exactly where everything would be planted. She was most particular about her herb garden. It was certainly thoughtful of Emrys, she mused to herself, to send her the herbs. She hadn't even thought about having to have herbs for cooking and medicine. She would never have thought of sending tansy for Lucy's summer fleas. Emrys was always surprising her.

She went to get Garfield and Edward to spade up the herb garden so she could begin getting the plants into the ground right away. Garfield muttered, but he and Edward went right to work on it. "Surprised the man would think of your herb garden, and him with no missus to remind him," Garfield said, hitting a chunk of dirt with the back of his shovel to break it up. "He should get married again. Everybody in the village hopes he'll have an heir before too long."

"I didn't know you were knowledgeable about village conversations," Sara said with a laugh. She had suspected that Garfield was making trips to the village pub after everyone at Saint's Haven was in bed. She couldn't resist teasing him.

"Good to know what's going on." He banged another chunk of dirt, and bits of loam fell everywhere. "Not that

I can ever add to what they say. I never know what's going on."

"Well, I can tell you a little," Sara said. "It's probably public knowledge as well, so Emrys won't mind me telling you. If he dies without an heir, the estates and title go to a distant cousin in Cornwall. Emrys said he hadn't seen the man since he was about four years old."

"Cornwall!" Edward stood up straight and looked into the distance. "Cornwall." He turned to Sara. "Where is Cornwall? I remember something about it." He frowned as he thought. "A house. The sea." he looked at her pleadingly. "Is that right?"

Sara's heart went out to him. "Yes, it is. You mentioned Cornwall once before, Edward. Do you think your family might be there? I've never been there, but I've heard it's a lovely place. Bleak to some, but lovely in its own way."

Edward shook his head. "It's no use. I get a vague image, but then it floats away." He looked at her, despair in his eyes. "I wish I could remember."

"It will all come back to you, Edward, I'm sure of it."

Later that day, Aunt Zell and Mrs. Jones went to Roger Chiswick's house to help with the burial preparations and returned shortly after noon. Mrs. Jones was distraught. "The poor woman," she said, mopping at her eyes. "She must have had a terrible life."

"She was probably quite happy until she was attacked by Perkin and his men," Aunt Zell answered. "That was a tragedy all right, but the one I feel for is Chiswick. The poor man has stretched himself to the breaking point trying to take care of that woman. He's done everything humanly possible."

Mrs. Jones nodded. "I know. Then to have all these ugly rumors. . . ." She began sobbing again. "It isn't to be believed, Sara."

Sara and Aunt Zell made Mrs. Jones go to bed with a

tisane, and Sara sat with her until she went to sleep. Sara lit a candle in the early twilight and watched her mother, worried. The move to Saint's Haven had been hard on Mrs. Jones. Sara had thought that her mother would be happy here, but that didn't seem to be happening. For a fleeting instant, she thought about packing up and returning to London.

No, she thought to herself as she pulled the quilt up over her mother's thin shoulders and tucked it in, she wouldn't do it. Saint's Haven was their home, and Papa had always planned to return here and live. They would be happy here; she knew in her heart that it would happen.

As Sara went to get herself a cup of tea, she heard Lucy whining at the back door. "Bad dog," Sara said as she opened the door. "Don't you know you're supposed to stay outside?" She broke off as Lucy raised her head and looked forlornly at her. Lucy's head was cut and bleeding badly. With a cry, Sara scooped her up and hurried to the pump to wash her off.

The cut looked worse than it was. Lucy was well-behaved, whimpering only when Sara probed the cut for dirt. There was a huge knot under the skin as if someone had hit Lucy over the head.

Garfield came in for a drink of water while Sara was cleaning the wound. "That's what's happened, all right," he said, peering at the wound. "You'd better sew it up, too. Looks like someone's hit her with a stick or something like that."

"Something with a sharp edge." Sara glanced up at him. "What do you mean—sew it up?"

"Better stitch her up or it'll go putrid." Garfield looked at Sara's horrified face. "This is the country, missy. You'd best get used to doing things like that."

Sara gritted her teeth and went to work with her sewing kit. She got James to hold Lucy while she stitched. She had thought Lucy would howl and try to run, but instead, she sat quietly, almost as though she knew Sara was trying to help her. When Sara had the ugly gash sewed up, she took Lucy upstairs to sleep on the rug beside her bed.

Outside a low fog was rolling in, and Sara glanced at the herb garden, then at the fog. Even if it was almost night, she could still see by lantern light. The herb plants needed to get in the ground, and if she hurried, she could get a great number of them planted. The fog and mist would be good for them. She snatched her brogans, an old coat, and a hat, then went to the shed for her gardening tools. Edward was there, inside, sharpening some tools by lantern light. Surprised, he wheeled around, then smiled broadly at her as she came inside. "You certainly look ready for work in the rain."

Sara laughed. "Every gardener has to be." She picked up her tools and put them in her coat pocket. "I thought I'd get some of the herbs planted."

"Uumm." Edward finished putting an edge on his axe and put it and the honing stone down. "I've wanted to talk to you some. I've been doing some thinking today."

She took a step toward him and smiled. "I hope you've remembered something."

"I have." To her surprise, Edward drew her to him and kissed her. At first, she was so surprised that she froze; but the pressure of his lips was warm on hers, and the feel of his body against hers was doing strange things to her. She found herself returning his kiss and enjoying it more than she ever thought she could enjoy anything. He released her, looked down into her eyes, then kissed her again, slowly and thoroughly this time. Sara heard a noise and realized she was making sounds deep in her throat as his kiss was doing strange things to her body. She felt cold and warm all at the same time. Her knees felt weak, and she leaned closer into Edward's strong body. His lips left hers and made a trail across her cheek to her ear, then down her neck. With each touch, she shuddered, losing all sense of time and reason. She wanted this man, no matter that she knew nothing about his background or his family. She wanted him for the way he was making her feel.

His fingers slid to her waist, then upward. She didn't care what he did; all she knew was that she wanted him more and more. From somewhere in the back of her mind, she knew that she should say no, but she was powerless. All she could feel was the overwhelming wanting.

"Sara, where are you?" Someone was calling her. She ignored it, concentrating on the feel of Edward's lips and breath on her cheek and against her ear. "Sara, are you in there?" The shed door opened suddenly, and Sara jumped back guiltily. She was breathing heavily and couldn't speak.

"What do you want, James?" Edward asked calmly, as though he weren't touched by the same need as she.

James looked from one to the other with huge eyes. "I . . . I just wanted to see Sara. I found Lucy wandering around the house, and there was a little blood still oozing from that terrible place on her head. I . . ." James let his voice trail off. His eyes hadn't gotten any smaller.

"Thank you, James." Sara got herself under control and stepped outside the shed. She couldn't breathe in there. The whole place seemed to pulse with Edward's presence. "I suppose it's natural for such a bad wound to bleed some, even after I sewed it up." She paused. "You know how distraught I was—I might not have done a good job."

"You did a wonderful job, better than I could have done. Lucy was down looking for water when I found her." James was still looking from Sara to Edward, thinking who-knew-what.

"That's all right." Sara finally felt she could speak and breathe normally. "I should have put some water in a dish beside her rug. I do want her kept inside."

"What happened?" Edward picked up his axe again.

Sara was caught off guard for a moment. "Oh, you mean to Lucy? Garfield thinks someone hit her on the head."

"Why would anyone want to do that?"

Sara shrugged. "I'm not sure. Maybe she was chasing someone's chickens. She could have been hurt anywhere. She just came into the yard already hurt."

James pulled a wrapped piece of candy from his pocket. It looked as if it had been there for a while and had partially melted and gotten fuzz on it. "Emrys gave me this. Is it all right if I give it to Lucy?" At Sara's nod, he ran off toward the house.

Edward propped the axe back against the shed wall. "I'm sorry we were interrupted." His voice was low and soft. "Would you like to come back inside and see if we can pick up where we left off?"

Sara stepped back. She was still having trouble believing that Edward's touch could have given her all those new feelings. "I think not, Edward." She took another step back. "I really have to do some things."

"Wait." Edward stepped out of the shed and fell in beside her. "I apologize if I did something you didn't want me to do." He paused, but Sara said nothing. She had wanted him to do all that and more.

"It's all right," she said, not looking at him.

"I wanted to talk to you." There was another pause. "Your question about Cornwall this afternoon triggered some memories for me. I think I may be remembering some things about my birth and my family." He stopped and looked at her. "I remember a house, a rocky path to the shore, and the name of a place." He held up a hand to stop her from speaking. "I want to go to Cornwall and see if what I'm remembering is true. Perhaps if I see the place, my memory will return." He took her hand. "If what I believe is true and I am the person I think I may be, I . . ." He stopped and began again. "I care for you, Sara. I've hesitated to press the matter because I couldn't ask you to listen to a penniless wanderer, but if I do have a good family in Cornwall, then perhaps . . . perhaps I could pay my addresses to you in a more formal way."

Sara looked at him and was struck by the sincerity in his voice and expression. "Edward, do go find out about your past. If you don't want to return, then we'll understand. If you do find out good things, I wish you all the best."

"But while I'm gone, will you consider the way . . . the way I feel about you?" His hand gripped hers harder. "I'm only going for you, Sara. If my family is of good birth and I can provide for you, then that's all I want. I'll return and then I want to—"

"Edward, please." Sara interrupted him and turned away. "I will think about this, truly I will." She looked up at him. "There are some things of my own that I need to resolve. I want you to go find out about yourself, truly I do. I hope the best for you, Edward."

"I'll go right away, then." He leaned over and kissed her quickly on the forehead just as Jack came wandering out of the stable. Sara blushed as Jack began to giggle. She knew that Jack and James would be swapping stories and dreaded thinking about their conclusions.

"Never a dull moment with the children, is there?" Edward said with a smile. "I'm going to miss them, but not as much as I'll miss you."

Sara cast a nervous glance at Jack and stepped back. "If you can't come back soon, write us." She caught the look in his eye and realized he was planning to kiss her again, right there in front of Jack. "Good luck, Edward." She fled.

Behind her, she could hear Jack chuckling in the early dark. For some reason, it reminded her of Emrys.

Chapter 14

Contrary to what Sara thought he would do, Edward didn't leave that evening. Instead, he waited until the next morning. She thought he was gone and brought Lucy out to the back so Lucy could attend to her necessities. While she was waiting, Lucy running in circles around her legs, Edward walked up behind her. Evidently he frightened Lucy as the beagle ran off, howling, her tail down.

"I hope I don't frighten you as much as I seem to have done to the dog." There was a hint of laughter in his voice. Sara turned to look at him. He was dressed in his uniform, ready to go. There was a bag beside him. "I thought I'd catch the morning coach," he said, following her gaze. "I have enough saved for a ticket. Now that I'm beginning to remember things, I'm impatient to find out for sure."

"I don't blame you." Sara glanced back at Lucy. The beagle was cowering on her stomach beside the shed, her paws on either side of her nose. She gave Edward and Sara a strange look, then jumped to her feet and ran toward the pond. "She must want more water," Sara said with a

sigh. "I'd better follow her and make sure she's all right."
She paused. "The early coach leaves soon, doesn't it?"
She turned to look at him, and it was almost her undo-
ing. She made herself take a step backward. "I've got to
go." She didn't trust herself around him anymore. "As I
said before, Edward, take care. I wish you good luck."

He reached out and held her arm. "As I said before,
Sara, I care very much for you and want you to think about
what I said last night."

His touch was different today, but Sara couldn't place
exactly how. This time, she felt the same physical attraction,
but there was something else, something she couldn't identify. Whatever it was, it made her uncomfortable. "I'll think
about it, Edward."

"Good. That's all I ask." He gave her a quick kiss on
the forehead, then hoisted his bag. "I'll be back as soon
as I can. Take care." He brushed her chin lightly with his
fingertips and went around the side of the house, whistling
softly.

In just a second, Sara could no longer hear him. She
turned to go fetch Lucy, but the beagle was running back
toward her, her tail wagging, and her tongue lolling from
one side of her mouth. She came to a screeching stop at
Sara's feet and rolled over to get her stomach scratched.
"You're a moody little thing," Sara said, laughing as she
bent to scratch the dog. "One minute you're running away
and then the next you're trying to be appealing."

Lucy didn't get far from Sara all morning and spent
much of her time dashing to the shed and back, digging
furiously there for a moment, then stopping to run to Sara.
Jack and James were working with Sara to finish the herb
garden.

"I'm telling you, Sara," Jack said as they watched Lucy
scratch in the dirt around the base of the shed, "you need

to train Lucy to work in the garden. We'd never have to spade again."

"What is this thing you have about the shed, silly girl?" Sara asked her as she stopped at the pump with her gardening tools. The herb garden was completed, and she washed the dirt from her trowel and small hoe, then went to put them away in the shed. "There's nothing here at all." Sara swung the shed door open. "See. Perfectly empty."

Lucy ignored her and returned to her large hole at the back of the shed. "Now, Lucy, I was going to plant hollyhocks there." Sara got her trowel out and began to shovel dirt back into the hole. The dirt was unusually loose, almost as though it had been dug over recently. "Emrys sent over pink, white, and violet. This will be the perfect place for them."

"He's coming over this afternoon, isn't he?" James asked, propping his clean hoe against the shed wall.

"Yes, I think so. Matthew and Mary said he was."

"I'd better go see. Matthew and Mary don't want to miss him." James started for the front of the house.

"You just want to talk horses with the man," Sara said, laughing. "I know you, James. Lucy, stop that." This last was said to Lucy as Lucy zipped in front of her and began furiously digging, making dirt fly behind her. Sara's lap was covered in an instant.

"Stop that this minute," Sara said firmly, but Lucy ignored her. Sara reached to grab her by the neck, but stopped as Lucy barked and began tugging on something in the hole. "A bone there?" Sara asked. "I assure you, Lucy, that I have absolutely no use for a bone, but I'll help you retrieve it if you promise not to try to bring it inside." She moved Lucy aside and loosened the dirt with her trowel. Lucy rooted around for a moment with her long nose, then turned to Sara, something in her mouth. Sara looked at it. She didn't know what it was, but she did know it wasn't a bone. It looked rather like a dull white, thin box. "Give it to me, Lucy," she said, tugging gently. To her surprise, Lucy gave up the object and flopped down in the moist dirt, exhausted by her exertions.

Sara looked closely at the object, turning it over in her hand. It was some kind of heavy, oiled cloth. She unwrapped it carefully and found another wrapped packet, this one in a cleaner cloth, also oiled. Inside the second cloth, she discovered a book, thin but expensive. The back was finely tooled leather, a rich red in color, trimmed with gold. There was no name on the outside, but when she opened the cover, she caught her breath. The book was inscribed on the flyleaf. *Elizabeth, Lady Emrys, Her Diary.* Sara put the book in her pocket and whistled for Lucy.

Inside, Sara hurried up the stairs, Lucy at her heels. In her room, she took the book from her pocket and put it on the bed. One part of her said that the diary didn't belong to her and was private—the only right thing to do was give it to Emrys. Another part said that she should read the book and perhaps decide what to do after she had seen part of it. The entries might be too difficult for Emrys to read. After all, the man was only now beginning to come out of his painful shell, and she certainly didn't want to do anything that would cause him more distress.

No, she told herself, she had no right to read Elizabeth's private thoughts. She put her hands on the book to put it away, but found herself opening it and beginning to read. She couldn't help herself.

The diary dealt with the last few months of Elizabeth's life. She talked freely about her love for Ned Perkin and of the many times they met. Every time Emrys went to London, Elizabeth slipped away to be with Ned Perkin, telling everyone at Brookwood that she was going to visit her father. Evidently Elizabeth loved living a dangerous life with Ned Perkin, and admitted frankly how delighted she was to be pregnant with his child. She wrote that Ned thought it the world's greatest joke that his child would be Emrys' heir and would inherit Brookwood and the title. Elizabeth seemed to revel in the deception she and Perkin were foisting on Emrys.

Sara closed the book and put it under her pillow. She went to the window and looked out. Emrys was there, walking with Matthew and Mary, giving them sugar lumps to feed to his horse. James was holding the big black and stroking its nose gently. Emrys laughed as Mary made faces when the horse ate the sugar from her hand and got her hand wet. *He wants nothing more than love,* she thought to herself, almost ready to cry. She turned away from the window and threw herself down on the bed, feeling the hard lump of the diary under her pillow. She got up and locked her door—she didn't want anyone coming in and asking her to go down and see Emrys. She couldn't face him right this minute.

When the clock struck four, Sara got up and looked out again. There was no one in sight, and Emrys' big black stallion was gone. Sara went downstairs to help with the evening meal, hoping that Aunt Zell and Mrs. Jones wouldn't notice her heavy sadness.

Sara made the excuse that she had a headache when Aunt Zell and Mrs. Jones asked what was wrong with her. In part, that was true. James was drawing a picture of a horse on a piece of paper, while Matthew and Mary were full of chatter about their afternoon. It seemed Emrys had held each twin and given them a ride on his big black. James had gotten to ride alone down the road and back. They were all excited. Jack sat there, glowering and jealous. "Some of us had to work and couldn't go riding," he said to James.

"He'll take you for a ride tomorrow," Mrs. Jones said. "He came inside and said that you two boys are to come to Brookwood whenever you wanted and he'd show you how to ride."

Jack and James looked at each other and said nothing. They didn't have to. Sara had never realized that the boys might like to ride and hunt. Emrys must have noticed that immediately.

Sara excused herself right after supper and went up to her room, determined to rewrap the diary and burn it. Or rewrap it and give it to Emrys. Or rewrap it and bury it. Instead, she pulled it from under her pillow and sat down, leafing through the pages, reading selection after selection, feeling more and more guilty. One thing she discovered: Elizabeth had never loved Emrys in any way. Even from Elizabeth's biased point of view, Emrys had done everything he could to be a good husband. Instead of appreciating him, Elizabeth and Ned Perkin had jeered at him behind his back. Even reading through the details of the diary, Sara could see that from the beginning, Elizabeth had been completely under Perkin's influence.

Sara skipped over most of the middle, thoroughly disgusted both with Elizabeth and herself. She glanced at an entry near the end, then made herself shut the book and put it back under her pillow. She refused to read the last entry.

After a few minutes, she got the thin book out, rewrapped it, and put it in the drawer of the small table beside her bed. Her father's picture was there, but now his eyes looked accusing.

"It's strange," she said to Lucy as she crawled into her bed, "that Papa can make me feel guilty even now." She sighed. "I shouldn't have read that, Lucy. I know better." She punched the pillow and blew out her candle. "The poor man," she said as Lucy whimpered and curled up into a ball beside her bed. "I don't suppose anyone knows how much Emrys has been through." She rolled over and looked down at Lucy on the floor. "I'm going to do the right thing tomorrow and take him the diary, Lucy. It's what I ought to do." She glanced at her father's picture in the moonlight. He looked as she remembered him, smiling.

From somewhere deep in sleep, Sara heard sounds she couldn't immediately sort out. There was the clock in the hall, chiming one o'clock; then there was Lucy whining and scratching at the door, and finally, there was a muffled whispering and knocking at her door. Groggily, Sara got out of bed and opened the door. Jack slipped inside.

"I heard something," he whispered.

"It's Lucy." Sara looked down at the excited beagle. "Stop that."

Jack shook his head. "No, I heard something outside; then, when I went to the window to look, I saw someone in the orchard."

"You're dreaming, Jack. We've determined that the ghost was really poor Mrs. Chiswick."

"Not a ghost. It's bright enough in the moonlight to see things, and this wasn't in white. It was dark." Jack reached behind her door and took her cloak from its peg. "This was something else. I'm going—are you coming with me?"

"No. Yes. You can't go out there by yourself. You need to go back to bed."

Jack walked to the window, looked out, but saw nothing. "I'm going, Sara. If you want to go with me, then I'll wait. If not, I'm going by myself."

Sara looked at him. He was almost a man grown by now. She sighed and reached for her shoes. "I'll go, Jack, but I don't want any more excitement than I've already had. I think you're wrong."

They had just opened the back door when they heard a shot ring out and saw a flash of light. Lucy ran from the house, ululating in full voice, her beagle's bay echoing across the quiet night. There was a rustling sound from behind the stables, and Jack shoved Sara to the ground. "I thought the flash came from there," he whispered hoarsely. They stayed on the ground a moment, but heard nothing else except Lucy's frantic baying and the sound of a voice coming faintly from the orchard. "I think we can get up now," Jack whispered, scrambling to his feet. At that moment, there was the sound of a crash from the stables followed by a quick flash of light. Jack fell to the ground.

"Jack! Jack!" Sara screamed, crawling to him and throwing herself on top of him.

"I'm all right." Jack's voice was hoarse. Sara started to speak, but heard another noise. It took her a moment to recognize it—the noise of someone running away. In just a second, the thudding footfalls had faded and the night was quiet again.

"Are you sure you're all right?" she asked, scrambling to her knees beside him. He sat up. "I'm fine. He didn't hit me." He looked up at the house, then back toward the orchard. There was a light in Mrs. Jones's bedroom. "Hide," Sara whispered, pulling Jack behind the shed.

It took at least five minutes for Mrs. Jones to peer out the window, then go back and put out her candle. Sara thought it seemed an hour. It was the longest time she had ever spent. In the quiet of the night, she and Jack could hear Lucy whining in the orchard, her noises punctuated occasionally by the sound of a muffled voice.

They gave Mrs. Jones a few minutes to go back to sleep. "I think it's safe now," Jack said.

"I believe I've heard those same words just recently." Sara grinned at him. "This time, I think we should take a shovel or an axe with us. Just to be safe."

Jack needed no prompting. He noiselessly slid the bar

from the shed door and opened the door wide so the moonlight could illuminate the inside. He took the new axe and gave Sara a knife and a hoe. They hurried over the dark ground in the direction of the orchard, guided by Lucy's whimpering.

"I don't see her," Jack said, standing still and trying to see through the dark shadows of the apple trees.

"There." Sara pointed. "I see the white tip of her tail wagging." She paused. "Wagging? Why would she be wagging her tail?" She started across the grass toward the wobbling dot of white. Again she stopped as she heard the muffled voice. She listened intently, trying to make out the words. "Jack, that's . . . oh, good God!" She threw down her hoe and broke into a run, almost slipping twice on the long, damp grass. At last she was close enough to see Lucy. The beagle was standing over a dark form crumpled on the grass, wagging her tail and whining. Sara was on her knees before she got completely stopped and almost fell over the dark form. She touched him tentatively.

"Dammit, you devil cur, you!" The words were weak, but Sara breathed a sigh of relief. She turned him over. "Lord Emrys, are you all right?"

Emrys tried to sit up. His head was dark, and Sara caught her breath. "Miss Jones. What did you want with me? Is this your idea of revenge?" He reached over for Jack's axe and used it as a prop to stand up. Sara tried to help him, but he waved her away. "I can take care of myself, thank you, Miss Jones." His voice was ice splinters.

At last he stood, a dark, glistening rivulet flowing down the side of his face. The blood looked black in the shadows and moonlight. "I repeat, is this your idea of revenge, Miss Jones? I thought we had reached something of an understanding." Bitterness twisted his mouth. "I see I was wrong."

"What are you talking about, Lord Emrys?" Sara moved

toward him as he tottered and the axe almost slid. "Let me help you."

Emrys swayed dangerously, then righted himself. "I do believe you've helped me quite enough for one evening, Miss Jones. Thank God you're not a better shot." He bent over and, with sheer willpower, stood straight again, blood dripping onto his coat.

"I don't know what you mean." Sara tried to keep from grabbing him as he wobbled perilously again.

"I think you do, Miss Jones." His tone was a mix of ice and bitterness. "I thought you might be someone who could—" he swayed dangerously, the axe sliding—". . . care . . . care for . . ." Emrys pitched forward. Sara reached out to catch him, terrified that he was going to fall onto the axe. His weight pushed against her, and she almost fell backward as his body slumped onto hers. Emrys slid slowly to the ground, blood from his head making a trail all the way down her dress.

Chapter 15

They tried, but Jack and Sara couldn't carry the unconscious Emrys. Sara was terrified of hurting him further and finally sent Jack back for help. "I'll have to wake everybody up," Jack said.

"Then do it, Jack." Sara knelt by Emrys and dabbed at his face with the hem of her dressing gown. "Just hurry. Get Garfield to bring something to carry him on."

"He's not going to like it."

Sara pinned him with a look. "Go, Jack. Emrys could very well die while you're here dithering about. Run."

Lucy sat down on the other side of Emrys. The night was quiet, and Sara felt a prickling up the back of her neck as soon as Jack left. Whoever had shot Emrys could very well still be out there, waiting. The person could shoot her as well. Unconsciously, she bent lower until her face was almost over Emrys'.

He was still bleeding profusely, the blood caking around the fringes of his hair and clotting in the tips. Even in the pale moonlight, he looked spectral, his face a ghastly white contrast to his black clothing. Blood was everywhere, dripping from his face onto her dressing gown. She could feel the warmth of his blood as it soaked through her clothes. She cradled his head in her arms. "Don't die," she whispered.

"Die," he muttered, trying to move, but only succeeding in pillowing himself closer to her. "Won't die."

"No, don't die," she crooned. "It'll be all right, it really will." She gently ran her fingertips over his hair and onto his face. He felt colder now to her touch, and she knew a minute of fear. Was Emrys going to die? Was he bleeding to death in her arms? She put her fingertips over his mouth to see if he was still breathing. His lips were warm, and she felt his breath, steadier than she had thought it would be. She glanced up, worried, and looked toward Saint's Haven. Every tree seemed to have a black shadow behind it, and she trembled, not from the cold. Emrys put his hand on her arm. Even with his injuries, he knew what she was feeling, and his touch was meant to reassure her, she knew, but his fingers were icy cold, and that terrified her even further. She held on to him, crooning reassuring words that meant nothing.

Lucy put a paw on her arm, and she looked up again. This time she could see a torch as several people hurried across the yard toward the orchard. "Thank God," she breathed, looking back down at Emrys. There was blood puddled in her lap, but Emrys was still breathing steadily, even though his skin was cold and clammy.

Garfield, Jack, and Aunt Zell came into view, all of them running through the grass. Garfield and Jack were carrying a door that looked as if it had been hastily ripped right off its hinges. Aunt Zell was trotting beside them, a quilt thrown over her shoulder. They ran right up to Sara and Emrys, and Garfield threw the door on the ground. "Put him on here and let's get him inside," Garfield said without preamble, shoving the door right beside Emrys on the ground so they could roll him onto it. "Zell left Briget to fetch water and have it ready, and James is set to go fetch the surgeon if need be." He and Jack carefully lifted Emrys' head and placed him on the door, covering him and gently tucking the quilt in around his body. "Don't want him to get cold. Worst thing that can happen," Garfield muttered. "Get that other end." He spoke to Jack, and the two of them lifted on a count of three and began carefully walking back to Saint's Haven, keeping the door even. "Here, Zell, light the way," Garfield called. "The last thing we want is to fall and dump him in the dirt."

Aunt Zell looked at Sara, then back at Garfield. She had taken Sara's arm to help her as Sara was standing wobbly, her clothing wet with Emrys' blood. Sara put her hand on Aunt Zell's arm. "He needs you more than I do, Aunt Zell. Go help them and carry the light. I'll make my own way." She took two or three steps to show Aunt Zell that she was all right.

"If you're sure," Aunt Zell said briskly, giving Sara a pat on her shoulder. "Might as well tend to the worse. I take it that blood all over you belongs to Emrys."

Sara glanced down at her ruined dressing gown and touched the cold, dark smears. "All of it. I'm not hurt at all."

Aunt Zell nodded and ran to take the torch from Garfield and light the way. As soon as she had gone ahead with the light, Sara fell into a puddle onto the grass, her knees jelly. She was shaking all over.

She stayed on the grass, Lucy beside her, until she could stand up. By that time, the torch was almost at Saint's Haven. She felt a prickling at the back of her neck as though someone were watching her. She picked up the axe and made herself stand and take one step after the other. If someone was out there, she wouldn't have the strength to use the axe, but she still felt better for having it. She was still trembling, and her body refused to work the way it should. Lucy walked right beside her, against her leg, as though to provide a prop.

By the time Sara reached the kitchen of Saint's Haven, Garfield already had Emrys inside on the table. The door, which Sara now recognized as the dining room door, was propped against the back. On the table, Emrys was as waxen as death. Sara hung onto the door facing and gasped. "He isn't dead, is he?" she whispered into the silence of the kitchen.

Briget glanced over at the door and Sara's blood-soaked clothes. She screeched and almost dropped the kettle she was carrying. "Grab that kettle!" Aunt Zell cried to Garfield. "Sara's not hurt."

Mrs. Jones, who had been standing at Emrys' head, took one look at her daughter. "Not hurt? With all that blood all over her? Oh, Sara." She fell quietly to the floor.

"I'm not hurt," Sara said, coming into the kitchen. She had no idea how pale and frightened she looked. She didn't even notice her mother on the floor. She had eyes only for Emrys. "He isn't dead, is he?"

"No, he isn't dead." Aunt Zell turned and ran practiced fingers over her. "Are you sure you aren't hurt?"

Sara shook her head. "No, I'm fine. Is Emrys all right?" She took a step nearer the table and almost stepped on her mother.

"Garfield," Aunt Zell ordered, "pick Sophie up and take her upstairs to her room. She'll come around in a few minutes." She looked at Sara. "You'd better go change and stay with your mother. She'll have to see you to believe that you're not hacked to pieces."

"I can't go right now." Sara moved as Garfield picked up Mrs. Jones and carried her out. "How is he? Is he going to be all right?'' She touched Emrys' head with her fingertips and looked at Aunt Zell.

By the time Aunt Zell had washed the blood from Emrys' wound, Sara felt that she had aged ten years. Emrys moved and muttered as Aunt Zell worked, every touch bringing him pain. ''Be still,'' Sara whispered to him, putting her hands on his shoulders. ''Be still.''

Emrys' injury proved to be a nasty flesh wound, a graze across his head and temple. ''Another inch this way and he'd be dead,'' Garfield said, inspecting the furrow. ''Someone was aiming to kill.''

''Miss Jones,'' Emrys muttered. ''I didn't think she'd do it.'' His eyelids fluttered. ''I thought . . . I thought . . .''

''What do you mean?'' Sara moved to stand beside him so she could see him better.

Emrys opened his eyes and looked up at her. ''Why did you try to kill me?''

''I did no such thing. Jack and I found you and brought you here.''

Emrys tried to sit up, held his head, and moaned. Garfield took one arm and Sara the other, and they helped him sit. ''If you didn't try to do this, then who did?'' Emrys said after he was upright. He put his hand to his head and felt Aunt Zell's neat bandage. ''You were the one who told me that it was urgent that I come to the orchard to meet you.''

''At this time of the morning? I certainly told you nothing of the sort.'' Sara glanced at the doorway, reminded that she needed to go upstairs to see to her mother.

Emrys reached into his waistcoat pocket. ''I saved this, Miss Jones. Perhaps you could explain it to me.'' He handed her a note written on a small sheet of paper. The paper bore Sara's initials. She had a box full of it upstairs in her room. When she opened it, she saw what appeared to be her handwriting, but she knew she had never written such a note. As Emrys had said, the note asked—no, she thought, the note *begged*—Emrys to come to the orchard after midnight as she had something important to tell him. It was signed Sarafina Jones, and the signature looked to her exactly like her own. She paled and handed the note back to him. "I have no explanation, Lord Emrys, and I own that the writing looks just like my own. However, I swear to you that I did not write that note, nor do I know anything about it."

Emrys looked into her eyes, his tawny gaze icy at first, then warming as she looked steadily at him. "All right, Miss Jones, I believe you. Now the question becomes *who did send the note?* It had to be someone who knew both of us well enough to know that I would answer a distress summons from you. Someone who wanted me dead."

"Someone who knew my signature and could duplicate it exactly." Sara glanced again at the signature. "I know I didn't sign it, but even I could swear it's my signature."

"Then who? The same person who forged your father's signature?" Emrys looked at the note again.

"One of your business acquaintances?" Aunt Zell suggested.

Emrys started to shake his head, but winced with the pain. "No," he said hoarsely. "Very few people would know that I'm acquainted with Miss Jones. Even fewer would know that I would be worried enough to come when she asked me to."

"I didn't—" Sara began, but Emrys touched her hand and smiled.

"I know, Miss Jones. I believe you when you say you didn't write the note. Still, whoever did has to know your handwriting and have access to your stationery box." He glanced back down at the letter in his hand. "I take it that this stationery is genuine."

"It is." Sara touched the paper with her fingers. "Mama

gave me a box of it for my birthday, and I've saved it for special letters." She put her hand to her head, as though hers ached as much as Emrys'. "Who would have been in my room? Who would know where I keep it?"

Emrys tried to stand. "Once we answer those questions, Miss Jones, I believe we'll have Ned Perkin." Emrys wobbled, and Garfield caught him and sat him in a chair. "You'd best stay here tonight," he said. "It'll just be until morning, but I don't think you'd better try to get to Brookwood in the dark." He glanced out the window. "Besides, whoever tried this may still be out there waiting to try again."

"Correct, Garfield," Aunt Zell's voice was crisp and brooked no disobedience. "You'll stay here tonight, and I'll take another look at that in the morning. You're going to have a sore head by then, anyway." She glanced at the ceiling as a screech came from upstairs. "You'd best get up the stairs to Sophie," she said to Sara. "I think she's come to."

"Oh, my Lord." Sara put her hand to her mouth. "I forgot about Mama." She wheeled to dash out the door and fell over Lucy. Lucy dashed under the table, squealing while Sara staggered and tried to catch herself. She couldn't grasp anything except air and crashed forward, falling onto Emrys, hitting her chin on his knee, and finally winding up on the floor at his feet.

Emrys held out a hand for her as she tried to make it to her knees. "Can you still say that you're all right, Miss Jones? If your chin hurts as much as my knee, then you've got a bruise."

Sara sat up on the floor, listening to her mother scream from upstairs. She had bit her lip when she hit Emrys, and there was blood dribbling from the cut down onto her chin. Before she knew what was happening, Emrys had cupped her chin in one hand and was dabbing at the cut with his handkerchief.

He smiled down at her, his eyes like liquid amber. "A little cut, Miss Jones, but I'm afraid you'll have a bruise. Should I apologize now or wait until your chin is blue?" His voice was like a purr, and his eyes got warmer and more liquid until Sara felt she was being consumed by them. She couldn't even answer him. "I'm fine, thank you," she stammered. "I hear Mama."

Emrys glanced up at the ceiling as Mrs. Jones screeched Sara's name again. "Yes, you'd better go alleviate her fears. She seems to be worried."

"Humph," Aunt Zell snorted. "Sophie always did carry on." Aunt Zell reached down and helped Sara to her feet. "Come on, girl, I'll go with you. If that dog gets in the way again, you're likely to break a leg on the stairs. Let's go tend to Sophie."

As soon as Mrs. Jones saw that Sara was unhurt, she promptly went into hysterics.

"Just reaction," Aunt Zell said, unperturbed, reaching for the laudanum bottle and a glass of water. "Sophie always was high strung." Deftly she mixed the drops in the water and held it to Mrs. Jones's lips.

"Sara, my dear," Mrs. Jones said between gulps, "you could have been killed! We must go back to London."

"Don't be silly, Mama. I'm more likely to be killed in London than here. Here, let me put a cool cloth on your head." She picked up the book beside Mrs. Jones's bed and turned to a chapter. "I'll read to you until you go back to sleep."

By the time Mrs. Jones dropped off to sleep, Emrys had taken Jack's bed and gone to sleep as well. Sara went to her own room and thought that she would never get to sleep, but as soon as she fell into her bed, she dozed off. The only time she woke was when Lucy hopped up on he bed, but she went right back to sleep and didn't wake up until the sun was streaming into her window.

Everyone else seemed to have stayed in bed as Sara rose to a quiet house. She opened the drawer to her bedside table and pulled the wrapped diary from it. She sighed. There was no choice, she thought to herself. She had to give the diary to Emrys.

She was just finishing her breakfast when Emrys came into the kitchen. He looked terrible. His face was swollen and purple-blue above and below the wound. Some blood had seeped from the furrow and had dried, caking on his cheek where a stubble of beard gave him a dark look.

"Does my appearance startle you, Miss Jones?" He sat down and touched his head gingerly. "You look fine—nothing except a small cut. I thought you'd have a bruise as well." He touched her chin with his fingertip, and Sara felt it down to her knees. Emrys didn't notice her reaction. "As for me," he said, touching his bandage, "I'm afraid to look in the mirror. If I look half as bad as I feel, I'm going to scare small children for weeks."

"You look fine. I really didn't notice a thing."

Emrys grinned. "Liar."

Sara blushed, caught. "All right. You look absolutely wretched."

"Good. If I feel this bad, I want to look it as well." He stood up shakily. "I'd best be getting back to Brookwood."

"You'll do no such thing until you've had some breakfast, and then Jack will take you in the cart."

"Heavens, Miss Jones, breakfast is fine, but as for the cart—do allow me a little dignity."

"The cart," she said firmly as she began cooking his breakfast. "I hope you're hungry."

Emrys paused a moment, considering. "Actually, since I feel so terrible, I shouldn't be hungry, but I'm ravenous."

He looked at her with interest. "I didn't know you could cook, Miss Jones."

"With all these children around, everyone has to pitch in." Sara got out a loaf of bread and some butter Aunt Zell had bought in the village. "Everyone here can cook, except Mary and Matthew, of course, but they'll learn when they get older." Sara poured him a cup of tea. When his breakfast was ready, Emrys proved he was ravenous.

"Excellent, Miss Jones." He patted his lips with his napkin. "I feel much better."

Sara toyed with a spoon and made circles on the tabletop. "I found something you should have, Lord Emrys."

He raised an eyebrow in surprise, but said nothing as Sara went over and picked up the packet containing the diary. "I know you've had a difficult time, and I hate to compound that . . ." Her words trailed off, but she had to finish. "I found this—or rather Lucy found it—buried behind the shed." Emrys unrolled the covering and saw the diary. "It should belong to you," Sara said.

Emrys ruffled the pages. "Did you read it?"

Sara wished the floor would open, but she couldn't lie. She met his eyes and was surprised that he wasn't angry. His gaze was warm. "Yes, parts of it. I didn't read everything."

Emrys snapped the book shut and slipped it into his pocket. "I doubt I'll discover anything I don't already know or suspect." His mouth twisted with bitterness, and he looked as if he was going to say something else; but Jack came into the room.

"Garfield says I'm to take you to Brookwood," he announced, feeling important.

"In the cart," Sara added. "He's not to walk, not in that condition."

Emrys grinned at her. "My keeper has spoken, Jack. Eat your breakfast and we'll go. I won't protest a whit, I promise you, but I insist we dodge main street in the village. All we need is for the gossips to line up for a look."

After Emrys had gone, Sara sat at the kitchen table for a few minutes, then went up to her room. She looked out the window and saw the faint smudge of Brookwood across the orchard and fields. Emrys was a rich man, she knew that. She also knew that she was nothing except a poor missionary's daughter, and she had no prospects. Then why was she allowing herself to be attracted to a man who was impossible to know, impossible to attain? Sara slumped down on the floor under the window and looked dejectedly at her room. It was plain, comfortable enough, but shabby. Was this how Emrys saw Saint's Haven? Why, why did she have to see those tawny eyes every time she looked at him? Why did she have to imagine. . . . She looked down as Lucy put her head in Sara's lap and looked up at her. "You love me, don't you, Lucy?" she said, putting her arms around the dog. Everything else was unspoken, and Sara forced herself to stop thinking about Emrys. He was beyond her touch.

Late in the afternoon, Emrys returned with two large men. He found Sara in the backyard, sitting on a rough wooden bench, waiting for Lucy to finish eating. "I've brought Timothy and Allan to guard the place at night. They'll be here from now on at night, one at the back and one at the front." He shook his head as she started to speak and motioned for the men to take their stations. As soon as they left, he sat down beside Sara. "No, I don't want to hear any objections. I could have been killed last night, you could have been killed, or Jack could have been killed. I don't think it's worth taking a chance. Too many things have happened recently, and I see Ned Perkin's hand in this. From what I've heard of the man, he'll stop at nothing." Emrys looked around, wincing slightly as he turned his head too quickly. "I just wish I knew what he was after." He paused. "There was no clue to that in Elizabeth's diary."

"You've read it, then?"

He nodded. "How much did you read?" He sat quietly beside her as Lucy looked up from her empty dish, wanting more.

"Nothing else for you, Lucy," Sara said. "You're getting fat already."

"She may be eating for four or five or more, you know." There was a touch of laughter in Emrys' voice. Then he became serious. "You didn't answer my question."

"I read parts of it, as I told you. I started to read the last third or so, but I couldn't do it. It was too private, and I felt as if I was prying." She hesitated. "I apologize for reading any of it."

"That's all right. I think you should have read it." He shifted slightly so he faced her. "I told you something of my marriage, but even I was shocked at some of the things Elizabeth wrote. I had spent a long time feeling sorry for her and thought perhaps I had misjudged her until I reached the end of the diary." He ran his fingers through his hair, then touched the bandage on his head with his fingertips. "This thing's a damned nuisance." He gave Sara the ghost of a grin. "Sorry, I forget that I'm not among men. I've grown unaccustomed to being around ladies."

"It's all right." Sara smiled at him and found herself looking into his eyes again. She felt dizzy, almost as though her world were spinning around her. Before she betrayed herself, she forced herself to look straight ahead on the pretext of examining Lucy.

"I want you to read the last section sometime," Emrys said. "You may be thinking that Elizabeth was trapped with me and unhappy, and she was. Still," he paused and took a deep breath, "she carried on her affair with Ned Perkin.

The baby was Ned's, and she wrote in her diary that she and Ned planned to kill me and make it look like an accident; then she would marry Ned, and they'd claim Brookwood for the baby.'' His voice twisted with bitterness. "They had it all planned. If Elizabeth had met up with him that night, I'd be dead today, and his child would be heir to Brookwood and all that I have.''

"Is that where the diary ends?" Sara still couldn't look at him.

Emrys bent slightly and propped on his knees. "With the plot? No. It ends with a scrap of paper from Perkin that tells Elizabeth that he's in jail; then there's a notation that Elizabeth has received word that he's been in an accident and she's going to him, no matter what.'' He paused. "That was the last sentence.'' He couldn't keep the pain from his voice.

Sara turned and put her hand on his arm. "I'm sure she didn't mean it. Often women get carried away and do things they regret. I'm sure it was that way with Elizabeth.''

Emrys covered her hand with his own. "No. She had been involved with Perkin for years. Elizabeth was just bad, Sara.'' Sara glanced at him, but he didn't even realize he had used her first name. "You probably don't understand that, but some women are just bad through and through. Elizabeth was, and I knew it at the time, although I tried to tell myself it wasn't so. It's time for me to admit the truth.''

Sara didn't know what to say to him. She glanced down at his hand on hers, strong, the fingers long and tapering. Most of all, she felt the warmth of his hand through her skin, a reassurance there that she was surprised to feel. Finally, she looked back up into his eyes and was lost completely. He looked vulnerable and open, and her heart went out to him.

"I don't know what I can say to you," she whispered. "I wish I could make things right."

He smiled at her. "That's what you like to do, isn't it—make things right for everyone? For the children, for your mother, for Lucy?" He moved his hand, and his fingers slipped up her arm. "That's a wonderful quality to a point. What about making things right for yourself?"

"I don't know what you mean." She looked at him in surprise.

"I mean that it's time to start thinking of yourself, Miss Jones. It's time to stop making things right for everyone else and start making things right for yourself." He grinned at her and stood up. "I think you'll discover what I mean after you've thought about it." He glanced around to see that the men were on guard. "I'll be checking by frequently and, of course, getting reports from Timothy and Allan. If you need anything, let me know at once."

"Of course. I do hope you're going home and go to bed. You need the rest."

Emrys chuckled. "There you go—making things right again. Just by way of information, Miss Jones, that's exactly what I plan to do. I hope you have a good night as well." He smiled at her again, put on his hat sideways to avoid his bandage, and went around the corner of the house where his carriage stood waiting. Sara followed behind him, but stopped at the corner of the house. "At least," she said to Lucy, "the man isn't gallivanting around on that horse, shaking his whole head with every step." She watched as the carriage pulled slowly out and went toward the village and Brookwood.

Sara stood there at the corner of the house for a long time, almost until darkness had fallen, just standing there and thinking. She tried to make sense of Emrys' words, but images of the man kept intruding: his smile, his eyes when he was angry and they were like ice chips, his eyes when he was happy and they were like liquid caramel, his hands with the strong fingers, his expressions. Darkness fell, and Sara finally went to sit on the bench in the front garden. She pulled Lucy up to sit beside her and put her arms around Lucy's neck, burying her face in the familiar fur as she finally figured out what Emrys meant. "For myself," she said. "Lucy, just thinking of myself, I know what I want and I want Emrys." She rubbed her cheek against Lucy's soft, floppy ear. "Oh, God, Lucy," she whispered as realization sunk in, "I think I'm in love with Emrys."

Chapter 16

Almost a week passed and there was no word from Emrys. Sara was beside herself, thinking that anything could have happened to him. She worried that he might have gotten an infection and a fever, worried that he might even have taken gangrene, worried that he might have decided that Elizabeth's revelations were too much and left the country, worried that he had even done away with himself. At last, she could stand it no longer and dressed to go over to Brookwood and find out for herself. She was going to take Mary and Matthew with her on the pretext of taking them there to look at the horses. It was a flimsy excuse, but, as she told herself as she dressed, better than nothing. She went down the stairs to get Mary and Matthew and ran into Chiswick, who was standing by the door, talking to Mrs. Jones. Something about the way they were standing caught Sara's attention, but she really couldn't say what was different.

Chiswick wheeled and moved toward the door when he heard her footfall on the stairs. "You startled me, Miss

Jones," he said with a smile. The man seemed to have aged five years in the past two weeks, Sara thought to herself.

"I apologize, Mr. Chiswick." She turned to her mother. "I was going to take Mary and Matthew over to Brookwood to look at the horses. Have you seen them?"

Mrs. Jones looked at her sharply. "Brookwood? Whatever for, Sara? Surely Emrys doesn't want to be bothered with children coming over. If you start that, it'll be difficult to stop it."

"Emrys won't care," Chiswick said. "He loves children and invites little ones from the village to Brookwood at every opportunity." Chiswick looked back to Sara. "However, it won't do much good to go over there today—Emrys left for London some days ago, and I don't know when he plans to return. It should be soon."

"It might be better," Mrs. Jones said. "You could take the twins over to see the horses while Emrys isn't there. That way, there will be no bother." She turned and called out the door for the twins, and Sara was obligated to dress the urchins and take them to Brookwood, even though she certainly had no interest in looking at horseflesh. The twins, however, had a marvelous time.

To Sara's surprise, Emrys came to Saint's Haven two days later. He came rather late in the evening after the lamps had been lit. When the knock came, Sara went to answer it as Aunt Zell and Mrs. Jones were busy with needlework. Emrys was there, dressed, to her amazement, in dark brown. It was the first time she had ever seen him in any color except black. "Do come in, Lord Emrys." She stepped aside so he could enter.

Inside, they sat down, and there was a small silence. "And how was London, Lord Emrys?" Sara asked.

"London?" Emrys was blank.

"Mr. Chiswick told us you had gone to London."

Emrys chuckled. "That was a ruse. You know how everyone in the village gossips, and I wanted no comment on my real purpose. Actually, I've been trying to track down Bekins, the younger. I thought he might be able to assist me."

"By telling you that we had really sold Saint's Haven?" Sara was annoyed. "Are you still trying to evict us from here? And to think, I was worried about you."

His eyes softened. "You were? What a nice thought, Miss Jones." He glanced around at the anxious faces. "No, I certainly had no idea of evicting you from Saint's Haven. I recognize defeat when I see it, I assure you. I was trying to track Bekins down because, if you remember, he's the one man who can identify Ned Perkin. I thought if Bekins could give me a drawing or some kind of description, then we could be on watch. I loathe having to pause and ascertain whether or not every person I see is Ned Perkin. I decided that I wasn't going to live that way—I was going to find Bekins and discover Perkin's disguise. Then I could deal with him."

Mrs. Jones leaned forward. "And did you find out anything?"

Emrys nodded. "I discovered that Bekins is in Newgate for bad debts. He simply can't manage money, it seems. At any rate, I do plan to go to London tomorrow and quiz the man. I want to engage an artist to accompany me and sketch Perkin. If I can get the authorities interested, and I think I can, there should be wanted posters of Perkin all over Britain within a month."

Sara had to keep herself from clutching his arm, but her voice was still anxious. "But isn't that dangerous—going to London, I mean. If Perkin knows you're going, he could waylay your coach and kill you. Worse, he could have someone set on you in London and kill you. Worse than that, he could—'' She stopped as Emrys broke out laughing.

"Do hush, Miss Jones. You'll have me dead and buried before I get back to Brookwood.'' Sara turned away, embarrassed, but Emrys moved in his chair so he could see her face. "Of course I agree that the trip could be dangerous. After all, look what Perkin did around here." He touched his head with his fingers. The bandage had been removed, and there was an angry red furrow running across the side of his head. "I will take care. I'm also taking along my man, two men from Brookwood, and, of course, the coachman." He stood and smiled at all of them. "I just wanted to come by and remind you to keep the doors locked and don't go out alone, even in the daylight. Until we know what Perkin looks like, every man is suspect."

Garfield grunted. "Been keeping an eye out myself."

Emrys clapped him on the shoulder. "Good. And I still have Timothy and Allan posted at night. I trust they're keeping good watch."

"Out there every night." Garfield nodded as he spoke.

"Good. They're able men, both of them. I'd trust them with my life." He smiled at the group. "I'll bring the sketch over right after I return from London. I hope Bekins is able to describe him well enough for someone to draw him accurately."

"What if he can't?" Sara's tone was dull.

"Then he can't." Emrys shrugged. "If that happens, I can probably pay off his debt and buy his release. I'll bring him back here and let him look for Perkin." He raised an eyebrow. "Of course, how long the man would last is an open point. I'd say Perkin would be ready to shoot him immediately." Emrys smiled at them again. "Of course, things won't get that bad. I bid all of you good night as I'm off in the morning. I merely wanted to remind you to be careful until I return."

"We're always careful." Sara walked him to the door, all the while trying her best to act normal. It was more difficult than she had thought it would be. She certainly didn't want Emrys to get a hint of her feelings. The man was far too perceptive.

Three days later, they had heard no word from Emrys, but just before dusk that evening, Jack ran inside to tell them that a stranger was coming up the road. The man was a swell, Jack said, riding a fine horse.

"A swell?" Sara frowned as she went to the window. "What have I told you about using slang, Jack."

"Well, he is. I could tell it wasn't Emrys because . . . well, just because the man's a swell."

"Don't use slang." Sara peered out the window as the man on horseback slowed his horse and turned into Saint's Haven. "Do you think something has happened to Emrys?" she asked anxiously, not even knowing if anyone was listening.

"Could be." Jack looked again. "He could be coming to tell us."

Something had happened to Emrys, Sara just knew it. She jumped from the window and ran outside, her hair flying. The man was dismounting and turned as she came dashing outside. "Did you miss me that much?" His smile was wide. It was Edward Moore, and he was wearing new clothes, tailored and made of the best blue superfine. He tied his horse and took Sara's arm. "You have no idea how wonderful your homecoming has made me feel." He walked with her to the door. "I can't wait to see everyone and tell you all my news."

Inside, Edward was greeted with enthusiasm. He had been correct, he told them, and had found his family in Cornwall. He didn't want to go into particulars just yet, as some family members hadn't been notified; but at least he recognized them, and they had welcomed him home.

"Odd that you should come to St. Claire, rather than stay in Cornwall," Aunt Zell said, placing a cold supper tray in front of him.

"There's a reason for that, but I can't divulge it right now." Edward tasted Aunt Zell's mutton stew. "This is always delicious. It's worth traveling from Cornwall just for this."

Aunt Zell laughed. "You've a silver tongue, Edward Moore. I don't care where you're from or what you do, you'll always make it through life on your turn of speech alone."

"I wish that were true." He ate and chatted about his travels and Cornwall until the others had gone to bed. Sara stayed up with Mrs. Jones, and they talked further. At last, Mrs. Jones nodded off in her chair, and Edward moved closer to Sara and took her hand. "I hope you remember our discussion before I left."

"Yes, I do, but . . ." Sara didn't know how to go on without divulging her feelings for Emrys. "Edward, I—"

He interrupted her. "Please, Sara, just let me say what I must. I just wanted you to know that my family is a good one. Not the richest in Cornwall, but one with prospects, and of gentle birth. I'm going to have to return to establish myself, of course, and regain my status in the family, but . . . ," he paused and looked at her a moment, "I still want you to know that I hold you in the highest regard, Sara. I wish to offer for you since I know I have a home and a family. It will be a while before we could wed, but you could have everything you ever wanted."

Sara glanced at Mrs. Jones, who was snoring gently, her head bobbing in her chair, and tried to think of a way to gently refuse Edward. "I don't know, Edward." She looked around the room. "I've always envisioned myself here at Saint's Haven with the children, Aunt Zell, and Mama. Cornwall seems a long distance."

"They could come as well." Edward put his other hand over hers and held it. For some reason, it didn't seem as reassuring as Emrys' hand had been. Sara shook her head, trying to rid herself of thoughts of Emrys. He was much beyond her, no matter how she felt. Common sense told her to accept Edward and make the best of the situation.

"You're shaking your head no," Edward said, turning her face with his fingers. "Don't do that yet. Think about what I've offered and remember that I could give all of you a good home. I would be good to you, Sara, don't doubt that for a moment." His face was very close to hers.

"I know, Edward." She was trying to work up the courage to tell him *yes*, and the word was on the tip of her tongue when he leaned further and kissed her. She waited for the sensations his kiss had produced before, but there was nothing. She moved closer to him, trying to find the feeling, but no matter that his kiss was expert, no matter that she wanted to care for him, there was nothing. Nothing except a different feeling that she couldn't identify. She pulled back and looked at him, the *yes* gone forever. She could never marry him.

"Please think about what I've said," Edward whispered, glancing over at Sara's mother. Mrs. Jones was rousing and fluttered her eyelids. "Promise me you'll think about it."

"All right." Sara knew she could give him only one answer, but she didn't want a scene here with her mother. She knew Mrs. Jones would want her to marry Edward, and that just wasn't possible. "Are you awake, Mama?" Sara asked, not wanting to have to say anything else to Edward.

"I haven't been asleep," Mrs. Jones answered, grumpy. "Although it's time." She stood and glanced pointedly at the clock. Sara stood as well. "Good night," she said with a smile. She felt awkward when it occurred to her that sleeping in the stable might very well be all right for Edward

Moore, hired man, but it was certainly no place for Edward Moore of Cornwall, gentleman. She didn't know what to say when Edward smiled and told her that he felt it was best if he stayed at the inn a few days until he went back to Cornwall. Sara gave him a look of pure relief and saw him to the door.

"He offered for you, didn't he?" Mrs. Jones said shrewdly as they went up to bed. "I know the signs." She paused. "And you said yes, didn't you?"

"I said I'd think about it." Sara tried to hurry down the hall to her room.

"You should say yes." Mrs. Jones was decisive for the first time in her life. "I'm convinced you should. You'll have a comfortable house, and I've heard that people in Cornwall love it there, although strangers have a time adjusting. You'd learn to love it, I'm sure."

"Good night, Mama." Sara scooted into her room just behind Lucy, then closed the door and leaned against it. As soon as she heard her mother's door close, she went to the table beside the bed and picked up her father's picture. "I can't marry a man I don't love, Papa," she whispered, "so that means I'll never marry. The boys, the twins, and Briget will have to be your grandchildren. I hope that's all right." She put the picture down and went to bed, welcoming Lucy when she jumped up on the bed and curled up. It was nice to have something to love that loved you back in return, Sara thought.

Edward returned late the next day, dressed expensively again, this time in a dark claret color. The clothes became him well, Sara realized. If she had never seen Edward working at the stables, she would never have known he had been anything but a gentleman. He must have remem-

bered his status as well as his family, as he acted the gentleman born.

"I've been tying up some loose ends," he told Sara as
they sat on the wooden bench in the back watching Lucy
down her evening meal.

All Sara could think of was the way Emrys had looked
as he had sat beside her there. She tried to block the image
from her mind, but it wouldn't go away.

"Have you thought about my offer?" Edward asked,
taking her hand. His foot got near Lucy, and Lucy growled
at him, then went on eating.

"I haven't had time today." That was a lame excuse and
she knew it. She had thought of nothing else except that
and Emrys' continued absence. "That's not true, Edward.
I have thought of it."

"Don't give me your answer now," he said softly, his
fingertips making little circles on the back of her hand.
"I want you to think about it and be sure. I'm sure."

"Edward, I have to tell you—" She stopped as his fingertips touched her lips, sealing them.

"No, not now," he whispered, "I just want to revel in
the thoughts that I know who I am and that now I'm worthy
of you."

Sara dropped her head and looked at the ground. How
could she hurt him? Emrys would never offer for her—he
himself had said that he would never marry again, and
besides, if he decided to marry, he'd pick someone from
his own class. Never in a million years would he marry a
poor missionary's daughter.

"Promise me you'll think about it, Sara."

"All right, Edward. I'll think about it."

"Good." Before she knew what was happening, he
turned her to face him and kissed her thoroughly. This
time Sara's body responded, but her emotions were dead.

I can't, she thought to herself. *I can't go through a lifetime like this. I can't marry Edward.*

Edward didn't seem to notice anything but her physical response and pulled back, a satisfied smile on his face. "I think I know what your answer will be, Sara."

Sara put her hand out to him. "I can't, Edward. I just can't marry you." She blurted the words out. That wasn't the way she had wanted to do it, heaven knew. The words just poured out, tactlessly.

Edward's face hardened, and for a second, Sara had a glimpse of something else, something she couldn't define. Then his expression smoothed. "Why not, Sara? I thought you cared for me."

"I do, Edward. I've been concerned for you since I first met you. I'm delighted that you've found your family and hope—"

He interrupted her. "Is there someone else?"

Sara didn't answer him immediately. "No," she finally said. It was true as far as it went—there wasn't anyone else because she could never marry Emrys. "There's no one else."

Edward turned her face so he could look into her eyes. Sara couldn't meet his eyes and dropped her gaze. "There is, isn't there?" Edward asked softly. "Who is he, Sara? I know you had no one in London because I asked. It has to be someone here." He thought a moment as Sara remained silent; then he tilted her face up with his finger. "It's Emrys, isn't it? You've fallen in love with that . . . that scum."

"And why do you call him that?" Sara rushed to defend him, forgetting to deny her feelings.

"Because he is." Edward's tone was bitter. "I suppose you've heard the stories about his wife—how Emrys hounded her and made her life a misery. There are those who say he killed her."

"I don't believe it!" Sara stood and glared down at Edward, hands on her hips. "I can't believe this of you, Edward Moore. How could you say such things?"

"Because they're true." He stood beside her and looked down at her. "Think about what I've told you, Sara, because Emrys is no good. Besides, he'll never marry you, you know that, don't you?"

"I know that."

Edward reached for her hand and clasped it. She tried to pull away, but he held her fast. "Emrys will never marry you, Sara. You're throwing yourself away on a dream. I can give you everything that Emrys has, believe me. You'd want for nothing, and you'd have everything Emrys could ever give you; only it would come from me." He hushed her as she started to speak. "I know that Emrys' wealth is an influence on you, but he won't have that long."

Sara's head snapped back as she looked into his eyes. "What do you mean? Do you know something about Emrys?"

Edward smiled, a strange, small smile. "Trust me—he'll have nothing left before long. I know. Don't think of Emrys—think about your feelings for me. I know you have them—I've had proof before."

Sara turned away, blushing. "I . . . I . . ."

Edward moved in front of her, almost stepping on Lucy. "I'm going to be at the inn for a few more days, so I don't want you to give me your final answer now. All I'm asking is that you think of what I've offered." He held her hands in his. "I can give you everything Emrys could ever give you, Sara. Think about it." With that, he turned and went through the house.

Sara knew in her heart that he was going inside to talk to Mrs. Jones. She couldn't face that tonight, not after refusing Edward. Instead, she whistled for Lucy, who was hiding behind the shed, and they went out to stroll through the orchard in the dusk.

Sara managed to escape her mother until early the next evening when Edward came back to visit. The day had been foggy, and with evening, the fog had settled into a thick cover. Sara hadn't even seen anyone coming up the walk. Edward was wearing a many-caped coat that fit him exquisitely. Sara could see that the coat cost more money than she had in a year. Evidently Edward's family in Cornwall was wealthy.

Luckily Aunt Zell was in the room and made no move to leave, no matter that Mrs. Jones dropped repeated hints. Edward was forced to discuss mundane matters, although he did elaborate on his family. They were wealthy, and he had prospects of becoming more so, he told them, although he didn't want to go into details. Mrs. Jones had just asked him whether he had brothers and sisters when Allan knocked on the door. He had a message from Emrys.

Sara took the letter and broke the seal, not waiting until she was alone to read it.

"Well, what does it say?" Aunt Zell asked, impatiently.

"Yes, do read it to us," Mrs. Jones said.

Sara glanced around at them. It would be all right to read this in front of Edward, she thought. After all, he was family in a sense. Allan was one of Emrys' trusted men, so that was all right as well. She unfolded the letter and read it aloud. It seemed that Emrys had paid Bekins' way out of Newgate and was bringing him back to St. Claire to identify Perkin. He also mentioned that he had some new information about Perkin that would bring the man to a hangman's noose.

That was all. There was no personal note, just an impersonal *Emrys* scrawled across the bottom of the page.

"Wonderful," Edward sighed with relief. "It will cer

tainly be a blessing to the neighborhood to know that Ned Perkin is gone.'' He chuckled. "No longer than I've been here, I've heard a dozen descriptions of him. I hope Emrys has the right one.''

"Oh, he does,'' Mrs. Jones said. "Bekins, the younger, can identify him." She looked at Sara. "I thought Emrys was going to bring a sketch back of Perkin and have some posters made up of the man. That would certainly ensure Perkin's captivity.''

"It certainly would." Edward nodded. "I just hope Emrys gets here with Bekins. That man's a scoundrel through and through, I've heard. He gambled away everything his father had.''

"Including the money Lord Emrys paid him for Saint's Haven.'' Mrs. Jones was indignant. "I'd like to know what happened to that.''

"All of us would." Edward picked up his hat and smiled at her. "When do you expect Bekins and Emrys?" he asked Allan.

Allan looked at him blankly, so Sara once again unfolded the letter. "They left London day before yesterday,'' she said, a worried frown on her face. "They should have been here already.''

Edward bit his lower lip. "I hope they haven't met with an accident. I'll go to the village and ask if they've returned." He smiled down at Sara. "I'll let you know as soon as I find out anything.''

Sara closed the door behind Allan and Edward. "Mr. Moore is a fine man,'' Mrs. Jones said. "You'd be quite lucky to wed him, Sara.''

"I know, Mama.'' Sara glanced back at her mother and led up the stairs to her room. It seemed the only place he could be where she could think of Emrys. Tonight,

though, she could only worry about him. What if he had
met with an accident? What if Ned Perkin knew what Emrys
was doing? A thousand thoughts careened through her
head. She finally crawled into bed with Lucy for company
and cried herself to sleep.

Chapter 17

Sara was awakened in the middle of the night by Lucy's howling and another noise she couldn't immediately identify. It wasn't until Jack began calling for her that she recognized the sound of someone beating on the front door. Jack, Sara, and Mrs. Jones went down the stairs together, carrying candles. Jack peered out the window, but could see nothing. The knocking continued, and someone outside called out, "Mrs. Jones! Miss Jones! Open the door!"

"That's Emrys!" Sara cried, rushing to the door. Mrs. Jones grabbed her and held her back. "It may be someone else, Sara. Remember what Lord Emrys said about keeping an eye out for strangers. Even Roger warned me to be careful and not let strangers inside."

"I recognize his voice, and Emrys is no stranger, Mama." Sara disentangled herself and rushed to the door, throwing it open just as Emrys was getting ready to knock again. He caught himself just before he hit Sara in the face with his fist.

"You do give one pause, Miss Jones," he said, coming out of the heavy fog into the house. He wore a caped greatcoat which was dripping water. Emrys was followed by a younger man and two other men Sara had seen at Brookwood, and they were similarly attired, with hats to keep the water from their faces. "I apologize for the hour," Emrys said, shutting the door behind them and checking the lock, "but I felt this was urgent. I've hurried from London as fast as possible." He looked at Sara. "Did you get my note?"

Sara nodded. "Yes, tonight. I wondered when you'd be returning, but I had no idea you'd be arriving here at three o'clock in the morning." She glanced down at her old, faded dressing gown. "We're hardly prepared for company."

Emrys took the candle from her and went into the front room, setting the candle down and taking care to pull the drapes tightly. He went around the house, checking that the doors and windows were all locked, then came back. In the meantime, Mrs. Jones had gone to make some tea, Jack had gone to rouse Garfield and Aunt Zell while James built a small fire to warm the room and help dry out the men. Sara had taken advantage of the bustle and had gone upstairs and quickly slipped into a dress. She ran her fingers through her curls and tied them back with a ribbon, then hurried downstairs.

Emrys looked up from his tea as she walked into the room and smiled appreciatively. "I'm sorry for all the mystery and air of melodrama," Emrys said, "but this directly concerns each of you, and there may be some danger." He turned to the younger man. "Meet Mr. Bekins, recently of Newgate. I brought him here to identify Ned Perkin and tell his story to you." Emrys gratefully accepted a cup of tea and handed Bekins one. "If you will, Mr. Bekins." They all sat to hear the story.

It seemed that Bekins had been a gambler who played regularly with Ned Perkin. He had often suspected that Perkin cheated, but could never prove it. At any rate, Bekins found himself deep in debt to Perkin. Bekins had nowhere to go for money as his father had sworn not to give him another farthing for gambling debts. Bekins told this to Perkin, and Perkin said he would take care of the aging Mr. Bekins. Here Mr. Bekins, the younger, stopped, overcome with emotion. He had gone in the next morning after Perkin had said this and had found his father dead. From all indications, the death was natural, but Bekins always knew in his heart that Perkin had been responsible because there wasn't a single farthing left in the office. Bekins knew his father had kept sums locked up carefully. Bekins didn't know how Perkin had killed his father and taken the money, but he knew that he had. What Perkin hadn't known was that Mr. Bekins, the elder, was a careful man who kept most of his money in the bank.

They waited a moment for Bekins to compose himself, and then he went on. Now the field was clear for Bekins to pay off his debts, which he did. However, it wasn't long before he was under the hatches again. The only asset he had that could be used to raise money quickly was Saint's Haven. Perkin first mentioned the scheme and assured Bekins that the Jones family had been gone so long that they wouldn't know what had happened. Bekins knew it was wrong, but Perkin kept after him, relishing an opportunity to defraud Emrys. In addition to his other talents, Perkin was a master forger. Bekins prepared the deed and brought an old letter from Mr. Jones. Perkin forged the signature, and it was perfect. Even, Bekins noted, Chiswick, an old friend, couldn't tell the difference. Emrys was glad to pay the money. Here Bekins stopped and looked at Emrys apologetically. "I'm really sorry," he said.

"I understand how you were led to it," Emrys said. "Go on."

That night, Bekins told them, he hid the money he had received from Emrys, knowing Perkin would want it. He had determined to leave since he knew what happened to most of Perkin's accomplices. Bekins visited Perkin at Saint's Haven and told Ned that Emrys was going to give him the money in the morning. Bekins assured Perkin that he would stop by and give him the money as soon as he received it from Emrys. At the time, Perkin was drunk and grieving over Elizabeth's death. Perkin blamed Emrys for her death and the death of his child. He told Bekins that he was going to kill Emrys and was enough into his cups to show Bekins the money he had hidden. Bekins knew then for a certainty that Perkin was responsible for the death of his father.

The money was labeled and carefully wrapped. It was the money and certificates that the elder Bekins had saved and invested for Clayton Jones over the years. Bekins knew that when Perkin sobered up and remembered what he had told, Bekins would be the next on his list. That night, he took the money Emrys had paid for Saint's Haven and fled to London where he hoped to start again. He had been living there under another name, terrified every moment that Ned Perkin would find him. He had finally lost all the money gambling and had been thrown in Newgate.

"So you mean that there is money hidden somewhere at Saint's Haven. You've seen it?"

Bekins nodded. "Every penny of it was labeled with Clayton Jones's name."

"So you mean the money Perkin is after belongs to us?" Sara asked slowly.

Bekins nodded. "Every penny of it. He had it on the table and told me that he kept it hidden in the house.

don't know where, but I suspect that he's trying to get it back." He paused. "It was a very considerable sum. I have no idea how much, but I do know that my father was pleased with his investments."

"Forget the money for now," Emrys said, standing and looking out the window into the fog. "There's something more pressing at hand." He turned to Bekins. "Describe Perkin for them. Tell them exactly what you told me."

Bekins began, and Sara had a vague sense that she might have seen the person he described. When Bekins finished, Sara looked in puzzlement at Emrys.

"Do you know that person?" Emrys asked, removing a folded sheet of paper from his pocket.

"I should, but I can't really place him. He sounds like someone I've seen. The hair, the expression . . ." Her voice trailed off as Emrys began unfolding the sheet of paper.

"I had an artist sketch Perkin from Mr. Bekins' description." Emrys showed the paper to Bekins. "Is this the man you've identified as Ned Perkin, Mr. Bekins?"

Bekins nodded. "That's him. Line for line, just like he is in life."

Emrys turned and held up the drawing. Mrs. Jones screamed, and Sara felt the blood drain from her face as they looked right into a drawing of the face of Edward Moore.

"He knows," Sara said in a strangled voice.

"What do you mean?"

"Edward—whatever his name is—was here when your note arrived, and I read it aloud to everyone. He knows you're bringing Mr. Bekins back to identify him."

"I'm a dead man," Bekins whispered. "Dead."

Emrys wheeled on him. "You're no such thing, Bekins. You're going to Brookwood and stay there. I doubt that even Perkin can get to you there."

"Oh, but he can. You don't know that man. He's the devil, he is."

Emrys came over to Mrs. Jones and Sara. "Come to Brookwood. Let the man come here and we'll set a trap for him."

"He's at the inn," Sara said, standing. "He said he was going back there."

Emrys ran to the door, motioning for his men and Bekins to come with him. "Timothy and Allan are still here, so we'll go to the inn and apprehend Perkin. He'll be thinking that we'll be back tomorrow, and we can catch him while he's sleeping."

Sara walked to the door. "Be careful," she whispered. "He'll kill you if he can."

"I know that." Emrys paused. "I'll come back, I promise."

Sara shut the door behind him and checked the lock. "I'm glad that Allan and Timothy are there tonight," she said wearily. "Edward knows every inch of the grounds and this house. He could get in here at any time if we don't keep watch."

Sara went back to bed, but sleep was impossible. She kept thinking of Edward Moore. She knew, just knew, that he would return to Saint's Haven. She knew as well that he would kill Emrys if he possibly could. After a while, she got up and went downstairs to fix herself some tea. The house was dark and quiet, and every sound reverberated.

In the kitchen, she found Jack sitting asleep in front of the door. With a smile, she got a quilt and covered him. He woke up and looked at her. "Not much of a sentry am I?" He stood and wrapped the quilt around him, then sat at the table to have tea with Sara. "I think he'll come back, Sara."

"So do I, Jack. We'll just have to watch for him and be ready."

"He may try to lay low for a while, just to get us off guard. That's my guess, anyway."

Sara sighed and sipped her tea. She was getting a headache. "You may be right. I'm not very perceptive—I thought the man was a war hero who had lost his memory. I accepted everything he had to say, even that tale about his family in Cornwall." She took another sip. "Where do you think Perkin went during his absence?"

Jack shrugged. "Maybe to London, maybe to one of the ports to recruit some men. Who knows? Most likely he was trying to find Emrys."

Sara nodded. "That thought occurred to me." She reached over and put her hand on Jack's arm. "I think he's going to try to kill Emrys, Jack. He has . . . personal reasons."

"The late Lady Emrys?"

"How did you know about that?"

Jack smiled, and Sara realized once again that he was becoming a man. "Everyone in the village knows part of it, Sara. I heard the gossip, guessed at other parts, and came up with a reasonable answer." He laughed. "I didn't spend years in the stews of London without learning how to add two and two."

"I thought you had forgotten that past, Jack."

"I have." He paused. "Thank you."

Sara looked at him, startled. "For what, Jack? You know how Papa felt about you and all of God's creatures."

"I know, but he chose me, and that made all the difference." He sipped his tea. "I could have been another Ned Perkin. I could have been swinging from the end of a rope or on a transport ship."

Sara patted his shoulder. "But you're not. You're here at Saint's Haven, and we're depending on you." She looked at him. "Sometimes I think we depend on you too much, Jack, but you always know just what to do."

Jack beamed and went back to sentry duty at the door. Sara washed up the tea dishes and went to the front room to read until daylight. Shortly after sunrise, Emrys rode up. He looked terrible, mud-spattered and weary.

"Perkin was gone," he said without preamble when Sara opened the door. "I don't know how he knew we were coming, but he did. There was no trace of him anywhere. We scoured the country." He followed Sara into the kitchen for a cup of tea and smiled broadly at the sight of Jack fast asleep against the door, huddled in his quilt.

"He seems to be a good boy," Emrys said softly, sliding into a kitchen chair.

"One of the best." Sara fixed the tea tray and put the water on. She sat down across from Emrys. "What now? What do you think Perkin will do?"

"I think he'll go after either Bekins or me. Odds are that he'll try to get into Brookwood, but he may try here if Bekins is correct. I don't think he'll leave his money if it's still here. I'd feel better if all of you went somewhere else for a few days."

Sara looked around. "We have nowhere else to go."

"Brookwood." Emrys paused. "I assure you that all of you will be well cared for there. I've brought in extra men, so I don't think Perkin will get in there. If he comes after me, it'll be when I'm out somewhere." He shrugged. "Perkin may well wait for months or even years, but I think he'll try to get his money right away. That's why I want you out of this house." He paused. "Money really doesn't mean much, compared to life."

"I know. I'm not worried about the money. We'll manage, we always have." Sara sipped her tea. "I'll talk to Mama, Aunt Zell, and Garfield about staying at Brookwood." Sara frowned. "The children are just accepting this as their home. Do you think we'd be able to return soon?"

"I think so." Emrys finished his tea and stood. "I'll be back in a couple of hours for your answer. I know you really don't want to move to Brookwood, but it's as safe as I can make it, and I do feel there's danger here." He walked to the door, then turned around, smiling. "I think we've passed a milestone, Miss Jones. I just suggested you leave Saint's Haven, and there was no argument about ownership."

"Merely because you've recognized our rights, Lord Emrys."

He laughed. "Correct, Miss Jones. I'm merely a guest here now." She got up to walk him out as Lucy wandered over to them, sniffed at Emrys boots, then led the way to the door, her tail wagging.

"She's an opinionated woman," Sara said with a laugh.

"Aren't they all?" Emrys paused at the door. "No arguments, Miss Jones, I apologize." He became serious. "Please convince the others to come to Brookwood. I'm certain Perkin will come here for his money. Think of the children."

Sara nodded and closed the door, locking it firmly behind Emrys. As soon as everyone was up, she told them of Emrys' offer and the reasons behind it. "Heavens, yes," Mrs. Jones said, fanning herself. "I couldn't sleep a wink in this house if I thought that man would return. I think we should go immediately."

"I think this afternoon will be soon enough," Garfield said. "I don't think Moore, or whatever his name is, will come today. Tonight is more likely."

"Then we should come here tonight and nab him." Jack stood up in his excitement.

"No." Garfield was emphatic. "Leave that to the magistrate. We'll just keep an eye out today and stay at Brookwood tonight." He finished his tea and stretched. "Right now I want to go search Moore's room. I doubt he's left a thing, but I want to be sure." James and Jack were out the door almost before Garfield.

They found nothing, not even a scrap. Even though they were all watchful and on edge, the day was peaceful, broken only by a quick visit from Emrys. He left as soon as he learned they were coming to Brookwood, telling them he would expect them at five that afternoon.

As usual, Mrs. Jones was late, Matthew fell and had to have his clothes changed, and Jack begged all the way over to be allowed to stay the night at Saint's Haven so he could capture Perkin. It was half past six by the time they arrived at Brookwood, and already dusk was falling.

Brookwood had all the appearances of an armed camp on the outside, but inside Emrys had made every effort to make them feel at home. Supper wasn't a formal affair, and Emrys insisted that the children eat at the table with everyone as they were accustomed to do at Saint's Haven. After supper, the children and Emrys went off to organize a treasure hunt, while Aunt Zell and Mrs. Jones retired to the front drawing room for some needlework they had brought along. That was when Sara missed Lucy.

"We didn't bring her with us, I'm sure," Mrs. Jones said. "I recall seeing her go up the stairs as we were getting ready to leave. I suppose she went up to your room." She paused. "It isn't a good idea to encourage animals in the house, Sara."

"Lucy's no animal, Mama. That is, she is an animal, but she's more like a person." She thought a moment. "She doesn't like Edward and never has. I think he's the one who tried to kill her by hitting her on the head." She turned to the others. "I've got to get her here, Mama. Edward—Perkin—will kill her if he finds her. I know he will."

She went searching for Emrys but couldn't find him, then decided that was probably a good thing. Emrys would tell her to leave Lucy, citing the danger in going back to Saint's Haven. Sara went to the door and asked Timothy if he would go with her to Saint's Haven to get Lucy. "It will only take a moment, Timothy," she pointed out, "and we'll hurry. All we have to do is dash inside, pick up Lucy, and come back." Timothy hesitated, saying he needed to speak to Emrys first. Sara knew that Emrys wouldn't allow either of them to go, so she promised Timothy it would be all right. She went back to the drawing room to leave word with Aunt Zell.

"Zell had a headache and went on to bed," Mrs. Jones told her, searching for her emerald silk thread.

"Mama, Timothy has agreed to go with me to Saint's Haven to get Lucy. We're just going there and back, so tell Emrys that it's all right. Don't forget to tell him."

"Of course, dear. Take care. There it is!" She pulled a tangled mass of emerald from the basket. "I don't understand how silk can get so tangled. Do you have time to help me?"

"I will when I get back, Mama. That shouldn't be long. Don't forget to tell Lord Emrys." Mrs. Jones nodded and attacked her silks while Sara grabbed her shawl and went to get Timothy.

The night was pitch dark, and even with a lantern, Sara and Timothy had trouble seeing as they went across the field and the orchard toward Saint's Haven. It seemed to take forever to get to the house, and it was so dark that Sara had trouble getting the lock to turn. "I don't know what's wrong with it," she said, finally shoving the door open. Inside, the house was dark and quiet. "Lucy," Sara called and heard an answering whimper from the upstairs.

"I'll go get her," Timothy said, picking up the lantern.

"No, she doesn't know you. I'll go." Sara took the lantern and hurried up the stairs, going to her room where she could hear Lucy. Sara kept calling Lucy's name, and the beagle was howling in earnest now. When Sara opened the door to her room, she didn't see Lucy, but heard her under the bed. Sara put the lantern down and got down on the floor. Lucy was huddled at the far end of the bed, whimpering again. "It's all right, girl, come on." Lucy took a tentative step, then cowered back. It took several minutes before Sara was able to coax her out. Sara leaned back on her heels and took Lucy into her lap. "Good girl. Now we're ready." Before she could stand up, she was grabbed from behind, and a hand covered her mouth. She twisted and tried to scream, but it was no use.

"Don't bother screaming for your bodyguard." It was Edward Moore's voice. "He won't be answering anything for a long time." He fumbled in the top drawer of Sara's small chest and dragged out a long scarf which he used as a gag. "There," he said as he stepped back and turned her around. "That should hold you for a while. I'll take it off if you promise to behave. Do you promise?" Sara nodded, and Edward—Ned Perkin, she reminded herself—came close to her and took off the gag. Then he kissed her. "A much better way to silence a woman, don't you think?" he said with a smile. "Hold out your hands." He tied her hands together and pushed her down on the bed. Lucy brushed against his boot, and he kicked her savagely. The beagle crawled back under the bed, whimpering.

"I've come for what's mine." Ned picked up a hammer from the table and went over to the mantel of the small fireplace in Sara's room. He used the thin end of the hammer to pull the mantel from the wall. Behind the mantel, two bricks had been removed, and there was a metal box in the space. Perkin removed the box and flipped open the lid. "Looks like it's all here," he said with a satisfied smile. "Now there's just one thing left to do."

"And that is . . . ?"

He snapped the lid shut. "Kill Emrys, what else? I have it all planned. I'm going to be the cousin from Cornwall. Edward Moore was going to be, but Bekins scotched that. However, a mustache and a little hair dye and a change of mannerisms, and no one will know I'm not the Cornwall connection. After all, that man's dead already."

"Did you kill him?"

Perkin turned, his handsome face sinister in the lantern light. "Of course. It was ideal. The man was practically a hermit and lived in Cornwall with only two retainers. A bookish sort, it seemed. It was quite easy. Unfortunately, I had to dispose of the retainers as well. I'll have to bring in someone who can vouch for my identity, but that shouldn't prove difficult."

"Why do you hate him so?" Sara slid from the bed to stand and face him. "If anything, you're the one who's wronged him."

"He killed Elizabeth," Perkin said flatly. "If he hadn't, I'd be at Brookwood today. He has to pay for that."

"You'll never get away with it."

Perkin laughed. "Oh, but I will. A little audacity goes a long way, my pet. I learned that long ago. If I kill Emrys and walk in here claiming to be the cousin from Cornwall, then everyone will agree that's who I am. People rely on their expectations. If they expect Ned Perkin to be the next Robin Hood, then that's who he'll be."

"What if everyone expects Ned Perkin to swing from the end of a rope?"

Perkin's handsome face twisted, and he slapped Sara hard across the face. "Let's go," he said harshly, shoving her ahead of him out the open door. "You're my bait for Emrys." He pushed her down the hall, and she stumbled. She thought about screaming, but knew it would be no use—if Perkin had killed or silenced Timothy, there was no one else. She went down, hearing the soft thud of Lucy's footfalls behind them.

"In the kitchen, the lantern outlined Timothy's dark bulk on the tile floor. "Is he dead?" Sara asked, wanting to go to him.

"I don't think so," Perkin said, without a glance at Timothy. "At least, he was alive when I left him." He laughed wickedly. "Do you want me to check? I could accomplish that quite easily."

"No." Sara stood impassively. "What do you want me to do?"

"Out to the shed." Ned opened the door and pushed her outside as Lucy slithered out next to Sara. Perkin opened the shed door and shoved Sara inside. "No chance of you leaving, Miss Jones. Give me your shawl." He took the shawl and tied Sara firmly to a ring in the wall that had been used to hold tools. Then he took the scarf from his pocket and stuffed it in her mouth. "I don't mind you yelling for Emrys to come help you, but I certainly don't want you making a sound to warn him until he gets here."

Sara made a muffled noise behind her gag. Her whole mouth was already strained and dry. Perkin just laughed. "I suppose you're telling me that Emrys won't be caught, but I can tell you, my lady, that not only will he get caught, he'll be finished." He chuckled, picked up the lantern and went out, bolting the shed door behind him.

The darkness was so thick it seemed to close around Sara. She tried and tried, but she couldn't make a sound. The gag made her retch, but stayed firmly in place. She heard Lucy outside whining and scratching at the back of the shed, but could make no sound to call her. After a while, the scratching and whining stopped, and Sara thought Lucy had gone away.

She was all alone with no way to warn Emrys.

Chapter 18

Sara thought she slept, but she had no idea. She might have been passing in and out of unconsciousness. The darkness was almost palpable, and the strain the gag put on the muscles of her face and jaw was painful almost beyond bearing. Worse, she kept listening for a noise—anything to tell her that Emrys was at Saint's Haven. That was the sound she dreaded because she knew it would mean Emrys' death.

Finally, she heard a noise, but it was Lucy's whimpering and scratching at the shed door. Unable to make a sound, Sara threw herself against the wall of the shed, knocking down some tools and creating a clatter. Lucy began clawing at the door and barking. In just a moment, the door opened, and Sara was blinded by light from a lantern. The flame was shuttered on two sides, but Sara had been in the dark so long that even the feeble light was too much. She squinted to try to see who was there.

"Thank God you're safe!" Emrys' voice was ragged as he came inside, set the lantern on the floor, and pulled the gag from her mouth. "Poor sweetheart," he said softly, cradling her swollen face in his hands. "Are you all right?"

Sara tried to nod yes, but began sobbing instead. Emrys pulled her to his shoulder and rocked her back and forth for a moment. "It's all right, it's all right," he crooned. "I'm here now."

"You've got to leave. Hurry." Sara had trouble saying the words. Her face was swollen and stiff. "Perkin's going to kill you."

Emrys reached behind her and began to untie the knots that held her fast. "I know," he said calmly. "I've known that since I got his message."

"Message?"

"He sent an urchin to Brookwood with a note that you were in the house and if I ever wanted to see you alive, I would come to Saint's Haven alone. If I brought anyone, you'd be dead before we came through the gate." He leaned back on his heels and chafed her wrists. "There. Does that feel better?"

"Perkin said I was in the house? How did you know to come here to the shed? Have you already met him."

Emrys reached over to pat Lucy. "You can thank the devil dog for leading me to you. I would have barged right into the house, no doubt right into Perkin's trap." He grinned. "I wasn't thinking very clearly." He stood up and pushed the shed door closed.

"You've got to get away, right now." Sara tried to stand and wobbled, but Emrys caught her and pulled her to him. "I'm going nowhere without you, Miss Jones. Don't even consider it." He looked down at her, and Sara was caught up in the expression in his eyes. For an instant, she thought it was love, but knew it couldn't be.

At that moment, the shed door crashed open, trapping Lucy behind it. "What a tender scene," Perkin said with a laugh. "Just like a novel, I'm sure. The dashing hero

comes to the rescue of the virtuous maiden." The pistol
he held looked huge, and Sara cringed.

Emrys stood still, his arms around her, protecting her.
"You can't get away with this, Perkin," Emrys said quietly.
"I came alone as you instructed, but others are waiting for
you outside the gate."

"They'll never catch me. I've slipped in and out of more
places than you know. I could have gotten into Brookwood
if I had wanted, but I thought this would be more fitting."
Perkin sneered. "It's time for you to pay for Elizabeth's
death."

"I had nothing to do with that, as you well know." Emrys
moved so that his body shielded Sara. "Elizabeth heard
you'd been in an accident and was on her way to you. She
took a horse instead of a carriage because a horse would
be faster. Evidently, she didn't worry about the baby—or
her neck. The horse threw her and she died instantly."

"You killed her!" Perkin came into the shed, shouting.
"I know you did! She didn't love you—she never loved
you."

"I won't argue with that." Emrys' voice was quiet; but
every muscle was tense, and Sara could sense that he was
ready to spring whenever he got the chance.

"I could have been master of Brookwood right now."
Perkin waved the pistol. "I still will be. Meet your new
cousin from Cornwall. The one who's going to take over
your title and estates when they find you dead." He
laughed shortly. "The man couldn't have run Brookwood
and all you own—he was a bookworm."

"What did you do to him?" Emrys' voice took on an
edge.

Perkin shrugged. "What does it matter? He is no more.
Those cliffs in Cornwall can be treacherous if you're not
careful." He waved the pistol again. "Enough of this."

"One thing yet, no, two," Emrys said. "What about the

man at the back of the shed and Gwendolyn Chiswick? Were those two your handiwork as well?''

Perkin's laugh was low and hard. ''Minor irritations, those. Yes, Black Tom had once been my man, but somehow he got Elizabeth's diary. Stole it from her maid, he said. Then the fool went to church, and God told him to give the book back to you.'' Perkin shook his head in disbelief. ''He came here to tell me that he was taking the book to you. I told him I wanted to see it that night before he gave it away. He refused, so I killed him then with the axe, but never did find the diary on him. I understand he had already buried it and Miss Jones found it.'' He raised an eyebrow. ''I was surprised. I didn't think Black Tom was intelligent enough to hide the book.''

''And Mrs. Chiswick?'' Emrys was controlling himself with an effort.

''The loony? She'd been a thorn for years. She was sane enough to recognize me when I was at Chiswick's, and I was ready to kill her then. I didn't get the opportunity, so I waited, knowing if she said anything, no one would pay attention. Who's going to listen to a loony? She would have been all right if she hadn't spent her nights wandering around. She was out rambling the countryside pretending to be a ghost that night and saw me do in Black Tom. I had to wait until she wandered back this way, and then I killed her. I meant to drown her; but she put up a fight, and I had to bash her head in.'' He laughed. ''No matter, she was just as dead either way.''

Sara closed her eyes tightly, imagining Gwendolyn Chiswick's final moments. She hoped it had been over quickly. She opened her eyes and caught a movement behind the door. It was Lucy. ''Here, girl,'' Sara said softly.

''What?'' Perkin asked, looking to the side, but seeing nothing. Lucy worked her way from behind the door, bounding forward, and shoved the door open, right into

Perkin. He turned, ready with the pistol, and Emrys seized his chance. He leaped forward and grabbed Perkin. They fell to the floor and rolled on the dirt. Sara snatched the lantern up and held it, then put it on the shelf that held the small tools while she searched for something to use to help Emrys. Perkin rolled over and pinned Emrys down on the dirt floor, then began beating him on the head with the butt of the pistol. Sara grabbed a shovel and came down with all her might on Perkin's back. It hurt him enough for him to roll off of Emrys and aim the pistol at her. Lucy began barking and trying to bite him. He scrambled to his feet and backed out the shed door as Emrys drew his own pistol. Perkin saw the pistol in the lantern light and fired, the bullet going wild and ricocheting off the shovel Sara was still holding. Emrys fired back.

Perkin dropped his pistol and looked at Emrys in a dazed way. He tried to take a step forward and say something, but couldn't. He grabbed for the doorway of the shed and slowly sank forward to the ground. Emrys rolled him over as Sara held the lantern. Perkin's eyes were slowly clouding. He looked up at Sara in the lantern light. "Elizabeth," he whispered as he died.

Sara turned, dazed, as the yard filled with men. She had no more chance to speak to Emrys. She made someone go check on Timothy and heard with relief that Perkin had only knocked him unconscious. Sara sat huddled on the back bench, holding Lucy close to her until daybreak.

Emrys came up to her and sat on the bench, putting his hand on Lucy's head and scratching her ears. "Are you all right?"

The yard was still full of men, Squire Sherman and Chiswick among them. Sara nodded. "I'd like to go back to Brookwood if no one minds. I want to make sure Mama knows I'm all right."

"I sent word." He paused. "I'm sorry you had to go

through this." Emrys didn't look at her, but instead looked out at the yard and the sheeted figure of Perkin prone beside the shed.

"Did you tell Squire Sherman and Roger Chiswick what Perkin told you?"

"Yes, although Sherman will probably want to get a statement from you to corroborate." He stood up and held out his hand. "Come, Miss Jones. I'll get you to Brookwood and bring some men over here to clean up. I know you'll be glad to get back into your house and know that there's no longer any danger."

It was true. By the time they got back to Brookwood, Sara felt years older. She told her mother, Aunt Zell, and Garfield everything. "Poor Gwendolyn," Mrs. Jones had said in distress when Sara finished.

"I know, Mama. I had hoped the end was quick."

"It was." Garfield's voice was gruff. "It had to have happened instantly." He looked out the window. "Do you think we could go back home now? I'd say they're through there by now." He looked at Mrs. Jones. "Will it bother you to go back?"

Mrs. Jones shook her head. "No, I think it will seem like home now that the danger has passed. The children are anxious to return." Gratefully, they packed up the children and their belongings and went home.

When they entered the house, Squire Sherman was just leaving. Before he went out, he handed Mrs. Jones the box that Ned Perkin had taken from behind Sara's mantel. As soon as the door shut behind the squire, Mrs. Jones took the box to the table in the front room and opened it. There was more money there than they had ever had. Each packet had been carefully labeled by Mr. Bekins as to the ownership and origin. All of it belonged to Clayton Jones.

"We won't have to worry about money again," Mrs. Jones said.

"Does that mean we can stay here forever?" Matthew asked.

Sara hugged him and assured him that they would never have to leave Saint's Haven unless they wanted to. Even Jack was of the opinion that the country seemed to be more exciting than London. Besides, he added, Emrys had promised to send him to school. Sara stared at him openmouthed. "School? You, Jack? The person who swore he'd never open another book?"

Jack blushed. "Lord Emrys says only educated men get ahead in the world."

Emrys. He seemed to be everywhere. Sara went up to her room and looked out the window toward Brookwood. Since they had arrived at Saint's Haven, Emrys had always seemed to be there in one capacity or the other. That was over now, she thought. There would be no more Emrys, no more seeing his eyes change, no more hearing his voice. "He called me sweetheart in the shed and held me," she told Lucy. "He was worried about me, but it wasn't love. It was just worry." She looked at the smudge on the landscape that was Brookwood. "He could never love a missionary's daughter, Lucy. He needs a fine lady from London."

She sat down on the bed and pulled Lucy close to her, burying her chin in Lucy's short fur. "From now on, it's just the two of us, Lucy. I love you and you love me and that's all." Lucy reached up and licked the side of Sara's cheek. "I know," Sara said, stroking her, "I know. No one will ever know how we feel about Emrys, Lucy. I can tell you, but no one else. We love him, don't we?" Lucy snuggled closer to her and put her nose on Sara's lap. "Love is really a hard thing, isn't it, Lucy?" She wiped a tear away and put her hand back down in her lap. Lucy licked the tear away and wagged her tail, but it didn't help Sara at all.

Chapter 19

The days afterward were busy ones. They must have been busy as well for Emrys, Sara reflected, as he came only once to Saint's Haven, and that was to speak to Mrs. Jones. The most frequent visitor was Roger Chiswick, closely followed by Squire Sherman. Sara told her story so many times that she could almost do it by rote. Bekins, the younger, stopped by to make sure all of Clayton Jones's money was there and had been returned to them. He ran his fingers over his father's careful notes.

"He was a good man, although I never knew it until lately." He looked at them with bleak eyes. "I have a great deal of atoning to do. The first thing I plan to do is try to make things right with Lord Emrys." The money Emrys had paid Bekins for Saint's Haven was all gone, gambled away. Bekins told Emrys he would make every effort to repay him, but Emrys told him not to worry about it. Emrys told Roger Chiswick that he considered the sum a small amount to pay for ridding the world of Ned Perkin. Chiswick told the story with relish when he came to visit.

Chiswick was at Saint's Haven so often that Sara felt compelled to talk to her mother about it. Unfortunately, she had just gotten two sentences into the conversation when Chiswick walked in.

"Roger," Mrs. Jones said with a laugh, "Sara is taking me to task about your visits. Isn't that sweet of her?" She turned to Sara, still laughing. "Only a perfect daughter would be so concerned, but I must tell you that you have no worry."

"Not after a year, at any rate." Chiswick came to stand beside Mrs. Jones and handed her a bouquet of early flowers.

"A year?" Sara was puzzled.

Chiswick looked at Mrs. Jones. "Why don't you tell her, Sophie? She has a right to know."

Sara's heart thudded to her knees. She knew exactly what her mother was going to say. Mrs. Jones was going to marry Chiswick. "You can't," Sara blurted. "It wouldn't be right, not so soon after Gwendolyn."

"My goodness, Sara!" Mrs. Jones was incredulous. "We would certainly do no such thing. After all, Gwendolyn deserves her mourning period." She looked up at Chiswick, clearly in love again. "Roger and I plan to wait for a year and then marry."

Chiswick looked at Sara hesitantly. "I've always loved Sophie, you know. Even when she spurned me to marry Clayton." He paused. "Is this all right with you? I know how much your father meant to you, and I have no intention of ever trying to take his place. Still," he stopped, groping for words, "I'd like for you to look on me as something of a father."

Sara took a step backward. It was too much for her to grasp all at once. She looked at her mother, the woman who had loved Papa so much and had been so devastated when he died. With a choked sob, she ran from the room and dashed up the steps.

She was still in her room, petting Lucy, when Aunt Zell walked in. "I didn't knock because I knew you'd refuse me entrance, and then I'd have to come in anyway." Aunt Zell pulled up a chair and sat down. "Isn't it time you realized that your mother is the kind of woman who needs a man to make her happy? Roger Chiswick will spend the rest of his life trying to do just that."

"I thought she loved Papa."

"She did. I'd say she still does. No one will ever take your father's place, but, to be blunt, Sara, he's dead and she's not. She doesn't need to spend the rest of her life moping about when Chiswick can coddle her."

Sara sighed. "I know you're right, Aunt Zell. It's just that I didn't expect this."

Aunt Zell stood up and put her hands on her hips. "Marriage is a fine thing for some people—you, for instance, and your mother."

"Me?" Sara was indignant. "Whatever do you mean?"

"You know what I mean, Sara. I wasn't born yesterday. But it's your mother I'm worried about right now. Do you know what she did when you ran up the stairs? Do you know?" Aunt Zell paused for breath and went on. "Of course you don't know, so I'll tell you. Your mother turned to Roger Chiswick, told him that she could never marry him if you didn't approve, and sent him away."

Sara put her hand over her mouth in horror. "She didn't!"

"She did. Then she took to her bed. I daresay she's in there now, crying her eyes out."

Sara jumped up and flung her arms around Aunt Zell. "Thank you for telling me. I'll make it right." She ran out of the room, Lucy right behind her, but instead of going to her mother, she ran down the stairs.

"I told you your mother's in bed. Where are you going?" Aunt Zell called after her.

"I told you—I'm going to make things right." Sara jerked open the door and ran outside. Chiswick wasn't in sight, so she began walking down the road as fast as she could. Before long, she saw him. He was walking slowly, leading his horse. His head was bowed, and he looked the picture of misery. Sara called out, and he stopped.

"Is there something, Miss Jones, that—"

Sara didn't let him finish his sentence. She threw her arms around him. "Yes, there is something. You can accept my apology and come back to Saint's Haven with me to tell Mama that you still want to marry her. I'm truly sorry." She stepped back, a little embarrassed at being so effusive.

Chiswick was smiling at her broadly. "Do you mean it, Miss Jones?"

"Call me Sara. After all, we're going to be family." She linked her arm through his and nudged him back toward Saint's Haven. "Yes, I mean it. I apologize for running away like that. I was just surprised, although I should have known."

By the time they reached Saint's Haven, Sara knew she had done the right thing. She would make her own apologies to Papa later. Right now, as Aunt Zell had pointed out, life was for the living. After all, wasn't that the same thing she had hoped for Emrys—that he would put Elizabeth's death behind him and be happy.

Mrs. Jones was happier than Sara had seen her in years. Aunt Zell, as usual, had been right. The only problem was Saint's Haven. Mrs. Jones planned to move into Chiswick's house when they married and had no use for Saint's Haven. "I don't know about turning the place into an orphanage, Sara. I want to deed the house to you so you'll always have a home," she had told her daughter. "I've already spoken to Lord Emrys about helping me with the deed." She laughed. "He told me that he'd taken to reading deeds very carefully lately, so he'd see to what I wanted."

"But I want Saint's Haven to be an orphanage, Mama. There's room enough here for me and the children, too."

Mrs. Jones tapped her chin with her finger. "All right, Sara, if you insist. I'll send word to Lord Emrys. I'm sure he'll take care of it."

True to his word, Emrys came to Saint's Haven with Chiswick and brought a carefully worded deed that gave the property to Sara to use during her lifetime. If she died without heirs, the property was to be used as an orphanage forever. "This means," she said to Emrys with a laugh, "that Saint's Haven is out of your grasp forever."

"I'm reconciled to that, Miss Jones." He smiled at her. "Just keep it full of children so I'll have plenty of visitors at Brookwood." He disentangled Mary's sticky fingers from his hair and set her down. Sara noted that Mary had gotten part of her bonbon on Emrys' coat, but he merely rubbed at it with his handkerchief and forgot it. "Of course, you'll always be the chief visitor to Brookwood. I want you to come over often."

"I'll probably be busy with the children." Sara absently rubbed Lucy with the side of her foot. Lucy was getting as fat as a stuffed sausage. "I'd say the Saint's Haven-Brookwood liaison is about to produce some offspring," Emrys observed. "Several pups, I'd say."

Sara looked at Lucy's girth with wide eyes. "Good heavens!" She could think of nothing else to say. Emrys laughed as he stood to leave. Mary and Matthew came running to beg him to come back soon. Emrys laughed and threw them up in the air one at a time, catching each one as they squealed with delight. He promised to return and took his leave. Sara watched him go with sadness. Surely Emrys would find happiness with someone. He was a difficult man to get to know, but once he was a friend, he was warm and caring. *But he's not for me,* she thought as she turned back to Saint's Haven. She would, she decided, never marry.

That night, Sara went outside after supper to sit in the warm dusk and smell the wonderful garden smell of fresh dirt and beginning flowers. Lucy went with her and draped herself across Sara's feet. "You're too heavy for that, you little roundheels," Sara said with a laugh, moving her feet. She kicked off her shoes and propped her feet against Lucy. She heard a noise and turned. Emrys was coming into the gate. "You look very comfortable, Miss Jones."

"I am." She smiled at him. "I'm afraid you're too late. Mary and Matthew have already gone to bed."

Emrys sat down beside her. "Actually, I rather hoped they were asleep. I wanted to talk to you, Miss Jones." He paused. "This really isn't the right way, but our entire relationship has been unusual, wouldn't you say?"

"Well, yes." Sara was puzzled. Was the man going to try to buy Saint's Haven again?

"You're an unusual woman, Miss Jones." Emrys seemed to be searching for words.

"I suppose I should take that as a compliment." Sara smiled at him. She had never seen him so disconcerted.

"Yes, you should." He said nothing else, and the silence lengthened. Sara waited.

Emrys slapped his gloves against his thigh. "Oh, hell," he said in disgust. Sara stared at him. "Pardon me, Miss Jones. I do appear to be making a colossal botch of things."

"What things?" Sara moved her feet and felt around for her shoes. She was vaguely aware of Emrys standing up beside her.

"Miss Jones." He sounded strange.

Sara finally located her shoes and glanced up at him as she slipped her feet into them. "Yes?"

"Yes? You knew?"

"Knew what?" Sara stood up, wobbling in one of her shoes that wasn't quite on. "I don't know what you mean, Lord Emrys."

He threw his gloves down and took Sara's arms. Before she knew what he was doing, he pulled her to him and kissed her thoroughly. Sara felt as if she were spinning, whirling, and falling all at the same time. She heard a strange noise from somewhere and realized that she was making odd sounds deep in her throat. She found herself holding him, running her fingers through his hair, molding her body to his. Emrys stopped kissing her, and she stepped back, ashamed of herself. She was proving to be nothing but a wanton.

"I . . . I . . .," she began.

"Hush, sweetheart. I've got to say this now or I'll never get the words out." He tilted her chin up so he could look into her eyes in the moonlight. "I love you, Sarafina Jones, and I want to marry you. Will you marry me?"

"Marry you?" Sara thought she was dreaming the words. "Lord Emrys, I can't. There are the children, and I'm not . . . I'm not suitable."

He kissed her nose softly. "No, you're not merely suitable. I would say you're extraordinary. The children, I hope, would come with you. I want them as well. And our own children, of course." He traced a line of kisses across from her ear to her lips. "I love you, Sara."

She put her hands on either side of his face and looked at him. His eyes were warm and loving. "You do, don't you? I see it in your eyes—they always give you away." She smiled at him. "I love you, too. Did you know that?"

Emrys threw back his head and laughed, then picked up Sara and whirled her around. "No, I hoped it, but I didn't dare believe it could really happen. Tell me again." He put her down on the ground.

Sara cast away all worries about being a wanton and

slipped her arms around his neck. "I love you, I love you."
She couldn't say more because Emrys kissed her again.

"And you're going to marry me and love me forever,"
he mumbled against her ear. "Tell me."

"I'm going to marry you and love you forever," she
whispered back.

Emrys sat down on the bench, pulling Sara down beside
him. He reached for her again to kiss her, but Lucy hopped
up on the bench, right between them, her bulk pushing
them apart. She sat there, quite pleased with herself, wagging her tail.

"I think we're offending Lucy's sense of propriety." Sara
giggled.

Emrys looked down at the pregnant beagle. "You've had
your turn, Lucy, now scat!" He pushed Lucy from the
bench and proceeded to kiss Sara again until she moaned
and held on to him. Lucy shook herself, glared at him,
then decided that such odd human behavior was quite
beyond her and stretched out with a yawn, plopping her
bulk across Emrys' boots.

WATCH FOR THESE REGENCY ROMANCES

BREACH OF HONOR   (0-8217-5111-5, $4.50)
by Phylis Warady

DeLACEY'S ANGEL   (0-8217-4978-1, $3.99)
by Monique Ellis

A DECEPTIVE BEQUEST   (0-8217-5380-0, $4.50)
by Olivia Sumner

A RAKE'S FOLLY   (0-8217-5007-0, $3.99)
by Claudette Williams

AN INDEPENDENT LADY   (0-8217-3347-8, $3.95)
by Lois Stewart

ROMANCE FROM JO BEVERLY

DANGEROUS JOY   (0-8217-5129-8, $5.99)

FORBIDDEN   (0-8217-4488-7, $4.99)

THE SHATTERED ROSE   (0-8217-5310-X, $5.99)

TEMPTING FORTUNE   (0-8217-4858-0, $4.99)